STRIPPED

STRIPPED

A HAPPY ENDINGS NOVEL

ZOEY CASTILE

KENSINGTON BOOKS
www.kensingtonbooks.com

KENSINGTON BOOKS are published by

Kensington Publishing Corp.
119 West 40th Street
New York, NY 10018

All Kensington titles, imprints, and distributed lines are available at special quantity discounts for bulk purchases for sales promotion, premiums, fund-raising, educational, or institutional use.

Special book excerpts or customized printings can also be created to fit specific needs. For details, write or phone the office of the Kensington Sales Manager: Kensington Publishing Corp., 119 West 40th Street, New York, NY 10018. Attn. Sales Department. Phone: 1-800-221-2647.

Kensington and the K logo Reg. U.S. Pat. & TM Off.

eISBN-13: 978-1-4967-1525-8
eISBN-10: 1-4967-1525-X
First Kensington Electronic Edition: September 2018

ISBN-13: 978-1-4967-1524-1
ISBN-10: 1-4967-1524-1
First Kensington Trade Paperback Printing: September 2018

10 9 8 7 6 5 4 3 2 1

Printed in the United States of America

For Sarah Elizabeth Younger,
a true friend and champion of love stories.

1

The Thong th-thong thong thong

ROBYN

The thong is covered in red, white, and blue sequins reminiscent of the American flag. Though I know it can't be *exactly* the American flag. One, because it's a sign of disrespect to wear the flag as an article of clothing, let alone a shimmering strip of fabric that gets wedged all up in your private bits. Two, I just went over this in my class when Freddy Dominguez asked how many times the flag has changed since Betsy Ross's original design. One thing led to another, and I suddenly found myself explaining to a class full of ten-year-olds why they could not make a dress out of the flag for an extra-credit class project.

Here, now, at seven o'clock in the morning, I hold the thong up to the light, like an archaeologist might hold a particularly curious desert find. Upon further inspection of the G-string, I don't think it'd be possible to fit all fifty stars and stripes on the triangle attached by flimsy elastic fabric. It's a rather large piece of fabric, all things considered. Either the owner is packing a lot of junk or has a huge vagina.

I take a deep breath. What a way to start the morning. I slept through my alarm, and while my coffee was brewing, I ran down in my pajamas to pick up my laundry bag from the place next door. Since the first item I took out was a thong I don't remember buying, I'm going to go out on a limb and say I was given the wrong bag.

It's pouring outside, and the ink on the receipt attached to the bag is too smudged to read the name on it. In twenty minutes, I'll start the countdown for being late to work. It's probably frowned upon for an elementary teacher to be late to class for the third time this week. It's only Wednesday. Unlike in college classes, my students don't get to pick up and leave after fifteen minutes of me not showing up. Plus, since my lateness is, uh, *recurring* the last couple of weeks, my little devils have taken it upon themselves to booby-trap my desk with pranks. Lately, it's been whoopee cushion central in room 412. Yet another generation has discovered the hilarity of fart noises. #Bless.

Anyway, when I opened up my laundry bag, I knew it wasn't mine. This leaves me with a few problems. One: I don't have any clean underwear or clothes, other than the ones I'm wearing now. Two: I'll have to run back in the rain and swap them out, leaving me with a desperate need to shower again after sweating my face off and getting soaked in dirty New York water. Three: Wouldn't the sequin itch once it got all up in the owner's butt crack? Finally, on what occasion, other than the Fourth of July, would someone wear something like this?

My second alarm buzzes, but at least I'm awake now. Murphy's Law is kicking my ass. No clothes, no shoes, no service. Well, I do have shoes, I suppose. I could be an Internet sensation. In local news, fifth-grade teacher shows up in pajamas and rain boots. My mother always said I have a face for TV.

Also, what is that dripping noise?

I slide across the living room in my dirty socks (better than Swiffering!) and get to my kitchen. My toe hits the river of coffee snaking across the slanted floor.

"*Breathe,*" I tell myself, looking down at the sight. "*Breathe.*"

There was once a time when I was a hopeful twenty-one-year-old ready to graduate college early with honors. I woke up before the sun, without the help of six alarms spaced out by ten-minute intervals. *That* Robyn wouldn't wait for all her clothes to be dirty before sending them out to the wash. Hell, she would've walked the extra ten blocks to the Laundromat and sat there while paying her bills early. That Robyn was never late. Didn't even use the word *late* in her vocabulary, not even when commenting that *other* people were late to meet her. That Robyn had her shit together. That Robyn didn't forget to put the coffeepot *in* the coffee machine before it started percolating.

That Robyn was a fuzzy memory, replaced by this Robyn: twenty-eight and with a severe case of "chicken without a head." It's a very technical term, and it's real, my students are sure of it.

"Dammit!" I shout at my apartment in Astoria, Queens. I repeat it until I work myself up into a cocoon of anxiety. I'm answered by a truck horn, dozens of children screaming in the street, and the general cacophony that is my block at any time of day.

New plan: Clean this up. Run downstairs in the rain and swap out bags. Beg Principal Platypus to not fire me. Teach students how to not be a disaster using self as an example. Perfect. Great plan.

I step over the puddle of coffee and shove the empty pot in place to salvage at least one cup of precious java. Then I go to grab a fistful of paper towels. Empty.

I open the drawer for a dishrag. Empty.

I remind myself that the dishrags are in my gray laundry bag, which this is not. It is, however, *someone's* clean laundry.

"I can't do that," I tell myself, hopping back over the stream of caffeine. I do always tell my students to think outside the box. Sometimes the solution is right in front of you, and my solution might just be this.

I pull open the drawstring and grab a fistful of items off the top. The star-spangled thong, a black tank top too small to fit a human person, and a pair of giant gray sweatpants. As I place the so-fresh-and-so-clean clothes on the river of coffee, I consider that this person must have an unusually disproportionate body.

But who am I to judge? I'm cleaning my floor in nothing but my panties and socks. All of my bras are dirty. If I hadn't spent my after-school time yesterday trying to salvage my friendships, I would've gone to Target to buy new underwear and socks.

Aside from a temporary solution to my wet floor, maybe the bag contains something that would fit me.

I wring out the clothes in my kitchen sink and let the water run a bit. I look back at the laundry bag open in my living room. Why stop at three items of clothing? There might be a clean top that fits me. It could be like the Sisterhood of the Traveling Laundry Bag. They'll never know. I'll come straight home, wash everything, and return it.

Then again, the day I show up to class in semi-stolen clothes will probably be the day I start on a downward spiral. What's to stop me from stealing someone's grocery bag or underwear?

"Maybe I should take an Adulting 101 class," I tell myself as my third alarm *and* a knock on the door interrupts me. "Or maybe get a cat so I'm not talking to myself."

I take off my wet socks and tap the phone alarm silent. The knock on the door is quick and cheerful. I like to think that you can tell a lot about people by the way they knock on doors. At seven fifteen in the morning, no one should be that damn peppy.

I throw on my silky robe that's hanging from the couch and make my way to the door. The person on the other side knocks again in the fifteen steps it takes me to get there. I'm pretty sure they're trying to tap out the tune of "Single Ladies," which is *always* a great song to have stuck in your head.

"Who is it?"

"Hi, it's your neighbor," a male voice answers. "I think I got your laundry bag by mistake."

My stomach does a weird flip-floppy thing, like I've been caught doing something wrong. That's probably because I *am* being caught doing something wrong.

"Just a second!" I shout to buy myself time. I look around the room, but there's nothing I can do except answer the door. I clear my throat and undo the bottom lock, then the middle, and leave the chain lock intact.

"Hi," I say in my best attempt to be nonchalant, as in, "*Hi, I didn't just use your clothes to clean my floor.*"

At first, he's just a tall and blurry blob that my brain can't process because this is a terrible, terrible morning. It takes me a second to notice him. *Really* notice him. The door creates a shadow that obstructs his features. Then, he steps slightly to the right so we face each other through the three inches of open door and the morning light behind me illuminates him.

His strong chin rests just above the chain lock. He's smiling, and I was right. He *is* too damn peppy for this early in the morning. He's also too damn fine to be standing at my door. I rub one eye, just to make sure I'm seeing right, and, yep, he's still there—the most beautiful man I don't remember ordering.

I almost forget why he's here when he holds up a pink laundry slip with my name on it.

The back of my mind is going, "*All the single ladies—*"

He smiles and my brain forgets the rest of the words to the song. I zone in on his face, though I'm pretty sure the rest of him doesn't disappoint. I love faces. How unique and different every single one is. I love *his* face. His smile crinkles at the corners of his lips. It pushes all the way up his face, like he's truly happy to see me, despite this ungodly hour of morning. It's a shameless smile because he knows, he *has* to know, the effect it has on people. On me.

"Uhm," I start to say, trying to wade through the fog of thoughts.

"Your apartment smells amazing," he tells me, looking past me and inside. "Is that a Colombian roast?"

I can feel my face scrunch up with confusion. Then, I'm completely aware of how quickly this stranger looks at my toes, the long stretch of my bare legs, and tries not to linger at the silky robe that clings to my breasts. I self-consciously pull the robe closer. The dull pulse of a caffeine-deprived headache starts to ebb its way into my brain

"So," he says, because I'm just staring at his face. I'm shamelessly staring. "Are you holding my clothes hostage? Is that what this chain is for?"

Playful. Charming. It's too early to be those things, but he's managing it. When he smiles again, my belly drops straight through my body and down the six floors of the apartment building.

Dammit. Not now, I scold my mind. At least I still have a slightly reasonable part of my brain that works.

"Right! Give me a minute." I shut the door in his face and run across the living room where his open bag of laundry is. I face a decision: Come clean (pun intended) and tell him that I used his clothes as a mop. Or, I shove the clothes back in there and let him find the caffeinated surprise later on. At least I know he likes the smell of my coffee.

He knocks on the door twice.

I realize I don't like either of those options. There's a third. I could take a page out of my students' proverbial books. This option would make me both deceptive and a thief, but that is what I'm going to go with. Besides, I'll return everything later on. He has plenty of sweatpants in there. I don't even need to know about the thong anymore. I just want to get dressed and go to work. That is if I still have a job to go back to. So, I kick the soaked clothes into a corner of my kitchen, and drag the bag toward the door.

I undo the chain and face him.

"Here you go," I say, my heart racing from sprinting back and forth. My heart could also be racing because looking at him now without the door obscuring my view is twice as startling as just the sliver of him. It could be that it's been eighteen months and counting since I've met a man who made my pulse throb. Or because he's equal parts rugged and charming, which is my favorite combination.

In his navy-blue sweats and white ribbed tank, he looks like he could've just left the gym. A duffel bag rests on the floor right behind him, next to my laundry bag, and I realize the tank top I "stole" from him can't be his. His chest is too broad, too solid. I catch myself staring at the curve of his shoulders, and mentally bite him, while trying to restrain myself. Who needs self-control when you're already in a tailspin, amirite?

Down, girl, I think. I realize that there is only a thin sheet of silk between us. And a door. And, well, our laundry bags. Whatever. We are really, really close to being basically naked together.

He lifts his Red Sox cap and runs his hand across his soft, light-brown hair. There's a question marring his features. He doesn't ask it out loud but I'm sure it's along the lines of "Are you crazy?"

Instead, he says, "Thanks, darlin'."

I hate pet names. But when my neighbor says it, I don't seem to mind at all. Hell, I'm even getting warm and tingly. He shakes his head, as if dispelling the thoughts in there. I wonder what he was thinking. He picks up my laundry bag and swaps it out with his.

The exchange has been made.

"You're a lifesaver," I tell him. "I'm officially out of clean clothes."

He laughs, and I decide it's the most wonderful sound I've ever heard.

"I don't know," he says. "That silk robe is a pretty good look."

I feel the burning blush creep up my neck and settle in my cheeks. It's not that I'm impressionable. I'm not. Well, I don't think I am. It's that he's caught me off guard. It's early and I'm late for work. If I'm going down that road, I'm late for my life in general, but that's a can of worms I'd rather not open.

"*All the single ladies,*" my mind singsongs.

Then, my fourth alarm goes off.

Panic replaces my attraction to my handsome neighbor. I start to shove him out of my doorway. He budges easily, taking a step back when I take a step forward, like we're doing some sort of morning tango.

"Thanks again, but I've got to go. I'm late for work and the new principal is probably going to fire me, so thanks but—" I start to close the door when he interrupts.

"Where do you work? I could give you a ride."

"Why?"

"Because you're late and the new principal—"

"Don't you have somewhere to be?" I cut him off.

He shakes his head once, and I wonder if I'm imagining the

glimmer in his eyes. "Just got home. The only place I have to be is my bed."

I can't help it. The mental image of him on his bed overpowers my thoughts. It's probably a very, very big bed. He looks like he spreads out on it completely naked.

I clear my throat and point to the window. "I teach up here by Astoria Park."

"I can drop off my things while you get dressed. I just moved into 5A a couple of weeks ago."

"You're right under me," I say. Then wish I hadn't.

"I am." He smiles his crooked smile and he leans a little closer to the door, careful to not step back in the doorway.

I recognize the implication in his grin, and suddenly, the silk robe I'm wearing feels more like a fur coat in the middle of July. I wonder where he's from and what his favorite song is, and whether he's a model or an actor because he's not normal-person attractive. He's a little too big and muscular to be the thin, European models in the latest issue of my *Vogue*. But his face. Damn, *dat face.*

God. I have to stop eating lunch with my fifth graders.

"You should wear the red dress," he says and winks.

As he picks up his laundry bag and slings it over his shoulder, I find myself stuck between being indignant and flattered.

"You went through my clothes?"

"Did you go through mine?" He laughs good-naturedly.

I cross my arms over my chest. "No."

I realize I sound more like one of my students than the twenty-eight-year-old child I truly am. Deny until you believe your own lie, right?

He bares his teeth and I swear that he's letting me get away with it. That's when I realize that I really, truly can't get a ride from him. Not just because he went through my undies (Hey, Pot! Meet Kettle!), but because it would be harder to return the clothes that are bunched up in a corner of my kitchen floor. I don't want anything to do with him after the laundry exchange. I can already feel the warmth of his smile creeping along my skin and that just can't happen. There is no room for this feeling in my life right now. Plus, how do you look a man in the face and say, "*Btw,* here's your sparkly thong. I washed it."

Plus, plus! Stranger danger. How can I caution my students about getting into strangers' cars when I'm minutes away from doing the same?

"It's really nice of you to offer," I start. I want to close the door and get to work. I want to hit the restart button for the hundredth time this week. I want to stay and talk to him because I feel a bud of something wonderful flowering in my chest. And that can't happen. Not right now.

"But?"

"But, it's totally fine. I usually walk. I'm not very late anyway. Sorry about the laundry mix-up."

He nods once, a suspicious grin on his lips. It turns to a yawn, which he tries to stifle.

"Sorry, long night," he says. "Okay, 6A. Have a good day at work."

He walks away, and I start to close the door when he whirls around. I catch the doorknob just before it slams on the hand he reaches out to me.

"Would you want to get a drink Saturday night?"

I want to say yes.

For the past year, I've been complaining about how hard it is to date in New York City. All of the dating apps in the world weren't able to give me a One True Match. I've waded through a Sea of Douche Bags for so long that I haven't just lost interest in going on another bad first date—a part of me has lost all hope in finding any semblance of love.

Could it be this easy? I give him a quick glance from head to toe. Honestly, he deserves more than a glance. He deserves a thorough inspection.

"All the single ladies," my mind hums.

Single ladies. That's when it hits me. "I'd love to but I have a work thing."

"On a Saturday night? Where's that New York hospitality you never hear about?"

My fifth alarm goes off.

My mind is frazzled, tugging between the mess in my apartment and the potential in the hallway.

"*Say yes,*" my heart urges.

He has a sequin thong in his laundry bag. And a girl's shirt. *DO NOT ENTER,* my mind practically screams.

When there's a war between my heart and my mind, then my mind always wins.

"I really have to go," I say.

I'm too old to date guys like this, anyway. He just got home at seven in the morning after partying. Then, a ray of light hits the beautiful stranger standing in my hallway. It's downright angelic, is what it is. He doesn't even look tired. His eyes have a mischievous glint, like one night with him could turn my world upside down. His body is tan and the sweat that's dried on his skin fills my senses. His lips—they're full and slightly parted as he patiently waits for me to close the door. His foot taps ever so slightly, and it's the only sign that he's perhaps nervous. But then I see something else that adds to the decision that, no, I should not be seeing a guy like this. I did not imagine the glimmer in his eyes. The glimmer is, in fact, everywhere.

"Also, you have glitter on your neck," I say.

He looks confused for a moment, then gives me an understanding closed-lip smile. An understanding that the glitter had to come from somewhere, someone. He nods again and watches me close the door.

"You know where I live if you change your mind," he says quickly.

After I shut the door I wonder if I've made a mistake. I look through the peephole and my heart gives a little tug because he's still standing there. He looks like he might knock again, but he hesitates. Instead, he smiles and shakes his head. He picks up his laundry and shoulders the weight, grabbing his duffel bag with his free hand.

Then he's gone.

I don't have time to pine for him, even though a sick, twisted, sexually deprived part of me wants to.

But my phone goes off again. This time it's not my alarm. It's my best friend, Lily, calling. Lily teaches in the classroom next to mine. I told her if I wasn't in the teachers' lounge by seven thirty, to call me.

I let the phone go to voice mail, and hurriedly pour the salvaged coffee into my travel mug. I rummage through my laundry while scalding my tongue with coffee. It's okay. Taste buds are overrated. So are hot men with glitter on their necks and bedazzled thongs and women's clothes in their laundry.

I shoot Lily a text. *Traffic! Cover for me, please!*

Lily responds with a side-eye emoji. *Hurry up. Principal Platypus is patrolling the halls.*

That's when I see it, and an involuntary grin spreads across my face.

At the top of my laundry stack is my favorite red spring dress. I put it on.

FALLON

"She totally went through my clothes," I tell Yaz when I walk into my apartment.

Yaz, my five-month-old husky pup, barks in response. She runs around the laundry I drop at the foot of my bed. I take my clothes off on the way to the bathroom, leaving a bread-crumb trail for no one. Once upon a time, this Prince Charming wouldn't be coming home alone after a night of work. Wouldn't have gotten turned down for a "work thing."

" 'Also, you have glitter on your neck,' " I say, trying to mimic 6A's voice. It isn't high-pitched, the way her sweet, soft face gives the impression it would be. It's a perfect, rough alto. The kind of voice I can picture whispering dirty nothings in my ear.

Having spent the night surrounded by hundreds of women with high-pitched screams, the sound of her voice is a welcome reprieve.

I kick off my sweatpants and run the water. I've started a downside list of living in New York. My place in Boston was brand-new and three times as big for the same price. Astoria's got its charm, I suppose. Greek coffee and baklava at any time of the day is a pretty sweet deal.

Downside #1 is that it takes five minutes for the water to turn hot. I love hot showers, and I'm not just talking about the times I have someone in there with me. I'm talking scalding-hot water. Feel the steam in my pores. Feel my muscles unwind after a night of acrobatics.

It's the only way I feel clean after having bills shoved down my pants. Don't get me wrong. I love money. I love having it launched at me from willing MILF hands, fingers that have mapped every inch of my hard-earned muscles. I work for that paper. But I still need a shower.

Fucking glitter. Ruining my life one sparkle at a time.

I scrub my face and neck, knowing how hard it is to get rid of this stuff. Glitter is the herpes of the makeup world. On that note, I think of 6A in her pretty silk kimono instead.

Wrong. Not pretty. Not pretty at all.

Her in that robe was the hottest wet dream I've ever had come to life; it was a gift from the gods themselves. She kept pulling it tighter around her full breasts and tiny waist, like she thought I had X-ray vision. I wish I'd been able to say something clever.

Well, if I'm wishing for stuff, I'd wish that she'd said yes. I pause and marvel at that. *She* said *no* to *me*. I must be losing my edge.

After a night of "yeses" I finally have one no. And it sucks. I haven't had a girl turn me down since I shot up a foot and had my braces removed in the eleventh grade.

I push the bath curtain aside and pull the cabinet mirror toward me. I wipe away some of the steam and take a look at myself. I've got some serious dark circles under my eyes. I resigned myself a long time ago to a life of sleeping in the day and working at night. It's part of the glamorous life I live.

I wink at my own reflection. That wink has gotten me out of

speeding tickets, brought in thousands of dollars in tips, and earned me passing grades up until I dropped out of high school. There was a time when I didn't have to say a single word to get a date. A wink, a smile, and it was over.

Zac Fallon, lady-killer. Not literally, of course.

What has New York City done to me? I don't have the attention span. I work, I go home, I go to the gym, I go to work again. Lather, rinse, repeat.

My buddy Ricky likes to remind me that at thirty, I'm over the hill. Ricky himself is thirty-nine, but still thinks like a horny nineteen-year-old. Maybe I am old. Maybe I look tired. Maybe I'm overthinking it. Maybe I'm just *not* for her.

As if sensing my distress, Yaz barks from the living room.

I push the mirror back into place, leaving a soapy trail on the glass.

Once I've rinsed the glitter out of my pores, I replay my interaction with 6A. Incredulous. Judgey. She was *so* fucking judgey. You know what? I probably dodged a bullet with that one. There's no point in getting tangled up with someone when I don't know how long I'm going to stay in this shit city.

As the waterfall of metallic New York water washes the suds away, I truly convince myself that I was never interested in her. Not in her high cheekbones that turned perfectly pink when I winked at her. Not in the thick, long black hair that tumbled around her shoulders like waterfalls of ink. Not even in the round and perky tits she kept trying to cover with that flimsy robe.

I hope she'll wear the red dress.

I turn off the faucet and watch the tiny whirlpools of suds and glitter run down the drain.

"Fuck." I'm hard. I'm hard just thinking about her in that silk robe. In that red dress. I don't even know her name and I'm hard as fuck.

It's not that I don't enjoy a good hard-on. I spent six hours with hordes of women grabbing at my dick and nothing happened. There was a time ten years ago when the touch of a woman, any woman, during one of my sets would have me saluting my flag.

That went away right quick. Self-control and all that.

But here I am, like a maypole reaching toward the sky, and I blame her. Judgey, rude, messy, gorgeous, sexy—

She wasn't just the girl who stole my laundry. She was the girl who saw right through me. My dick is a fucking masochist.

I turn the water back on. Hotter this time so steam can rise. It's been a while. Not because I don't have opportunity. I always have the opportunity. But because, lately, I feel worn and torn most of the time.

I groan into the rising mist. I rub my hand up and down my shaft. I hold on tighter to myself and to the fleeting memory of a woman who doesn't want me. Think of the way her nipples pushed against silk. If that thin tie had come undone around her waist I would've been able to see everything that she was hiding.

"Oh shit," I grunt, and shiver despite the heat, releasing my load into the drain as 6A's full dick-sucking lips come to mind.

When my legs stop trembling, and the water rinses me clean (well, relatively clean), I dry off and jump into bed. Tomorrow is the beginning of June, and the New York chill refuses to let go. I stare at the ceiling and try not to think about the fact that the hottest girl I've seen in this city has been living one floor above me. Then, I think about work—there's so much that needs to get done. So much to decide. The show gets bigger every day. . . .

Yaz barks, then climbs up on my chest and passes out. At least Yaz wants me.

Rick and the club will have to wait until Monday. I haven't had more than three days off in a row, let alone a weekend, in about five years. I give myself permission to think of 6A once more.

That heart-stopping, breathtaking, world-changing face.

Okay, that's it. No more. Tomorrow I can forget about her.

Okay, once more. "She could be the girl," I say, touching the chilly part of my bed. She could keep my sheets warm. She could be a reason to be in this damned city. I could be charming and sweep her off her feet. I can't wait to see her again.

But another voice, a strange, sensible voice that's been quiet most of my life, whispers, "No. *It's just the past coming to haunt you. She's just the girl who took your laundry.*"

2

You Give Love a Bad Name

ROBYN

"I'm here!" I shout down the hallway.

My voice echoes in the empty corridor of P.S. 85. Lukewarm coffee trickles down my wrist as I grip my travel mug like it's the Olympic torch and I'm late to the finish line.

Thirty minutes late to be exact.

The only medal I'm going to win is a gold in Being Fired. Principal Platypus is nowhere in sight, and so I run where Lily is, pacing between our classrooms.

My soles are like horse hooves clopping on cobblestones. The closer I get, the better I can see the disappointment and anxiety in Lily's brown eyes. Lately, I don't know who I'm more afraid of letting down—Lily or my parents. Lily is like the sister I never had. She's an only child, too, and we've been best friends since we both tried to start our own Spice Girls cover band in junior high school. She's been taking care of me more than I'd like to admit. Covering for my recent string of tardiness is just another thing on the long list of favors I have to pay back.

There was a time when our roles were reversed.

Adulthood, thy name is Lily Shang . . . soon to be Lily Cohen.

I stop suddenly, dropping my weekender purse on the ground. It's full of uncapped markers, a packet of birth control pills, notebooks, worksheets for today, and an extra cardigan.

When did Lily and I trade places? Was it only four years ago

I was holding her hair back while she puked her brains out on the F train platform?

I try to catch my breath before taking a long, desperate drink of coffee.

"Nice dress," Lily says, almost surprised that I'm wearing something other than the black slacks and button-down look I've been recycling for days.

I force myself to not think about my neighbor, Sexy Glitter Neck. The red dress was at the top of my laundry bag, and that's the only reason I wore it. It's a simple cotton dress that comes up to my knees, but the color is rich, and with the cardigan over it it's the most professional I've looked in a while.

"I'm so sorry," I blurt out.

"Don't thank me just yet." Lily silences me with a glance toward the doors. "Principal Papadopoulos is in there."

"Shit," I hiss at the floor. "Shitshitshit."

"Robyn," she says, sounding concerned. "What is going on with you? You've been late practically all month. Do you *want* to get fired? I can only take advantage of Lukas and David's friendship for so long."

"Of course I don't *want* to get fired. What kind of a question is that? I just—"

I don't want to get into it, but I know she's worried about me. Me who was always on time. Me who wouldn't leave the house if my eyeliner wasn't even on both eyelids, and everyone knows how fucking hard that is. Me who promised to plan her bachelorette party and then dropped the complete and total ball.

"Not now, Lily," I say, too tired to argue. "Please. You can yell at me during brunch on Sunday."

"You only say that because I can't yell at you in front of David's family."

"This is true."

"Here," Lily says, resigning herself to the "we'll talk later" that has overtaken our friendship in the last year. She wets her thumb on her tongue, and wipes off some of the blush on my cheek.

I grimace, feeling more like one of her students, only these kids have their shit together.

"Deep breaths," I tell myself. I'm probably not fired. Platypus can be nice, I've heard . . .

"Wish me luck," I say.

But Lily has already left me to go back to her classroom.

I have yet to have a one-on-one with Principal Platypus.

Shit! I am not a ten-year-old and therefore cannot get away with that. It's Papadopoulos!

I straighten up before I open the door to my classroom, trying to think of the excuses I can give for being late.

Insomnia. I forgot the worksheets for the day. I couldn't leave the house without makeup to make me look less *tired*. Damn the patriarchy! While I'm at it I can blame the subway, because the N decided to skip stops and go express. I could blame the cyclist who got in my way, the dogs that tangled their leashes around my legs, the crossing guard who was on her cell phone and definitely about to cause a traffic accident with me at the center, and the weatherman for making my hair frizz. I might as well blame the stars. Yes, I blame the stars. In their astronomical distance, I blame them most of all.

When I look down at my dress, there's a coffee stain. That, the stain, I will blame on myself.

When I open the door, all eyes turn to me.

"Ah, Miss Flores," Principal Papadopoulos says cheerfully. "Thank you for joining us. I do believe this was meant for you."

Some giggles and jitters break out among my kids because the principal is holding a whoopee cushion in his hand.

I turn to them. "I am so sorry. I will definitely have a conversation about this."

"Not to worry, I've taken care of it," he says, getting up from my desk. He buttons his suit jacket and extends his hand.

I reach out to shake his hand, but I'm too late because he's not actually trying to greet me. He's gesturing to the hallway, but I can't stop moving forward, so I end up karate-chopping his gut.

My students cringe visibly as Principal Papadopoulos clutches his stomach where my hand dug in.

"Oh my god, are you okay?" I clap my palm over my mouth.

He clears his throat, and tries to give me a reassuring smile. "I'll live."

"I'll say," I say nervously. "It's like hitting a ton of bricks—I mean because of your abs—I mean—oh no."

My students lose it. They're reveling in my embarrassment. My sheer stupidity. My chaos.

"I think we should take this outside," he tells me. He isn't smiling. Why would he? I just accosted my boss and then pointed out how hard his abs were in front of the *most* mature ten-year-olds in the world.

I follow Principal Papadopoulos out into the hallway. The minute the door closes, my students rush it. Their faces are plastered against the glass. Now I know what fish in the aquarium feel like. Exposed, on display, with nowhere to hide, and people tapping their fingers on the glass to get their attention. I'll never tap the glass at the aquarium ever again, I can say that much.

"I'm so sorry," I say. I swallow the dryness in my throat and squeeze my hands into fists. My entire body flashes the way it does when you get in trouble. I've only been in trouble twice in my life. Once for shaving off my cousin Sky's eyebrows. Another time for getting a B in Chemistry.

Principal Papadopoulos holds up his hands in an attempt to silence my stream of verbal diarrhea. His face softens now that his back is to the students, watching us from the window. "You don't remember me, do you?"

"Huh?" is my response. Four years of English undergrad and a master's in Education from Columbia, and I, Robyn Flores, go with "huh?"

"We met once before," he says.

I strain my eyes trying to recall having met him. I've seen the new principal before, walking down the hall or from the back of the assembly auditorium and behind the rippled-glass window of his office, but in the few months since he took over after Principal Roth had a heart attack, I've never had a reason to see him face-to-face.

It never occurred to me that our new Principal Papadopoulos was so young, and so attractive. I mean, he's my boss, so, no.

Up close I can admire the sharp square of his jaw. The meticulous trim of his short dark beard, and his styled jet-black head of hair. The sumptuous honey brown of his eyes. Is that what people mean when they say "Roman nose"? I wonder. He's breathtaking, really. And the tailored suit does wonders for his upper body. Why would the universe surround me with two hot guys on the day when I'm the biggest mess this side of the Hudson River?

And yet, I have no memory of having met him before. Not even a little.

"Lily and Dave's engagement party last year," he says casually. "I told you I was applying for jobs."

"That's right! What a great party," I say, and it hurts to keep up this smile. No wonder I can't remember. I drank so much champagne that night, I remember a blur of a man talking about having graduated from NYU with David, and then getting his master's at Harvard. A terribly distorted memory surfaces, like seeing something behind warped glass. Did he give me his number? No, that couldn't have been him because that would make this terribly awkward.

"I suppose I'll be seeing you at their wedding," he says, his bearded smile tilting at one corner.

"Yup." I nod, and wish he'd just tell me if I still have a job or not. "Thank you for looking after my class. I'm really terribly sorry I'm late."

"Look," he says, shoving a hand into his pocket. "I get it. You've been having a rough couple of weeks."

"Try months," I blurt out.

"Months, then," he says. His face expresses concern. This man hardly knows me. How can he be concerned? "I don't know what's going on. It seems personal. But whatever it is, you have to deal with it. It doesn't set a good example for the kids. I need you to show up on time."

"Mr. Pap—"

"Lukas," he interrupts me. "It's a lot easier to remember than Papadopoulos or *Principal Platypus* as the kids have so charmingly decided to name me."

My face feels like I have a third-degree burn. I'm so happy I could cry. Instead, I settle for a half-snort and half-hiccup.

"So, I'm not fired," I say, just to clarify.

"Fired?" Lukas says. "These kids love you. Besides, I've been there."

I shift my weight to the side. I feel more comfortable with him now that we're on a first-name basis. Plus, according to him we've met, even if I have no memory of it. He made me laugh, and is trying to chip away at my clearly professional exterior. I recognize the technique from school. But I won't be talked to like I'm one of my problem students. I cross my arms over my chest.

"Tell me, Lukas. What am I going through that you've been there?"

Lukas shifts uncomfortably under my unwavering stare. Now it's his turn to blush. He laughs nonetheless. "I've been a little scattered . . ."

I look at his shiny black leather shoes, the tapered cut of his pants, the *pristine* ironed white shirt that I'd never be able to keep stain-free. *Scattered* is not the word I'd use for him.

"Robyn," he says, this time dropping the understanding grin. "As much as I'm trying to not be *that* guy, this is still a warning."

"I understand."

"Don't just say you understand. Be here. Okay?"

I nod, feeling that this is such a strange way to get reprimanded, but at least I still have a job.

"And . . ."

"There it is," I say, smiling. I was waiting for the catch.

"I need a volunteer for Sunday's bake sale."

"I'm there." I have Lily's wedding stuff, but I'll be there. Late.

"I'll let you get back to class," Principal Platypus—Lukas—

says, switching back to his smooth, cool persona. I try not to think of how easy it is to be two kinds of people.

For now, I take the hand he extends, like an olive branch.

FALLON

I wake from strange dreams. I was in the middle of my best set. The Yankee Doodle bit always gets the most hoots, hollers, and, most important, dollars.

In the dream, I was in the middle of a dance when the scenery changed. I was naked, except for my thong. I was flanked by Revolutionary War soldiers. Everyone has the naked-in-public dream. Doesn't that mean anxiety or something? Well, in the dream, I'm in a field with the founding fathers. I need to stop drinking at work and beg Luis to stop listening to the *Hamilton* sound track during practice.

I shake my head, and grimace at the taste in my mouth. I feel the bed for Yaz, but she's abandoned me in the middle of the night for her more comfortable bed.

Typical.

I pull the white comforter off me and lie there spread out ass-naked on my king-size bed.

Though I'm not much for having girls spend the night (the morning after is never not awkward), I wish I could turn on my side and wrap my arms around another warm, equally naked body.

Plus, my morning wood is aching. I drag myself out of bed and take a piss.

I shake, flush, and groggily move to the sink to brush my teeth.

I've been in Astoria for a little over two weeks, and New York for a month, but it still doesn't feel like home. Before this we were in Miami, and before that, Vegas, and before that, Atlanta. Atlanta was by far one of the dirtiest cities I've ever been to. Sex dirty, not hygiene dirty. But that's a different story.

I want to go back to Boston. It's been years since I gave myself time to see my brothers and sister, not to mention show my face to my old man. Fallon Senior has never approved of my lifestyle. Not the girls or the drugs or the money. I don't care for drugs anymore, but there's still the money and girls and booze. My family is staunchly Catholic, and even though my siblings don't go to church on the regular, they still aren't strippers.

I'm a stripper and I fucking love it.

At least, I did for many years. The last ten months have been a series of existential life-crisis moments that have snuck up on me. Crisis or not, I ended up in New York, New York, following Ricky and the boys because they're my family.

I go into the kitchen to make a shake. I scoop vanilla protein powder into my bottle, and shake until there are no clumpy bits left. It's not the eggs and bacon I want, but it will do. These muscles weren't built in a day. Plus, I haven't exactly bought anything to cook with. There's a neat pile of takeout bags near my garbage I have to remember to throw out.

Usually, I'd room with a few of the guys, but this time around feels different. I was glad I'd picked this apartment out of the shit show that was Craigslist. The girl in 6A makes it worth it just for the eye candy, even if she does have a sexy Tasmanian devil thing going on. And, well, isn't actually interested in me. But a man can dream.

At that moment, I get a text from Ricky. Rick Rocket is our leader. He'd probably describe himself as our alpha, but I don't like to think of myself as following a pack. Ricky was the one who scouted out the members of Mayhem City, all-male revue. My whole life changed one night because of Ricky. I owe him everything. Back then I was bartending at a dive tucked away in Somerville. We got a mix of truck drivers, locals, and college kids who couldn't afford to live in Cambridge proper. Saturday nights were the wildest because it was all college kids. The bouncers looked the other way at fake IDs as long as the girls were cute. The hotter the clientele, the more dick-bag dudes would come in and try to buy them drinks.

On that night, Ricky and his crew waltzed right in. I was

busy slinging drinks. I'd been bartending since I was seventeen, when I realized bagging groceries for $5.75 an hour wasn't going to give me the kind of life I wanted. I was good at bartending, too. Even now, I can make two drinks at the same time and light your cigarette while throwing the shakers in the air. At least that's what I tell myself.

It wasn't my proclivity for bartending that made the girls turn up on Saturday nights. It was simply just me. I was slimmer then, but still built. I'd been a runner all my life, and in many ways, the vagabond life of a touring male stripper just made sense to me. I loved the attention, and I loved giving it right back. My biggest rule was that I was never fake. I just love making women smile. There's something beautiful about every single one of them. The shape of their eyes. The color on their lips. The way they flip their hair or twirl it around their fingers. I love that they *take time* and that is a gorgeous thing.

At the bar, I loved the way the girls would lean into me and say their drink. Loved the jealous irritation on the poor schmo *paying* for the drink, because most of the time, the girl kept looking over her shoulder at me.

Around midnight on every shift, things got crazy. Two hours till closing time, and I knew which songs to pick to keep the vibe going. I was never supposed to, but I always did give out free shots. I'd hop up on top of the bar and invite a handful of girls to bring along with me, like Coyote Ugly and shit. Somehow, I'd end up with my shirt missing and my bar full of dollar bills.

That was the night Ricky noticed me.

Sometimes I wonder where I'd be if Ricky's car hadn't gotten a flat tire down the road. If he hadn't decided to walk to the nearest bar and look for help. If he hadn't stayed because he's a make-lemonade kind of guy. If he hadn't picked me and given me a job that would change my whole world.

Life's just funny that way, I think as I get a text from the man himself.

Ricky: *Wake up, Princess.*

Me: *What?*

Ricky: *You still mad about the new guys? I'm just testing them out . . . You'll get your spot back.*

Me: *K.*

Ricky, like most people, hates one-letter responses. They aren't responses. They're dismissive. But I do it anyway because I want any excuse to be passive-aggressive.

Ricky: *Stop being a dick. I need you to cover a party this weekend.*

Me: *Fuck that.*

Me: *Get Wonderboy and his twin.*

Me: *What's his excuse this time?*

I knew before Ricky could answer that the latest member of Mayhem City was flaky. I didn't want to hire Vinny and Frank Suave in the first place, but I was outvoted. Whenever a new member of our group is added in a new city, all of the six original members have to vote unanimously since we add new guys in every city. For New York, because the location is bigger, we hired on six more guys, plus a couple of emergency backups. I was fine with the first four, but Vinny and Frank are twin brothers so they came together like obnoxious, fake-tanned salt-and-pepper shakers.

Ricky: *Always jumping the gun. I double booked Vin and Frank by accident.*

Me: *It's my first Saturday off in months.*

Ricky: *You're off today! We were off for a week last month.*

Me: *Driving cross-country in a van with you smelly fucks isn't a vacation.*

Ricky: *Will you do it or not?*

I wait a half hour before answering.

Me: *You know I will.*

Ricky: *Then why you gotta give me so much shit?*

Me: *See you at the gym?*

Ricky: *Nah, I have a date.*

Me: *The girl or the guy?*

Ricky: *Both.*

Me: *Dog.*

Ricky: *Someone around here has to get laid.*

I grunt and throw my phone on the bed and look for something clean to wear. I absentmindedly smile at the memory of 6A this morning. Well, since I wasn't going to go on a date with my super-cute and incredibly intense neighbor, I might as well work. This apartment is one of the nicest places I've ever lived in, but people did not kid when they talk about New York rent.

I rummage through the laundry bag for my favorite sweatpants. My entire wardrobe is sweatpants, windbreakers, and white and black T-shirts. I'm well aware that I'm a walking ad for a sports magazine, but I like to keep a low profile. As soon as they started making money, some of the other guys bought $800 shoes and $100 T-shirts. The temptation was there, but I just put that money in the bank. And by bank, I mean a fireproof safe in my closet. There's over ten years of savings and almost half a million dollars in there. I'd have more if I hadn't bought my car outright, and if I wasn't paying for my sister's private school and my father's medical bills.

Those things mattered. Those are the reasons I want to keep doing what I'm doing.

But after Mary finishes school and after my dad gets better, then what am I supposed to do with all this cash? I push the thought out of my head, though it's getting harder every day. Everything in life is just a countdown to whatever comes next.

Once, I felt like I was working toward a goal, but now? Now I'm just going through the motions.

"Where the fuck is it?" I dump all of the neatly folded clothes onto my bed. My favorite sweats are missing. Not just my sweats, but also one of my outfits for work. I go back to the hamper to make sure I hadn't left something out. I understood a sock being missing, but then it occurred to me—6A.

I dress quickly, hook the leash to Yaz's collar, and head out the door in search of my ridiculously gorgeous neighbor.

3

Lady in Red

ROBYN

I keep looking at the clock all day. My students were extra well behaved after they'd seen my one-on-one with Principal Lukas. There is nothing worse than the pity of thirty-five ten-year-olds.

When the bell finally rings, I grip the sides of my desk. I made it through another day. Why is it getting harder to just *make it through the day?*

I shove my things in my purse, and get ready to leave.

"Hey," Lily says, knocking on my door.

I take a deep breath and turn to my best friend. Unlike Lily, I don't look as polished as I had in the morning. Not that *polished* was a word I'd use to describe myself today. Lily's white blouse fits her slim frame, and her high-waist plaid pencil skirt gives her the look of an extra on *Mad Men.*

My hair has come undone, and my dress had acquired a collection of stains. If I weren't in an elementary school, they would be questionable.

"Is there *glue* in your hair?" Lily asks, reaching for a clump on my head.

I duck. "Is it doing a *There's Something About Mary?*"

Lily shakes her head. "I think you're more in *Ghostbusters* slime territory. Know what? I'm going to leave it before I give you a giant bald patch."

I laugh. It feels good to laugh like this, and the thought almost makes me want to cry. I hoist my overstuffed bag onto my shoulder. It makes me lean to the left with its weight. I wish my insurance covered a chiropractor. Otherwise I'll look like a question mark before I hit thirty.

Lily and I walk out of school.

"You missed lunch," Lily says. "Want to get a bite?"

"I can't," I say. "I have to catch up on the lessons for tomorrow. What about tomorrow after work?"

Lily's face falls for a moment. Then, she gets that disappointed look I can't bear. "Tomorrow after work I have my next dress fitting, which you're supposed to go to."

I shut my eyes. We reach Lily's car. I grab Lily's hands and squeeze. "Right. I'm the worst maid of honor. I'm Made of Dishonor. I'll do better, I swear."

"You should write terrible puns for a living," she says.

"I switched my creative writing major for a reason."

We get in Lily's car. For a moment, I consider telling Lily not to drive me home. It's not far, but it's the least bit of time we get to spend together as our lives go in opposite directions. To get up and walk home would solidify that distance, and even if Lily's life is going to change forever in three weeks, we still have today.

"Okay," Lily says, pulling out of the parking lot and turning right. "Fill the bowl. What did Lukas say to you?"

"Why didn't you mention the new principal was a Tom Ford ad? I mean, he's a little odd. I can't put my finger on it."

"Are you serious? Haven't you heard all the other teachers talking about him? They're like cats in heat."

I roll my eyes. "Okay, but you're the only person I talk to."

"We have to do something about that. You can't alienate everyone in school."

"Fine, at your bachelorette tea party, I'll be extra chatty and make new friends."

Lily smiles and turns a corner. "I thought you'd met Lukas before. He was at my engagement party. Are you really that out of it?"

"You know, it's funny. He actually reminded me that we met there last year. Is that weird? That was the first thing he said to me. I didn't remember him at all. But some guy did give me his number and I'm, like, fifty percent sure it was him."

"That night was made of champagne," Lily says. "I have a vague memory of him popping in. I thought he had a girlfriend then, though."

"Then that makes it a triple-shot latte of awkward."

"Did he say that?"

"No. Honestly, it probably wasn't him. He did ask me to cover the bake sale on Sunday."

Lily's quiet for a long time, though I've known her so long I can feel her mental mechanisms working. "Are you sure you're okay? Anything I can help with?"

"I told you, I'm fine. I'm more scatterbrained than usual. I'm having a hard time sleeping. I start counting the hours. If I go to sleep now I'll get seven hours. If I go to sleep now I'll get five, and then two, and all of a sudden I'm late for work and Lukas is signing me up for the bake sale."

"So, it's Lukas now?"

I sink into the plush leather seat. The car was a wedding gift from Lily's parents since David's parents wanted to pay for the wedding. "I *had* to sign up. You know I can't say no to work things right now. Plus, it's hours before your brunch, so don't worry. I just plan on not sleeping all weekend. And he told me to call him Lukas this morning because he knows we all call him Platypus!"

"Oh my god, Robyn," Lily says. "Platypus likes you. You're going to be Mrs. Platypus. I'll ask Dave to ask about you."

"Do not! I swear. He's my *boss*. He was just being nice. And, you just said he had a girlfriend."

"Had. A year ago." She makes a sharp turn and blows a red light. There's a small thread of the playful, wild Lily Shang I grew up with. "Besides, men are never just being nice. Before you say no, let me just say it's about time you get back on the dating horse. Or get on the Platypus until you find a horse. Dave mentioned he's looking to settle down."

"You're the actual worst." For a moment, my thoughts go back to my neighbor. The sculpted muscles on his broad shoulders. The absolute trouble that sparkled in his blue eyes. And his neck . . .

I miss some of what Lily says next. ". . . I understand that. Just be there. Please?"

"Of course, I'll be there," I assure her. I have until the weekend to get myself together.

Lily's kind enough to not mention that I have been late to every wedding-related event since David proposed. It was almost like my messy streak had started the day Lily put the Tiffany's princess-cut diamond on her engagement finger.

No, that's just a coincidence. I'm really happy for Lily. I am.

The remaining five-minute drive to my apartment consists of us singing along to Beyoncé's latest single. Lily drives and I stew in my guilt and try to pick glue out of my hair.

"Do you want me to pick you up tomorrow?" Lily asks.

I lean over and plant a sticky kiss on my best friend's cheek. "I bet I'll be there before you."

"Twenty bucks?"

"Deal."

Before I can open the car door and step onto the curb, Lily whistles at something she sees. Someone.

"Damn," Lily says.

Confused, I follow the object of Lily's gaze. At the front of my building is a familiar face. More like a familiar body. My skin flashes hot, not just because of our exchange this morning, and not because his sweatpants seem to hug his posterior in the most flattering way, but because his clothes are still on my kitchen floor.

"That's my neighbor," I say, and quickly run down what happened. I'm still holding the car door open. My neighbor is busy curbing the cutest husky I've ever seen, and completely unaware of two elementary school teachers checking out his ass.

"Dude. *That's* the guy from this morning?" Lily slaps my arm.

"Ouch!"

"You need to take one for the team. The team being me because I'm a reformed slut and going to be someone's proper wife."

"Reformed," I say, using air quotes.

Lily barks out laughing, and for a moment, things are like they've always been.

"I'm serious," Lily says. "Damn. He probably has a huge—oh my god, he's looking over here. Oh my god, he's coming over here."

"Drive!" I shut the door and lock it.

"I'm not going to drive," Lily shouts. "You're already home. Go talk to him."

Lily unlocks the door from her side, and starts to push me out of the passenger seat. The two of us wrestle all the while 5A and his husky stare.

"Robyn, I'm serious!" Lily says. "Go. Be a person. Who knows? Maybe instead of being Mrs. Platypus you'll be Mrs. Husky."

"I hate you right now." I huff and try to compose myself as I get out of the car and act as if I wasn't just practically slap boxing with my friend. I slam the door harder than I intended. I turn around once to give Lily a very stern glare, but Lily just smiles devilishly and peels off at the green light.

"Hey," he says. His husky pup runs circles around me so that I'm tangled around the ankles and have to reach out and grab on to his shoulder to keep my balance.

His hand reaches for my waist and grabs hold firmly, and I'm forced to look up at him, at those sky-blue eyes. In the early-evening sun, I can see there's a bit of green I hadn't noticed before.

"Sorry," he says, kneeling down to unravel the dog leash from around my ankles while keeping a hold on the ultra-excited puppy. "She's got a lot of energy."

I fight the urgent need to run from him, even though he's being perfectly polite. There's just something about him that sets my senses on edge. His hands brush my ankles, and I'm keenly aware of how close he is to the lower half of my body. His touch is soft and gentle. I feel like I've fallen into the Victorian era, and I'm letting a man I don't know graze my skin, and the feathery way he touches me has my heart racing.

He looks up and smiles at me with those deliciously full lips. "Cold?"

"Yeah, I left my sweater at school," I say.

When he stands up he's inches from me. It's like he knows just how to move, just how to look at me to make me nervous. I'm not short on confidence, but the feeling this stranger instills in me is new. It's the way a predator looks at his prey. It's like he's undressing me with his eyes and I'm letting him, reveling in it. No one has ever looked at me the way this man looks at me.

I haven't decided if I like it just yet, but I'm not ready for it to stop.

"I'm glad I bumped into you," he says. He's all smiles. He knows what he's doing to me and he loves it.

"You are?" I try to contain the nervous swirl at the base of my stomach.

"Yeah, I was looking for you. Is there any chance that my clothes might've gotten mixed up with yours?"

I feel a tug-of-war between the truth and a simple white lie. Little lies aren't so bad, are they? *Your baby is so cute! That shade of blond looks totally natural. Your novel is so Vonnegutesque!* Sometimes they're necessary to save people's feelings. Sometimes they're self-preservation.

But this has the potential to get more complicated. I resign myself to the truth. I come clean in a long, run-on sentence that probably makes me look like the Psycho-est Psycho in Psycho Town.

Then I ask, "Do you want to come upstairs?"

FALLON

To be honest, I wasn't really paying attention to my neighbor's frantic explanation about my clothes. Something about life being weird and coffee. I was too busy being mesmerized by the way her lips moved. She has the most full, luscious lips I've ever seen, and while she was still talking, all I could do was try to keep Yaz from leaping out of my hands, and me from leaping onto her face.

The thing that broke me out of this trance was her final question. "Do you want to come upstairs?"

"What?" I ask, dumbfounded.

"And get your stuff. Do you want to come upstairs and get your things?"

In the split second between her questions I've already fabricated a hundred different scenarios of what we could do upstairs. Laundry wasn't really one of them, though we could always get creative.

I've been infatuated a thousand times over. I love women, more than sleep and money and performing. Though all of those things go hand in hand with my work. But this girl. This woman. I don't even know her name. Her frantic, electric aura gives me a spark I haven't felt in so long. It takes me a minute to recognize it for what it is—raw attraction. I want her the way a drowning man wants to breathe. And I'm not sure I want to feel this way. She already turned me down twice in the same morning, and I'm getting too old to play games.

Still, I follow her into our building.

"Here, let me carry that," I say, taking her overstuffed bag.

She gives me an off look. It lasts for a moment, but I saw the mistrust there. I understand that she'd be wary about me. I know what I look like, and what people—especially women—think when they see me. Player. Man whore. Slut. Sex in a blanket. Sex on the beach. Sex on 6A's leather couch . . .

Get back on track, Fallon, I think to myself.

"So, do you always get into slap fights before you get out of cars?" I ask as we climb the steps. The super just mopped the floors and there's the strong smell of lemon cleaner on the stone tiles.

"That's just my best friend, Lily, being Lily." She laughs nervously, and flips her hair over her shoulder. If I were standing two steps up, she could've gotten me right in the eye and I would've liked it because I'd be closer to smelling her.

That's not creepy at all, dude, I think.

Yaz's tiny barks echo in the hall. I like to imagine that she's saying something like, "Are we there yet?!"

"How long have you lived here?" I want to keep her engaged. I want to keep her answering my questions because she's an enigma I want to unravel.

"About four years," she says, taking her keys out from her tiny purse slung across her body. I've always been fascinated by how many bags women carry. I'm holding her heavy purse that's brimming with papers and pencils and books. From where I stand I can see the red mark on her shoulder that the bag left, and I want nothing more than to reach out and massage it. Then, she has the tiny purse where she probably keeps the things she needs to reach right away—her keys, her ID, her lip gloss, and her birth control (I hope). I'd found out the rough way when I went into my little sister's purse for gum and fished out the rectangular strip of pills. I ate Monday, thinking it was a mint. They should teach these things in school.

She opens the door of her apartment, and I linger because she hasn't told me to come in yet. But I want to more than anything.

"Have a seat," she says, pointing to her black leather couch, then looks at Yaz. "Is he housebroken?"

Yaz barks in response as I set her down but keep her leash on. "Yaz is a girl."

"Is that short for Yazmine?"

I laugh harder than I want to. Yaz takes off with a run toward the couch, pulling me along. "Yastrzemski. He was my granddad's favorite Red Sox player."

"Oh, yeah," she says in this cute, sarcastic way. "I *love* sportsball."

She shakes her head and stands there. Her hair is coming undone from its ponytail and her warm whiskey-tan skin is flushed. I'm not sure about what to do with my hands, other than rein Yaz in. I want to reach for her, this lovely, fine woman. I want to see if her hair is as thick and soft as it looks. Feel her skin, starting from her delicate ankles again. I'm possessed and it scares the shit out of me.

"I'll get your clothes," she says. "I'm really sorry, again."

"It's fine. Just a misunderstanding."

The best misunderstanding I've ever had because it brought me here. I try to snoop without snooping. I crane my neck toward her bedroom. The whole place has the same layout as mine, but it looks more lived-in. The floors are scuffed and weathered. There's a spot on the ceiling where the paint is chipping off. There are portraits and replicas of artworks I don't know the names of but have seen before. I walk around the round table in the living room. It's stacked with unopened mail addressed to a Robyn Flores and books and a notepad with monogrammed initials. RF. *Robyn,* I say the name in my mind. I start to pick up the notepad, but stop myself. Instead I admire the curved slant of her handwriting that lists the things she needs: milk, coffee, socks, underwear. I grin like an idiot.

I pick up Yaz and she climbs up toward my shoulders. Sometimes I'm not sure if she's full husky or part monkey. Yaz jumps back down on the table and scatters papers and envelopes everywhere.

"Yaz!" I hiss.

I start to gather everything up and come across a photo of her. In it she's with another girl who looks like a relative. They're in pretty dresses holding up champagne flutes.

"That was at my uncle's wedding last summer," she says.

I jump and set the photo on the mountain of paper. "Sorry, Yaz is still—"

"Don't worry about it. Are you sure I can't wash this?" She's handing me a plastic bag with my missing clothes. Then, that's it. It's almost my cue to leave and I don't want to. I want to spend one of those amazing days with her, where I find out everything about her life. Those kinds of days always end with a kiss, and I desperately want to kiss her.

"Oh, please," I say nonchalantly. "This stuff happens all the time."

"Girls use your clothes as coffee rags?"

"Well, not all the time. Actually, never," I say, suddenly nervous. I want to run my hands through my hair, but I have to hold on tight to my pup or she'll wreck the place.

Robyn smiles. "The strangest day of my life is now officially over."

"It doesn't have to be," I say. "Are you hungry?"

She looks unsure. How can she resist me? I'm holding a wolf pup and wearing my most revealing gym T-shirt. As we stand facing each other, I see the moment when she gives in. Her eyes soften and her posture relaxes, as if a weight has been lifted from her shoulders.

"I'm starving."

"Me too. How does pizza sound?" I feel stupid asking again, let alone on the same day. I'm so accustomed to women trying to devour me at work that I never considered the real world is not a nightclub. Maybe I'm losing my touch, not just at work but in life. *Don't go down that spiral,* I tell myself. I feel my chest constrict as I hold my breath while she answers.

"Sure," she says. "But only if we order in. I'm a mess."

"You're the most beautiful mess I've ever laid eyes on," I say, and it's too late to take it back.

"I'll be right back." She dismisses my comment with a flick of her hand and a chuckle. She excuses herself to her bedroom. I feel proud of myself that I didn't gloat about her wearing the dress I suggested. It doesn't matter, because she said yes! Actually, she said *Sure,* which was a less enthusiastic yes. But it's a start.

"Do you have a local?" I ask and pull out my phone to call.

"Oh! Get the meat lover's from Rizzo's. And mozzarella sticks. And garlic bread."

My stomach does a strange fluttering thing that could be because of Robyn or because I haven't eaten anything since my protein shake when I woke up. Whatever. For a moment, I have the girl of my dreams all to myself. Third time's the charm, and all that. I place an order on the phone and hang up. I sink into the plush couch. Her TV looks ancient, but there's a stack of worn novels on the coffee table, along with five coffee mugs. I can picture her sitting right here, reading her book and setting down her drink. She probably sets it down and forgets and goes back to the kitchen for another. I try to picture the way this girl lives day by day and I try to picture myself sitting right here beside her. *Relax, Fallon,* I think, *it's just pizza.*

Wherever these thoughts are coming from, they fucking scare me.

"Hey, I'm Robyn, by the way," she shouts from her room, after a while. "What's your name?"

"Fallon," I say and Yaz barks as something knocks over onto the floor. There's a loud thump on the door, followed by a yelp.

"Are you okay?" I call out to her.

"Can you—uh—can you come in here?"

I push open the door and find her sitting on her floor. She's a wild beauty with her hair tossed around her shoulders and her hands trying to reach the clasp on the back of her dress. I want to tell her she looks cute when she's frustrated, but I also don't want to get punched in the face.

She looks embarrassed and annoyed, but not at me. She stands with her back facing me. "I'm stuck," she says. "Can you help?"

My heart races. My heart never races, unless it's cardio day, or I've had a sex marathon. I need to be cool. *Relax, Fallon.*

So I chuckle, and I say, "I've never met a dress I can't undo."

"I'm glad I have such an expert handy," she says dryly.

I unhook the clasp at the middle of her back. The metal is a little warped, which is why it resisted so much.

"There you go," I say, keeping my hands at my sides.

She pulls her hair over her shoulder and my heart stops. Her energy is frantic, like every little thing that has gone wrong in her day feels magnified, and I sort of get that. Her eyes look down at my lips, then at my pants, then settle on my face.

"Thanks," she says, but it's a whisper. "It's been a weird day."

I tell myself to step away. This is a dream. This is my wildest fantasy. But my feet feel like lead. My head spins. I'm frozen in place. This has to be a dream, because this perfect girl stands on her tippy toes and kisses me first.

4

What a Girl Wants

ROBYN

I feel drunk.

Not alcohol drunk. Drunk on something else. His scent. His eyes. The way his body fills the space of my bedroom. The way he's appeared since this morning in a way that makes me want to believe in signs. It's the way his lips fit perfectly against mine, savoring me, biting me until I have to press my hands on his chest and gasp.

I've never done this before. I've never kissed a stranger this way, like I need him. I've never been so discombobulated that I grasp for the closest lifeline I find. Part of me knows this impulse is wrong. But the rest of my life is out of order, so why not at least enjoy some of it?

Fallon.

His name is Fallon and all I know is that he's a fantastic kisser. No, I know other things. He loves dogs and he's a night owl and he's from Boston. I know he looks at me like he could eat me alive. It's that look that did it. It gave me a spark I haven't felt in so long. He picks me up and sets me on top of my dresser, and I wrap my legs around his waist to keep him pressed right against me. His sweatpants do little to conceal his erection pressing against my thigh. He groans against my mouth as I let my fingers wander toward the elastic band.

He pulls back for a second, pushes my hair away from my face, and looks at me with more questions than I can answer. What is this? How did we get here? Why does it feel right? But we don't speak. He holds my chin and leads my lips back to his, pressing them so gently I think this is what it might be like to kiss the sky.

The sky that then crashes around us when the bell rings and Yaz barks at the door like a hound.

"Pizza," I say.

"Pizza."

We're both in states of disarray. My hair is wild and the back of my dress is still open. Fallon's hard-on is nearly ripping through his pants.

"*I'll* get the door." I pull off my dress, no sense in being modest now.

Fallon turns to look away, a deer in headlights.

I smirk, throwing on a plain white T-shirt and shorts from my floor. "I could always let you get the door. But in your condition, the delivery boy might get the wrong idea."

With a wink, I leave him standing in my bedroom.

FALLON

The Bluest Balls, a novel by Zac Fallon.

Sure, that's not how the original book goes, but I might write my own. I'll dedicate it to Robyn. Robyn Flores. God, even her name drives me nuts. I have half a mind to shove the delivery boy out the door and finish what we started.

When I woke up this morning, this is not how I thought my day would end. I figured I'd see her in a couple of days and try my best to flirt my way into having her fall in love with me.

Instead, she lured me back to her apartment and shoved her tongue down my throat.

Fine, I know that's not what happened. But I'm still a little dazed. I pick up her dress and hold it up to my face. I breathe in the scent of her sweat and coffee and flowers, and . . . is that glue?

When I hear her shut the door, I feel like a dick. I'm standing in this girl's bedroom with a (now) semi, just having had the sexiest make-out session of my life, and I let her pay for takeout. My old man would knock me upside the head. My brother would say, *Her loss.* My sister would say something about feminism. Still, I feel like a jerk.

When the door closes, my erection is gone. It is a little painful to walk, but I make it to her couch. I sink into the soft leather and watch her. In the few hours that I've known her, she looks more relaxed. I don't want to brag, but I feel like my kiss might've had something to do with it.

"Order up," she says, setting the pizza on the coffee table in front of us, then she flutters away to her kitchen. I follow her tight, round derrière. The bottom of her pajama shorts reveals a crescent of her skin. Then she's out of sight.

"Can I help?"

"Red or white?"

I'd drink poison if she were serving it. "Red."

She walks back with two blue wineglasses and hands one to me. She sits on the opposite side of the couch and the distance feels impossible. Meanwhile, Yaz is taking a nap on a footstool.

"This is extremely weird," she says.

"Yeah, I don't normally do this kind of thing." After I say it, I realize how much of an ass I sound like.

She takes a sip of her wine, but looks amused. "That's supposed to be my line."

"I was actually talking about eating pizza," I say, trying to laugh away the tension in my balls.

"Sure, sure," she says, smiling that knee-buckling smile.

"I'm sorry I kissed you," she tells me, her voice tinged with sadness. She's saying it like an apology. Like it was unwelcome. Like I wouldn't have done it if she hadn't pounced on me first.

"That actually hurts," I say. "I'm not. I don't know anything about you except that you're kind of a liar and steal clothes from your neighbors."

"In my defense, I really have never stolen before today."

I drink. I don't know anything about good or bad wines, but I know that this is pleasantly bitter and fills my mouth with the taste of ripe fruit. I drink some more to settle my nerves.

"The way I see it," I say, "is that we can do the awkward thing, eat some pizza, and then finish what we started. But . . ."

"But what?" She smiles, revealing a dimple in her left cheek. The waterfall of her dark hair is tossed over one shoulder.

"But I really want to know more about you. Don't get me wrong. I'd hate to turn down someone when they fling themselves at me—"

She's so easy to tease. Her brows are drawn together and her voice gets loud and indignant. "I did not *fling!*"

"You physically flung your body on top of mine."

"Oh, whatever. Just for that, the flinging will stop."

I press my hand to my chest. "You just keep on hurting me, Robyn."

Robyn. I love the way her name sounds on my lips. Robyn. Robyn. Robyn.

What are you doing, Fallon? a voice in the recesses of my mind wonders. *Too fast. Too everything. Slow down.*

I open the pizza box, the cheesy, meaty steam filling my nostrils.

"What do you want to know?" she asks.

And I say, "Everything."

ROBYN

I'm going to regret this in the morning.

The morning! I still have a lesson plan to get through. Not to mention last-minute bachelorette-party planning and the dress fitting for Lily. I want to reach for my phone and text her. I want to tell her that there's a gorgeous man on my couch, and his baby husky is snoozing while we eat pizza and drink wine. She'd never believe me if I didn't include a photo. I hardly believe that he's real. I want to jump on top of him, but I already said I wouldn't be the one to start this again.

What was I thinking, kissing him like that? The answer is I wasn't thinking at all. I was following my instincts, which has never been a Robyn Flores thing to do. I wanted to *feel* something, and when he kissed me back, I felt *all* of him.

I can't remember the last time I've had people over. On one hand, the stacks of unopened mail and delivery boxes and laundry are a physical embodiment of my mind. On the other hand, I have nothing to hide. It was so easy to talk to him. Easier than it is to talk to Lily or my cousins or my parents. He's a blank slate and, in the end, I end up telling him more than I've ever told anyone in so long.

I tell him that I can't surface to save my life, my friendships, my career. That there was a moment when I stopped worrying about anything. Dates, friends, work. I stopped caring and I don't remember why or when. I was never chaotic as a teen or college student, but chaos has shown up with a vengeance, ready to shake up my perfectly tailored life. Chaos is my name, and I have no idea how to get back the nice, stable Robyn I used to be. I tell him about how weird it is that Lily is getting married. Lily, whom I was the exclusive DD for all throughout our years at Albany State, has order. A fiancé. A plan. What do I have?

I tell him all of that because maybe it's the wine. Maybe some part of me expects to never see him after tonight. But he listens to every word and, somehow, the space between us on the couch disappears and we're sitting side by side with our faces close enough to kiss.

"So you're having a quarter-life crisis and you're one of those born and bred New Yorkers," he says, summarizing my life story. "You have six thousand cousins, but no siblings. Your best friend is getting married in three weeks. You teach the fifth grade. And you're the best kisser in New York."

"I never said that," I say. We've demolished the pie and are now demolishing this second bottle of red. "Though I'm glad to represent my state in this category."

"You're my first kiss in this state," he confesses.

I don't know what to do with that information, so I shrug and smile and take another sip of wine.

"I think I hold the record for weddings attended in a year," I say, trying to change the subject.

"Do you want to get married?" he asks me. Then his face goes white with fear. "Not to me. I mean . . . fuck . . . I meant in general."

I laugh. "You're so cute. And ridiculous. If you're asking in general, then I have no idea. When I was younger, yeah. My parents have a really healthy marriage. It's weird. All of my other friends have parents who've been divorced, but mine are pretty much happy freaks. It's disturbing."

"So were mine, for a while at least," he says. His grin is easy and relaxed.

I remind myself I can't make the first move again. *Don't do it. Don't do it.*

My mind goes back to admiring his body. He isn't as shiny as he was this morning. He cleaned up well.

Hit it and quit it, the naughty receptors of my mind say.

He edges closer, his lips inches from mine. I reach out and rest my hand on his thigh, the heat of this touch instant. His sweatpants do spectacular things to his thighs. He looks like a still life from the Hot Guys & Puppies Tumblr. I admire every line on his face. The smooth line of his jaw, the wrinkle on his forehead, the laugh lines around his mouth, the tiny crinkles at the corners of his eyes. Each and every one is like a road map to his soul.

"Thanks for having dinner with me," he says, and I'm thankful he's changing the subject away from weddings. He's so good at this, so good at talking and making me comfortable. He's probably a bartender. "I was afraid I wasn't going to make any friends in the neighborhood. You know what they say about New Yorkers."

"That we've got the best sense of fashion and are amazing at everything?"

He playfully rolls his eyes. "Please. That you're all recluses who wear black clothes and ignore each other on the T."

"Excuse you. It's the *subway*," I correct him.

"Noted, again. So, this wedding. Is that what had you all hurricane-like in the morning?"

"Can we not talk about that?" I ask, closing the gap between us. Our thighs are pressing together, and he stretches his arm on the back of the couch to play with a strand of my hair.

"Okay. What do you want to talk about?" He leans back and looks at me. His stare feels as if I'm under a hot white spotlight. I feel like he's pulling apart my layers with those brilliant blue eyes.

"I—" Something clicks in my mind. "I want to talk about your choice of clothing. You've barely answered *my* questions."

"N-n-n-n-no," he says, wagging his finger in front of my face. "If we can't talk about what's going on with you, then I'm not going to tell you about that."

I take a deep breath. "Fine. Are you ready?"

"I've been ready since seven o'clock this morning."

This close to him, I have nowhere else to look but into his eyes. He twirls a strand of my hair with one finger and grazes my thigh with the other hand.

"I don't think it's the wedding. I'm happy for Lily. I just—I feel stuck, you know? I graduated at the top of every class I was in. I have two degrees. I come from a happy family. On paper, my life is immaculate. I feel ungrateful complaining about it. Lately, I'm just not sure. It's weird telling you that because I've known you for less than a day. But I've known Lily my whole life and I can't tell her the same, no matter how much I try."

"Am I allowed to interject?" he asks.

I think about it while he drinks more wine. "Yes."

"Then, let me ask you this . . . If you could give everything up. I'm talking just pick up and go somewhere right now, no consequences, where would you go?"

I take my time. I refill his wineglass and let my belly flutter with uncertainty. It's a luxury to dream like that. It's a dream to even dream.

"I don't know," I say.

"I know where I'd go."

"Vegas?" I guess. "South Beach?"

"I don't know if I should be offended or not," he says, but something flicks across his face and I think I've actually hurt him. I want to take it back, but he shrugs it off. He keeps talking. "But now I don't want to tell you because you already know me so well."

"I was kidding," I say.

"Machu Picchu."

"No way." I go to shove him, but we're so entwined on this couch that there's nowhere for him to move. I just rest my hand on his chest. "I love the Andes. My parents still have some family in Ecuador and Peru, actually. But I've never been to either."

"Yes way. Why is that so hard to believe? Every year I take a big trip. I take a month off and just go. Last year I went hiking in Chile. The year before that I spent a month backpacking across Australia. Did you know everything there has evolved to kill us?"

"Not evolved enough, because you're still here."

"At least I'm not afraid of those giant cockroaches crawling all over this city."

"You best respect this city while you're around me."

He bites his bottom lip and smiles at me. "Before that I went all around Thailand. I almost didn't come back because the beaches were actually heaven. I'm talking the most perfect blue you've ever seen."

I think I've already seen the perfect blue, and it's in the outer ring of his eyes. "You mean to tell me that you just take off for months at a time and your work just lets you? What do you do? Can I get in on that?"

He looks startled for a second. I can practically feel the wheels in his mind spinning. "You're a schoolteacher. You have the most vacation days of anyone who isn't a billionaire. Come with me next time."

"Okay, but without the billionaire salary," I correct. For the first time in a long time, I am at ease. How can I feel that way with a man I don't truly know? How can I let myself dream more in these moments with him than I have in years?

The feeling is short-lived. Out of nowhere, the reminders of everything I'm supposed to do flood my thoughts. I need to finish my lesson plan. I need to prove to Lily that she can still depend on me. I need to prove to myself that I'm still the same girl I used to be.

"It's getting late," I say, and it is physically painful to ask him to leave. "I have to finish work for tomorrow."

He nods an understanding. But his hand still rests on my thigh and our legs are tangled, feet resting on the coffee table. Neither of us makes the first move to get up. "Well, I already know you're busy this whole weekend. What about next weekend?"

"My calendar is free after the wedding. That's what my work thing is this weekend. It's the bachelorette party."

He laughs a little too hard. It even wakes up Yaz. "What's the plan for the party? Did you get her a lit-up crown and penis-shaped straws?"

It's my turn to laugh. "No. And definitely nothing gross and trashy like a bunch of male strippers or whatever you think bachelorette parties are like. I've been to five of them this year and I'm positive this one is going to be the tamest. Tea party and all."

I feel a shift in Fallon's body almost instantly. The most noticeable change is his smile. It's strained, almost like it hurts to keep it up. He looks at the door, like he's calculating how quickly he can get out. What did I say to upset him? I replay my words and can't think of it.

Fallon grabs me around the waist and lifts me off him. He picks up Yaz in his arms and stands.

"Thanks again for dinner," Fallon says, edging toward the door. Moments ago he couldn't seem to stay away from me, and now he's taking several steps back. He grabs the bag of coffee-soaked clothes, and reaches for the door.

"No problem?" I walk him out.

"I'm actually late for the gym." He touches my shoulder. It's different from all his other touches today. It's like he's trying to push me away. "I have to meet a friend."

I'm so confused. My eyes narrow, asking so many questions all at once. What happened and when did it happen?

"Bye, Robyn." He frowns, but leans down to press a kiss on my cheek, something sad in his eyes. Then he's gone, racing down the steps, putting as much distance between us as quickly as his legs will allow.

5

I Knew You Were Trouble When You Walked In

FALLON

"Gross and trashy." I bench-press 300 pounds.

My spotter, Aiden Rios, doesn't look impressed. Aiden joined Mayhem City when we were in South Beach. Aiden, Colombian-born and New York–raised, can twerk up a hurricane of dollar bills onstage. Though I've known Aiden the least amount of time, we're closer than the other guys in the crew. Aiden's twenty-four but an old soul, and easier to talk to because he isn't belligerent all the time.

I hold the barbell over my head for the full rep, my veins stretching against my skin like some Hulk shit. I'm on my third rep with no signs of slowing down. Robyn's words rattle inside my mind. They touch every part of me that feels not enough. I wasn't enough for my father. I wasn't enough for every teacher who told me I was a waste of time. I wasn't enough for Valeria, and maybe I'm not enough for Robyn, either.

"Oh, *come* on," Aiden says, holding his hands at the ready. "Don't be so dramatic, brother. She doesn't know what you do. She probably didn't mean it that way."

"How"—I grunt each word to the rhythm of the barbell— "Many. Ways. Can. You. Mean. That?"

On the last word my arms strain, and Aiden catches the barbell and hoists it back into place. I'm drenched in sweat and breathing hard. My little display has every man and woman in the weight room looking at us. A girl mid-squat straightens back up to flutter a wink at me. Two juiceheads switch their 50s for 100s and continue doing curls. It's a chorus of grunts and sweaty curses.

I let the pain in my arms wash over me. I'm stupid for pushing myself too hard. I'm going to be sore as hell the next couple of days. Still, this was the safest way I know to blow off steam. I sit up too quickly and regret the head rush that forces me to close my eyes. I feel the hard smack of Aiden's hand on my sweaty back.

"You need therapy, bro," Aiden says.

"I need to make better choices."

"Bad choices are the only way to live and learn, man. Remember what happened last time?"

I'm going to ignore the jab about *last time*. I know exactly what happened last time. But the rest, I'll acknowledge. "Is that from your daily wisdom app?"

Aiden slaps a towel on my ass. I hurt too much to do anything about it. I'm straddling a weird set of emotions. Instead of dealing with it, I decide to ignore it as best I can. I swap places with Aiden.

"Take two of those plates off," Aiden says, lying back on the bench. "I'm not trying to pop a vein like you, Winter Soldier."

"Nerd," I say, standing right behind his head. "Besides, I'm more Captain America."

"And *I'm* the nerd." Aiden wraps his hands around the metal bar and lifts. "Why do you care about what this girl thinks of you? You've known her for a day. A *literal* day. You haven't even tapped that. Forget her."

Aiden does five reps without stopping.

"Breathe," I remind him. "You're going to pass out."

"Thanks, Mom."

"Fuck you, bro." I grin. "And I know I've only known her for a day. She just got under my skin is all." Plus, she's the best kiss I've ever had. I usually share that with him, but with Robyn? I want to keep that to myself. Anyway, I don't need him ragging on me later.

"You got a picture or should I be using my imagination?"

"Sorry, I forgot to stop for a fucking selfie during dinner," I say.

"What's her name?"

"Robyn Flores."

"Is she my people?"

"I didn't ask for her DNA chart, either. But she said some of her family is from Ecuador."

"Paisa, son. Okay. Can I say something without you punching me in the throat?" Aiden laughs, does another couple of reps, and we swap places again.

"No promises."

"You should forget about her."

I grunt a response and resume my bench press. I'm not close enough to being tired. The more I think about her, the more my blood rushes through my body, until I have to stop my muscles from shaking.

Gross trashy stripper, I say in my mind.

"Listen, man," Aiden says, standing over me. "You're overthinking this."

"You *under*think things."

"Maybe, but at least I'm happy. You know who you are and what you do. She doesn't. My friend Clara was dating this guy and when he found out she was a stripper, he dropped her just like that. Clara's a nice girl and didn't deserve that, but she couldn't make him get it. Being a stripper doesn't come with respectability. It's easier when you're a guy, but still. Whether we like it or not, we're a joke. At least we're jokes who can pay off our credit-card bills."

"I don't want to be a joke anymore." I do five reps before my arms tremble and Aiden intervenes. We slam the barbell onto its metal post. I can feel my heart beating at the base of my throat.

"Do us all a favor, don't chase after her," Aiden says. "Don't waste your time, amigo. Remember your last girl?"

I let out a booming laugh. The gym's thinning out. It's a twenty-four-hour spot, which is perfect for our schedules.

"I have never felt as old as I did when I dated Valeria," I say. "Serves me right for thinking I should date a twenty-year-old."

"Hey!" Aiden says indignantly. It's no secret that Aiden's clientele are of the cougar variety. Aiden doesn't mind as long as they have deep pockets. "Sometimes older people need company."

"You do you," I say. "I just can't believe it took me so long to see."

"Maybe you just have bad taste in women. You have a type. The type that drags you through the mud and sets your heart on fire. Find a regular chick who needs love. She'll appreciate you more."

"You're not fucking helping." But I think back to the girl he's referring to. Valeria was a twenty-one-year-old waitress from Hollywood Beach in Florida. I met her after one of our shows. She was in the VIP section of some club that was pitch black except for the neon lights that cut through the air. She danced like her soul was on fire, and her dark hair and darker skin stood out among the orange tans and sun-bleached blondes trying to get my attention. She smiled at me and it was over. I took her back to my apartment and she didn't leave for a week. I was in love. Or I thought I was.

I didn't care when she asked for money to get her nails done, her hair done, her coffee. I was happy to buy her things. I was happy to make *her* happy. I didn't mind that she texted while I paid for dinner. I didn't mind that every now and then she'd vanish for a day or two without saying a word. Everyone needed their space, right? I thought I'd hit the lottery. A girl who was smoking hot and wasn't clingy? I was ready to sign on the dotted line.

Slowly, she'd come back. She needed a hundred bucks for something. She needed new shoes. She couldn't make her rent.

It was Aiden who'd made the joke first. "Where's your Sugar Baby?"

The other guys laughed at me. I really hadn't seen it. And then I stopped opening up my wallet and she got sad, then angry, then she pulled another disappearing act. When she reappeared, she was on the arm of a club owner twice *my* age.

Maybe I did have bad taste in women. There's a reason I'm

thirty and single, and I didn't want to believe it was my career choice. I always chose the wrong girl. Robyn will just be another girl in the long list of failed attempts at relationships. One friendly casual dinner didn't count as a relationship. One amazing kiss didn't mean anything. . . . As much as I want to deny it, Aiden is right. I *don't* know her. I don't have to pursue her. I have a type—beautiful and destructive.

I feel my arms shaking as I struggle to complete my final rep. That does it. I'm spent.

"Feel better?" Aiden asks, his white teeth bright against his brown skin.

I wrap my towel around my neck. "No."

"I know just the thing," Aiden says. "Come on. Let's get fucked up."

ROBYN

I check my phone for the third time in ten minutes. It reads 9:15 p.m. My dress, a lacy black number I got on sale a year ago, feels tight around the middle. I tell myself to pace myself on the drinks and appetizers. Every few minutes, waiters bring out new dishes of tiny meatballs, empanadas, and everything-on-a-stick. I didn't believe there was a way to make pigs in a blanket into a classy food, but somehow, Lily's future sister-in-law, Sophia, figured it out.

The bachelorette party is a moderate affair that started with an afternoon tea and has proceeded to cocktail hour. There's plenty of champagne being passed around the massive Park Slope brownstone. The guests are equally divided between Lily and my coworkers from school, classmates and friends, Lily's family, and David's family. I watch the pockets of social circles mingle from a designated wall. Being a wallflower is familiar and comforting, but not the thing that's expected from the maid of honor. I pick up a fried shrimp on a toothpick and another glass of champagne from the cute waiters who shove their trays in my face. Sophia did not spare any expense.

Part of me is glad that, ultimately, the party planning wasn't my responsibility. I'm the official maid of honor, but Sophia put herself in charge of the parties. Sophia is good at parties and she has time. Another part of me knows that I let Lily down once again, even if Lily won't admit to it. Not to my face.

The week that wouldn't end is still going. It's Saturday night and I'm not supposed to be drinking. Tomorrow's the bake sale I've "volunteered" for. Three nights ago, I'd shared the most dizzying and passionate kiss of my life. It was followed by a casual dinner with the most interesting, strange, and exciting man I'd ever met. I haven't heard from him since his sudden departure. Who goes to the gym after eating half a pie and drinking a bottle of wine?

Since then, I started lingering in the stairwell of our building. I rattled my key chain, as if he'd hear me and come out just to say hi. I even made sure I was in front of the building in the late afternoon when I'd last seen him take Yaz for a walk at that time. And yet, no sign of him.

Fallon ghosted me. Only it's worse because I don't have digital records of flirty messages. I have the fading memory of his sly smile, his dreamy blue eyes, and that spark that made my heart ache.

I don't want to think of him. He was not mine to start with. I tell myself I don't even have time to date, anyway. I tell myself that this is probably for the best because why go down that path when I don't know where my life is headed? He wants to travel the world, and I have to balance my checkbook. Still, it would be nice to know what I'd said to make him run away from me. Because he *did* run away.

I don't even know his full name. Is Fallon his first or last name? Is it a nickname?

"Having fun?" Lily asks. Her cheeks were flushed pink like the glass of champagne in her hand.

"Definitely!" I lie.

"You're checking your phone a lot. Still no word from him, huh?"

I put on my best smile. "Oh, I'm not worried about that. I just have to make sure I get enough sleep for tomorrow."

STRIPPED   55

STRIPPED   55

"Do you think everyone is having a good time?" Lily looks around the room with big, round eyes.

Every bride and groom this past year asked the exact same question. I realized that weddings are not for the bride and groom but for the people attending. Get a nice dress, show up and drink wine, dance a little. It's a reprieve from the banality of life.

I'm sick of it, and I hate that I'm sick of it. Lily's wedding was the one that was supposed to count the most, and here I am, pining over a cute guy and wishing I could get more than four hours of sleep a night.

Sleep, my most evasive lover.

"Sophia did a terrific job," I tell Lily.

Another thing I've learned from the number of weddings I've attended is that there is never enough reassurance that can be dished out. I could be dishonest about my own state of being. That didn't matter. What mattered was that Lily did not worry about a single thing.

"Sophia is a doll," Lily says. "I'm so happy with how this turned out. You're okay with it, aren't you?"

I bat my hands in the air. "Of course! I told you, don't worry about that. It totally worked out."

"It's just that Sophia has more time on her hands since her kids are off to college now."

As if hearing her name from the next room, Sophia turns a corner, and rushes to where we're standing. "There you are! Our cousin Liz from Florida just got here. She can't wait to meet you. She's putting her coat away in the guest room. Go say hi!"

Lily smooths out her skirt. As an only child, Lily is still getting used to being surrounded by so much extended family. *Her* family now. It puts a smile on her face and I'm happy for that. I take Lily's empty glass and wave to one of her friends.

Sophia, David's older sister, takes a long sip of her wine. "So, what do you think, Robyn?"

It's harder for me to fake a smile this time around. When I was little my father told me that smiles make people happy, and so I smiled at everyone. Too late did I realize that making people happy wasn't my job. Still, it's Lily's big day—big few weeks, really.

"I think it's a *great* party," I tell her, though I realize how fake I sound. "I can't believe it's only two weeks away."

Sophia puts her hand to her chest. Her eyes are done dramatically and her freshly manicured nails gleam in the light. "It's my pleasure. David's my baby brother and we know that Lily makes him happy. Besides, he's the youngest. It's been forever since we've had a party. *Wait* till you see the big surprise."

I sip my drink to stop myself from saying, "*Lily doesn't like surprises.*"

"It's almost time!" Sophia huddles closer to me. She checks the watch on her slender wrist and barely stops herself from squealing.

"Time for what?" So many of the women at the party are suddenly checking their phones. One of the waiters pulls a chair up to the center of the room. Women hold back giggles behind their champagne flutes. I look around the living room for Lily, but can't find her. At that moment, I realize that I'm not in on the surprise.

There's a heavy knock on the door downstairs.

Sophia turns to all of them and puts her finger to her lips. "Shhh!"

One of Lily's friends from grad school, Mindy Something, hands out eye masks covered in feathers and glitter. They remind me a little of Mardi Gras.

"Hurry," Mindy says, shoving the mask into my free hand. "Put this on. They're here."

"Who's here? What's going on?"

Mindy smiles from ear to ear. "Didn't Sophia send you the e-mail? We've been planning this all week."

"Right," I say, trying to save face.

Lily comes down the stairs, led by a woman with giant hair and tan skin. Cousin Liz. Cousin Liz wears a gold sequin dress better suited for a downtown nightclub. She pulls Lily by the hand and sits her down on the chair in the middle of the room. Everyone is wearing their masks and I quickly put mine on.

The energy has changed in seconds. It's as if everyone has been keeping this secret all night and now it's out in the open.

"Wait," Lily says nervously. She turns to me, clutching the sides of her chair. "You didn't!"

I shake my head, unable to stop what's about to happen. Her next word is caught in her throat as Sophia reappears at the doorway. I can see the four giant men standing behind her. It's like a Britney Spears video gone wrong. They're all dressed in SWAT uniforms and giant aviator sunglasses.

I grab another glass of champagne from the bar set up against the wall. I watch as Sophia steps aside and lets the men through. I can't watch this. Lily's face is a cross between terror and humiliation. Not only does Lily not like to be the center of attention, but she also doesn't like to be touched by complete strangers. I *told* Sophia that.

"Surprise!" Sophia tells me. She grabs my arm, like we're long-time friends.

I let my polite smile drop. I lean into Sophia's ear. "I told you—"

"I know, I know." Sophia rolls her eyes. "But we just thought—"

"No," I say. "Lily doesn't like people touching her."

"Well, that's not going to help things on their wedding night." Sophia looks affronted. She doesn't want to hear what I have to say and she turns away toward the show, and joins the other girls in hollering as the sexy SWAT officers walk in. I am overwhelmed with the need to slap her, but I have to behave.

The quartet of male strippers moves in slowly. There's something predatory about them. In the dim light, I think they all look the same. The glasses cover most of their face and their black caps are tipped low.

"Lily Shang," the leader says. His voice is deep and silky. I'm almost afraid to look at Lily, but I have to. "We hear you've been a *very* bad girl."

The music starts, a deep treble that ripples across the room.

All four men move the same way. They drop to the floor and undulate their bodies, then jump back up in formation. The tallest and most muscular one stands before Lily. His body moves with the music, and as if sensing how tense she is, keeps a careful distance. Instead, he dances around her, then bends over and rips his shirt off in one fell swoop. All the girls in the room lift their drinks in the air and shout, except for me.

All I can do is stare as I push off the wall and take slow steps toward the crowd.

Not at Lily or at Sophia or at the dozens of women howling like wolves. I stare at the man dancing for Lily. He throws his hat across the room, but leaves his sunglasses on. He runs a hand over his chest, the thrilled screams that cut through the music urging him to reach to his crotch. He pulls off his pants and they fly across the room right at my feet. The other men follow suit, and three more chairs appear beside Lily. The men prowl around the room for three more ladies. Hands go up, begging to be chosen.

When he turns around, we're face-to-face, and I have no doubt it's him. *Fallon.*

I recognize him before he recognizes me. How could he, when my face is hidden under this feather mask?

As his attention is focused on me, I feel frozen in place. I dreamed about him the other night. I spent all day fantasizing about seeing him again, bumping into him in the hall, seeing his number pop up on my phone.

A chorus of whistles and hollers goes up all around me. I wonder how long before the actual cops arrive. He takes off his sunglasses and throws them off to the side. He has no idea, and part of me is thrilled. For the next moment, I can be just any girl. I can have his undivided attention.

He points at me.

He grabs my hand.

He chooses me.

He gives me that smile that's like a slam to my gut. Damn that beautiful smile.

I take off my mask and watch his features constrict in the shadows. His smile falters and he withdraws his hand. He looks away from me, like he's never seen me before, like he didn't have his lips on mine three days ago.

He chooses Mindy instead.

As the bachelorette party gets into full swing, I turn around and do the thing I've been good at doing lately.

I run.

6

Tell Me Tell Me Lies

FALLON

I've danced through worse.

There was the time a customer's dress caught on fire. The bachelorettes had wanted to set the mood and, in a flurry of overexcited movement, she knocked over the candle and it went up in flames. Quick thinking on Ricky's part had the flames out in no time, and the rest of us soaking wet as if it had been part of an elaborate plan all along.

There was another time I sprained my ankle trying to pick up a girl and stepped wrong when my fingers hit a ticklish spot on her thighs.

The time with the black eye from a jealous fiancé who did not like how his woman screamed when she dry-humped Aiden, and the time someone's seventy-year-old mother walked in, and the time a customer sent us as a joke to his best friend's corporate banking office.

Public humiliation has never bothered me. That's the great thing about being shameless. I literally give no fucks about what people think of me. I thought I did.

When I catch sight of Robyn at the corner of my eye, leaving as if her life depends on it, something dark and regretful crawls under my skin and nestles there. A sick, twisted part of me wants to call out and turn the spotlight on her. Make everyone watch her the way they watch me. I suppose she doesn't want all of her swanky friends to know she has anything to do with a guy like me. *Trashy. Trashy. Trashy.*

"Fal," my buddy says beside me, nudging my elbow.

I miss a step and wait for the next beat to rejoin the routine. Only the boys notice. The women snapping open their tiny glittery purses don't give a fuck that I missed a step. That my whole vibe is killed. That my mind is trailing the ghost of a girl who just ran away from me. I grab the collar of my white shirt and rip it in half like a sheet of paper.

High-pitched, thrilled screams fill the room. Most of the waiters in the room stare at the tiny food on their serving platters. But one asshole is snapping pictures on his phone. I'll get him later.

Right now, the song changes. A slow R&B favorite with a hard bass and harder treble. In this routine, four girls get handcuffed. I can't help but think of what Robyn would've done if she'd stayed, if she let me pick her instead of this girl. This girl, she's pretty with brown eyes and a face turned fire-engine red as I take her hands and trace them from my pecs down my abs. She tries to ball her hand into a fist, but I keep it pressed to my skin as she lets out a cute squeal. Her legs bounce with excitement.

Ricky gives the cue when he takes off his sunglasses. Handcuff time.

I reach into my waistband for red furry handcuffs. I get down on my knees and hold one open.

"Can I?" I whisper in her ear. Because her voice is caught in her throat, she nods three times rapidly.

With the red handcuffs around her wrists, she stops squealing and sits back in her chair. There's always the moment when the embarrassed thrill goes away and is replaced by sheer pleasure.

And in the end, that's the whole point of this. To make them feel *good.* So good, they let go of their inhibitions, the stress that strangles their shoulders, the insecurity and uncertainty that's so easy to cling to.

Here, we freestyle. Each one of us taking our girls around different parts of the room. Jimmy likes to press them against the wall. Ricky likes to pick them up and flip them around, which is why his back is so shot to begin with. I lift my girl up. Have her straddle me. Her handcuffed hands around my neck so we're face-to-face. Then I lower her to the ground. Her fingers dig through the hair at the nape of my neck. Her body tenses with the sudden movement and she crosses her legs around my waist, afraid she'll fall.

But I never let them fall.

ROBYN

The moment I step outside, I regret it.

He saw me.

I take my jacket from the coat check in the foyer, the screams of every woman in the living room erupting when the song changes. My curiosity pricks at me, like dozens of little needles. I fight the urge to turn around and head right for the door. I'll have to explain to Lily later why I bounced early.

When I shut the door, the cold spring air whips my hair around. I throw on my jacket and head to the train, bracing myself for the long journey home. My heels are sharp clicks on the sidewalk, but I think my heart overpowers every other sound around me. The sirens in the distance, the drunken hollers from tourists and locals alike, the rumble of the train as it comes into the station, and the ding of the doors when they close. My heart is so much louder.

Of all the bachelorette parties in all the world, Fallon had to be a stripper at mine. Well, my best friend's.

I kissed him.

I wanted him.

And as I watch the sky darken over New York from the middle of the bridge, I realize—I insulted him.

I hit my head on the wall behind me so hard, other people on the car turn to look at me. Can they see my shame? Because I should be ashamed. I'm a terrible person. Not because I kissed a stripper, but because of what I said to him. *Trashy stripper.*

The look on his face. The way his mood did a 180 and he left my apartment like I'd spit in his drink. That's why he left. Because of my big, stupid, judgmental mouth.

I make a noise of disgust, scaring the passengers around me. I see myself reflected in the window in front of me. Long black hair parted at the center. Despite having gone to Sephora to do my makeup, my dark circles refuse to go away and are accentuated in the unflattering yellow light of the subway. The black dress that hugs my every curve is wrinkled and the AC makes me shiver. I left my sweater at Sophia's and I'm tempted to leave it there because I never want to go back.

I get off at the 30th Avenue station and walk down the deadly crooked steps that lead to the street. Crispy halal meat and the faint scent of beer greet me at the corner. I stop by a vendor and get a steak shish kebab, then hit up my next stop. Stress eating seems like the only thing I've got going for me, so that's what I'm going to do. I swing by the market and grab some oranges, then the liquor store for some Prosecco, and finally, the drugstore and get a bag of discounted Easter chocolates.

The tiny weird food Sophia catered has basically already evaporated from my body (#RobynScienceFact). I carry everything back up to my apartment for a typical Saturday night. Every step I take is heavier than the next because I don't have to close my eyes to picture Fallon. He's already at the forefront of my mind. So much so that when I pass his floor going up, I linger at his door. I can hear the tiny bark from Yaz, and that sends me running back up to my floor.

You're right under me.

Can I kiss you?

Trashy stripper.

I've got to go.

Why am I obsessing over this? I don't even know him. I can just add him to the list of ex-boyfriends who hate me after breaking up with them for various reasons, some unforgivable and some simply not my thing. Lily said that when there wasn't something wrong with someone, I wouldn't be happy until I found it, even if I made the flaw up. Let's see, I broke up with Jake for chewing with his mouth open, Henry for racist jokes when he got wasted, Kyle for wanting to have ten kids in the future, Lorenzo for trying to shove it in the wrong hole without my permission, Jared when I discovered be didn't brush his teeth, Bert for wanting me to dress up as Jabba the Hut, Marty for listening to jazz literally day and night, Nikolai for being prettier than me and because I was somehow *convinced* he was secretly a privateer, Trevor for being rude to waiters, and Chris for just being an asshole.

Fallon. Fallon was never my boyfriend, but I can't help but wonder what might've been if I hadn't made a snap judgment. Would I have kept it to myself if I had known who he was? Would I still have judged him in private?

I bite the last piece of meat with my teeth and slide it down the stick. Then I eat the bread, even though it's dry, and crumple up the foil into a tight little ball. I move on to my Prosecco. I cut the oranges in half and squeeze out the juice into a wineglass. I'm not going to pretend and use a champagne flute.

Who gets drunk by themselves on a Saturday night? This girl.

I make my giant mimosa and open the box of chocolates. I eat the ones I hate the most first, the ones filled with marzipan and cherries.

I check my phone and I have four texts from Lily, one from my mother, one from Principal Lukas. I ignore the texts and search for Fallon online. He doesn't have a Facebook or Twitter account, but I find him on Instagram because he tagged a photo at the café across the street. ZFFallon.

"Hm." I take another big gulp and move on to the second tier of chocolates, the crunchy ones that are covered in piped caramel. I'm glad it isn't something douchey like Gymguyxxx. And then I wonder, What do the Z and F stand for?

I scroll through his photos. There's one a few weeks ago of the New York skyline. The caption reads "I </3 NY. But third time's the charm." Photos of himself at the gym with others. I recognize a few of the guys from today's show. Their abs, at least. The caption reads "Workworkworkworkwork." The most recent ones are photos of Yaz on a fluffy white bed. Yaz in the park. Yaz

christening a fire hydrant. He should just make her an account of her own. The most recent photos are a stark difference from the ones farther down.

I refill my mimosa, scrolling with my thumb the whole time. Pictures of the beach. A gorgeous girl wrapped around his neck. He looks at her with reverence, and I feel a pang of jealousy. Who is she? What happened between them? It's the only one she's in. Why hasn't he deleted it? The rest are photos of South Beach. The audience of women on different nights. Snapshots of what must be the nights they have shows. Then, farther still, a different city every few months.

When I get to the end, it's a selfie of himself. He isn't as muscular as he is now, but the promise is there. His incredible blue-green eyes are sharper from some filter. His hair is longer, not as coifed and shaped and a little more blond at the top. He's young and smiling and there's a happiness in his eyes that startled me the first time we met. A spark.

I sigh, take another sip of mimosa, and go to my laundry bag. I still haven't put the clean clothes away but I rip off the pink slip attached. I find his number there and start typing. Then I delete. Then I type. Delete. Type.

How do I say, "I'm a jerk. I'm sorry"? I guess that's the simplest apology. But what if he doesn't want to hear from me?

I should take the silence over the last couple of days, since he left my apartment, as a sign that if he wanted to talk to me, he would've.

Or, I'm the one who needs to reach out because I'm the one who made the mistake. This is one of the things I'd ask Lily about. But it's her wedding time and I've already been selfish enough.

Speaking of Lily. Her texts read:
What happened to you?
Are you still here?
You missed Sophia getting a two-man lap dance.
Are you okay?
Two-man lap dance. I wonder if one of those men was Fallon.

And that right there is the snap judgment. I shake my head. There is no way I'd be able to treat him right. Not when my first reaction is to be bothered that he touches other women for a living.

I type back: *The shrimp-and-fish dip murdered me and I was not about to go in Sophia's porcelain toilet.*

I wait for Lily to respond, but I think she knows I'm lying. After a while I plug my phone in to charge and lie back on my couch. I replay every second with Fallon, each time wincing when I get to the moment he split. Why am I so shaken by him?

Then, there's a heavy pounding from downstairs and a chorus of salacious hollering. I wonder if Fallon brought a girl home. I don't move, and listen intently. Oh my god. There's tons of girls. I wonder if I know any of them.

"Let it go, Robyn," I order myself.

I refill my mimosa and take off my clothes to jump in the shower. The perks of being alone are that I don't have to feel bad about being messy. My apartment is a reflection of my life.

"It's over," I say out loud. Then realize, "Actually, it never even started."

But when I shampoo my hair, I think of Fallon. When I rinse, I think of Fallon. When I lather my skin with soap, I think of Fallon. My nipples get hard, and I turn up the cold water because I start to feel a flutter between my thighs. Fallon. His pristine blue eyes. The soft waves of his light brown hair. The way he walked into the room tonight with that shirt hugging every single muscle.

I turn off the water and slip into my favorite fluffy robe to dry. I look into the mirror. Clean and slightly flushed. With lust or embarrassment. Both, actually.

I go to my window that faces the street to pull the curtain shut. As a reflex, my hand goes to my chest, like it'll stop my heart from beating out of my skin, because it's Fallon standing at the curb, looking up at me.

I shut the curtain and slip into my sandals.

I grab my keys and polish off what's left of my mimosa on the counter, then I shut the door behind me and race down the steps.

I don't know what I'm going to say to him, but I can start by asking him to turn down his racket.

FALLON

Everyone is satisfied.

The client, the bride-to-be, the bachelorettes, the dozen friends of the bride and groom. Jimmy's in charge of collecting the money, and stuffing the tips into a blue bank deposit bag with a tiny lock on it. The bag is nearly bursting at the seams, and I remember why it was worth doing these house calls in swanky New York neighborhoods. The boys are all teeming with adrenaline, and the party is over, but the vibe is still lit and there's the scent of debauchery in the air. So it goes without saying that something has to go wrong.

I can feel it in my bones. A sixth sense for fights the way a ship's captain might sniff out a storm. Or maybe I'm the one who's looking for a fight. Something to release the anxiety and anguish locked up in my core. This anvil weighing me down. I need something to let it go.

A few of the women slow down on their way to the bathroom down the hall. They pause at the slightly ajar door and look in on us. We're getting dressed in a guest room the host provided us with. The boys stop slapping one another around and treating the place like a locker room at the sight of them.

"Hello, ladies," Greg says, and the girls break into giggles at the sound of his tenor voice.

I shake my head and pull on my shirt, trying not to notice the way one of the women stares at me. Heat radiates from her eyes, like she's trying to sear the memory of her into my brain before she keeps on walking. Any other time, I'd take more time to flirt with her. But my mind is occupied and it pisses me off so much that I just turn around and tug my T-shirt on.

Ricky shuts the door.

"What the hell is wrong with you, dude?" Greg asks me. He pulls on his sweatpants and yanks at the string to tighten them around his hips.

"Those fucking Giants sweatpants is what's wrong with me," I say, using my towel to slap his arm.

"Leave him alone," Aiden tells them. "He's licking his wounds."

"Get *over* it." Greg shakes his head and puts his jewelry back on. The beaded necklace is in the colors of the Jamaican flag, a black onyx cross that falls right between his breastbones.

I shoot Aiden a look that says, *I'm going to beat the shit out of you.*

"Aww, poor Fallon's got a new crush?" Rick asks. "Maybe we should add a Taylor Swift number to your routine."

They fall over in laughter, incredibly pleased with themselves, making lovesick noises in my general direction.

"You guys are useless," I mutter, and hold out my hand for my cut.

"Chill, my dude," Jimmy says. Ever since we got back to New York, his Brooklyn accent has severely increased and I'm not sure if he does it on purpose or not. He slaps the stack of bills on my open hand. He doles out the other shares and keeps the rest and the check in the bank bag. Then he secures that in his pack clipped over his chest.

"There's plenty of pussy in the sea," Jimmy says callously.

"We can't all be happy with being forty-five-year-old bachelors," I tell him. "And cats don't live in the sea."

"I'm thirty-nine, ya rat bastard."

I hold my hands up, all *my bad.* "Sure you are."

Jimmy has the temper of a flaming jalapeño. "Why you gotta do me like that, Fal?"

"As much fun as this is," I say, "I'm beat."

"Where do you think you're going?" Ricky asks. "I already invited some of the bachelorettes and it's your turn to host."

Fuck. Host. After every home call, we take turns after-partying at our apartments. That way the girls never know where we live since Ricky had a stalker problem a while back, and another girl basically set up camp outside Jimmy's house in Florida.

"I'm beat, man."

Ricky presses his hand on my forehead. He looks back at the other guys, all dressed with their duffel bags slung over their shoulders. "Hey, guys, I think he's really sick or something."

Aiden rings my neck with his arm and ushers me out the door. "Ignore them. You go home. Walk your dog. Both of them, if you get my drift. We'll go to my place."

I jab him in the gut and he jerks back. Now I don't want to seem like a dick. Besides, I don't want to be alone with my thoughts of her. I'll just keep replaying her literally running away from me tonight.

"No, you know what?" I say. "We're doing this. But you guys better refill my booze cabinet."

"Oh, is that the technical term?" Aiden says jokingly. "Booze cabinet?"

"Come on," I say, "before I change my mind."

The group of us stroll out of the room and wave at our host. The bride-to-be, pink-faced and smiling, sets her eyes on me. I recognize her as the woman who dropped Robyn in front of our building earlier in the week. Her eyes squint at me with recognition, but can't place my face. I swallow the ache that's lodged in my throat, and keep on going toward the door.

At the bottom of the landing, the bachelorettes are waiting for the guys. Not a single one of them hides the lust in her stare, the fantasy of taking home a stripper and then telling her friends about it the following day. All, "*Oh my god, you won't believe what I did.*" A moment of gossip. Fun. Thrill. Shock. Forgotten.

Jimmy throws me the backpack with our money to put in the safe in my apartment until I can swing by the bank in the morning.

One of the girls locks her brown eyes with mine. There's a devilish quirk on her full red lips, and I can feel her undressing me with her gaze. A few years ago, hell, a few months ago, I'd pick her up and bite the hell out of that lip right here in the middle of the street. I'd pin her against the car with a kiss, staining my mouth red with the taste of her. Her hair catches in the wind and blows around her angelic brown skin. Her breasts are pushed up to their limits, and when she breathes, it's the only thing the eyes fall to.

I smile at her, aware of how she reacts to my eyes on her skin. I might be different from how I was a few years ago, but I'm still not a saint.

"Party at my place," I say, and lead the way to our cars parked down the block. "But fair warning, I've got someone waiting for me at home."

And I do. When I walk into my apartment, Yaz runs circles around me. The boys are quick to set up shop, bringing out the plastic cups and blasting hip-hop out of a tiny Bluetooth speaker that looks too small to be so loud. I am definitely not going to win any "good neighbor" awards around here.

"This is a great space," Red Lips, I think her name is Anise, tells me. She pulls off the sweater that does little to cover her cleavage and lays it on the couch. "Want to give me the tour?"

I can't help but grin at that. There's nothing to tour. The one-bedroom is huge, and has the same setup as Robyn's. *Dammit.* I said I wasn't going to think of her, but there I go. Anyway, there's a big room, a bathroom, and a living room that came furnished with the sublet. But I already know what Anise wants, and she's not very subtle in the way she grabs hold of my forearm and squeezes.

Then, I'm saved by the husky. Yaz barks up at us, sitting at attention right at my feet.

"How cute!" Anise says, bending down to pet my dog.

Yaz hides behind my feet and avoids Anise's hand. If I can't trust my pup, who can I trust? Don't they say that dogs are great at reading people? I don't know who says that, but I'm sure it's a study somewhere. Anise looks disappointed.

Ricky is playing bartender. He knows where everything is more than I do, even though he doesn't even live here. He bought me a martini kit, which was more of a gift for himself since I don't drink martinis.

Between the heavy bass, Anise's too-sweet perfume, and Yaz

biting my pant leg, a headache blooms behind my eyelids. This is what I get for not wanting to let my boys down, I guess.

"I'll be right back," I say. Yaz needs to be walked before she goes on my floor again, and I need a space to breathe. I point at Ricky and shout, "Don't burn the place down!"

I hook the leash on her collar and race her downstairs. She sniffs the sidewalks until she finds a spot that she wants and pisses a river. The yellow light of the streetlamp makes her white fur look gold.

My phone rings and a strange strangling feeling takes hold of me. When I look at the screen, I don't recognize the number. I wonder if it's her. If it's Robyn. Though I don't underestimate the extremes some clients have gone to to get my attention. One girl got a separate phone to talk to me so her boyfriend wouldn't know.

I hit decline, and let Yaz drag me around the corner and downhill. She gets down on her hind legs and I swear loudly because I forgot to bring a plastic bag.

When I look up to curse the heavens and this literally shit day, I see her. Something twists in my gut at the sight of Robyn standing at her window. Her hair is tousled and wet, and in the golden glow of the streetlight, her skin takes on a bronze sheen. She's a goddess, her lips slightly parted as she looks down at me.

There's a pack of women ready to party in my apartment, but here I am, aching for the one who wants nothing to do with a guy like me. And despite trying to talk myself out of it, I can't look away.

But she does.

For the second time, she removes herself from me.

Yaz looks up at me, wagging her tail, her tongue sticking out in a way that makes it painfully impossible to be pissed at her. I look up and down the empty street. There's no one to see me leave this pile of shit in the middle of the sidewalk, but I'm not an asshole. At least, I try not to be. I take a step toward the tiny garden that wraps around the corner of my building. I pull a long oval leaf from a plant and scoop up as much of Yaz's *leavings* as I can. There's no trash can on this corner of the street, so

I'll have to take it to my place and flush it. I'm sure that'll thrill my guests.

"The things I do for love," I say to my dog.

"Who are you talking to?" she asks.

I turn around and take a step. I see this happening so quickly that I can't stop it. No matter what I do, I can't stop moving forward. An object in motion stays in motion. Robyn's eyes widen and fall on my open palm. The leaf on my palm. The shit on the leaf.

She can't step away from me fast enough and there is nothing we can do but collide.

7

Puppy Love

ROBYN

In my apartment, taking a second shower of the night, I scrub dog shit off my chest. I suppose I deserve it, even if Fallon apologized six hundred times as we headed back in to the building. Thankfully, it's the middle of the night and no one except for Yaz was there to witness our spectacular disaster.

My buzz has downgraded to a sugar headache, and my mind is now painfully clear and reprocessing the series of events that brought us here. Fallon is a stripper. Fallon slapped dog shit on my chest. Fallon is in my living room. Fallon.

I barely dry my skin, and throw on an old T-shirt and pajama shorts. I wish I owned something cute and silky to go to sleep in but this is all I've got. I pull my hair out of my shirt collar and look at myself in the mirror. My skin is dewy and I no longer look drunk, just a little tired. It'll have to do.

"You're missing your party," I comment as I open my bedroom door. Clearly, I want to ask a lot more than that. *Who is down there? Do I know them? Are you going to invite me now?*

"It's not really *my* party," he says, and I note a weary bitterness at the edge of his voice. "It was my turn to host. I didn't want to flake on my guys."

I linger at the doorway, a living room between us that feels as wide as fields. I watch him quietly. He's washing his hands in the kitchen sink. He's wearing a different T-shirt from the one I saw him in before. He must've gone to his place to change and come back. I follow that thought train all the way back to the bachelorette party. Fallon taking off his shirt in front of my friends and colleagues.

My belly does a somersault, and I'm not sure how to start parsing out the way I feel. I just know I have to apologize. Everything that comes after that is a roll of the dice.

I clear my throat. Yaz is sleeping on my carpet. I walk past her and into the open kitchen area. I stand on the other side of the counter from him so it looks like he's a bartender and I'm asking for a nightcap.

Though the kind of nightcap I want doesn't involve a drink.

Just one for the road, I think.

Still, because neither of us is speaking, I unstopper the Prosecco bottle I half finished before our shit-tastic meeting.

He follows my gaze behind him, to the shelf where I keep my glassware. He gets two champagne flutes and inspects them in the light. With his thumb, he brushes away a water stain and sets them on the countertop. He pours the bubbly liquid to the rim. Holds the drink up to me. The look on his face is unreadable. I can't tell if he's pissed at me or not. His brow is closely knit together, so I know he's a little mad and definitely confused. There's a tiny smirk on his lips, so I know he's at the very least *amused.* If he didn't want to be here he would've gone back to his apartment. He wouldn't have lingered while I showered. He would just let our stupid mistakes pass like ships in the night.

We don't owe each other anything. We aren't friends. We aren't lovers. We're in a city so big that even if we live one floor apart, we might never truly cross paths again.

But we're still here, and I think that means something, even if it's just a little bit of chance.

"What should we toast to?" I ask.

"To being hot messes," he says.

We clink our glasses and then an awkward silence settles. His blue-green eyes fall on my bare shoulder, where my ratty T-shirt falls to one side. Heat blooms across my skin, starting from that very spot.

"I'm sorry," we both say.

"I—" We both start again.

We drink at the same time. We lower our gazes to the floor at the same time. It would be cute if I didn't feel so pathetic.

"I should go," he says slowly, like he's testing out the words. "I'm sorry I smothered you with dog shit."

"I'm sure you didn't plan it. And I probably deserve it." I tuck my hair behind my ear and twirl a strand around my finger.

"True." He drinks his Prosecco, leaning on the countertop. The thin, delicate flute looks tiny in his massive hand.

"*Hey,*" I say indignantly. "I really am sorry, Fallon. What I said—I didn't know. I just talk too much. In high school I was awarded Most Likely to Put a Foot in Her Mouth."

An amused smile plays on his lips. "Look, I get it. I'm not exactly the kind of guy someone like you brings home to the folks. It's cool. I'm over it."

"Someone like me?" I set my flute down harder than I intended so it sloshes at the sides. I stand from the bar stool and stare into his eyes. "What's that supposed to mean?"

He shrugs and moves his hand up and down in front of me, like that's supposed to explain it. "Just—you know. Fancy degrees, nine-to-five, wholesome family, upper-crust types."

"I teach fifth grade!" I shout, my voice loud and shrill. I don't care if I'm shrill. I don't care if my entire building hears me. "I've got six figures of college debt. My mom's a dentist and my dad, who didn't speak a lick of English until he came to this country thirty years ago, is a pediatrician. So maybe, yes, I love my *wholesome family* and I work eight to three, and I went to Columbia, but I worked my ass off. You have no right to judge me."

"Like you judged me? Not so fun, is it?" Fallon drinks casually, then leans on the kitchen island between us, his face so close I can count the stubble along his jawline.

Over in the living room Yaz picks up her head and looks at us. The noise woke her up, but once I'm quiet, breathing hard and staring daggers into her owner's disgustingly beautiful face, she goes back to sleep. The heavy thumping of music and people dancing reverberates on the floorboards. Jesus, how loud are they?

I ball my fists. I point at his face. "What are you, a *Sesame Street* special?"

He grimaces. "I never liked *Sesame Street*. Puppets are an irrational fear of mine. But I'm just trying to make a point, Princess."

"Fine. I judged you. I said I was sorry. But I did it before I knew—that—what you did."

"That I'm a stripper?" he says plainly, smugly. "See? You can't even say it."

I feel my face burn. "I can, too, say it."

"So say it."

"I can't now."

"Why?"

"Because, it's no longer in context, that's why."

"But it's who I am."

"No," I say. "It's what you do."

"You're a teacher. It's part of your nature."

"I could teach you how not to throw shit at girls trying to apologize to you."

He pushes himself up from the counter, startled. "I didn't *throw* anything at you. You walked into me."

I shake my head. "You literally ran into me."

He throws his hands up. "Is this how you apologize to people?"

"How many times do I have to say I'm sorry? But you're worse."

"*I'm* worse?" He chugs his drink. His eyes are luminous and wild. "How?"

"Because you're judging me now, too. And you're sticking to it. You haven't even considered that you might be wrong about me."

He grips the edges of the counter, like he needs it for support. He's thrilling and terrifying to look at all at once. All muscle and anger making the veins along his throat pulse, and his chest rises and falls quickly from breathing too fast.

He walks around the island and my heart thunders with the thought that he might be leaving. *Don't go.* I can feel the words on the tip of my tongue. *Stay.* This feeling in my chest is new. It's the edge of a hurricane winding into a coil, my skin buzzing with his nearness, my breath falling short when he gets all in my space. I can't think of a time I felt like this. I want to hold on to it.

His hands grab my shoulders and a moan escapes my lips. His eyes search mine with a silent question. *Tell me to go.*

But I push myself up on my toes and meet his hungry mouth with my own. My life right now is chaos. I fear that anyone who gets too close might get hurt in the mess of it. I've already done it to my best friend, my last boyfriends, hell, even my family. It's wrong, maybe even cruel, to let Fallon into my life right now. Yet I can't seem to pry myself away.

Then, he grabs hold of my shoulders and pushes me at arm's length. He's breathless and his eyes rake across my face and he asks, "You're going to be the end of me, aren't you?"

FALLON

I want to hate her.

I want to leave and say, "*Fuck this.*" Fuck you. Fuck you and your stuck-up bullshit. Fuck this ridiculous feeling inside of me that shouldn't logically be here. Fuck these butterflies. Fuck your beautiful, unforgiving mouth. I don't need you.

But when she gets all up in my space, her hair wet, wild, and eyes as dark as midnight—I want to grab her harder and throw her onto the couch and break it in half with the force of our weight.

I realize, I need her.

When I kiss her, she tastes like regret, and the sliver of fear I'm only starting to discover. This girl might break me in a way I didn't think possible. I'm not a superstitious man, but I believe in this power she has over me. One I never asked for. One that has been thrown in my hands, against me. Right on my lips.

So instead of self-preservation, I choose to kiss her back. She's a featherweight in my arms, wrapping long bronze legs around my waist. I carry her to the couch, press her into the leather with my weight until she breaks the kiss to release a moan.

When she lifts her head back, I kiss the length of her neck. The underside of her chin. The tip of her jaw. All of it until I make my way back to her swollen mouth.

"I'm still mad at you," she says between panting breaths.

"I'm still mad at *you*," I say.

I push up her thin cotton T-shirt to the base of her ribs. Her lean muscles constrict under my touch; her skin is warm and soft and I wish I could touch every part of her all at once.

No one, *no one* has made me this crazy. It doesn't make sense, and part of me doesn't want an explanation. I just want to *be* with her, inside her.

She grabs at the hem of my shirt and pushes it up my torso so I have to pull myself away from her and finish taking it off. I fling it off to the side and give her my attention again. When I lower myself back to her, she presses her hands on my pecs.

I don't know what she sees when she looks at me like that. But I've never felt more exposed. Her dark eyes draw a path from my torso, across the tattoos on my shoulders, around my face, and settle on my eyes. She widens her legs, and I sink against her. My dick is hard and she pushes herself up so I can feel how wet she is through those tiny shorts. I whisper her name, *Robyn*, and rock my dick against her, and she digs her hands into the waistband of my sweats and rakes her nails across my ass.

I drag kisses along her jaw, her chin, and work my way back to her mouth. The swollen pink of it gives way to my tongue, and I think, *I could kiss her forever*.

She moans again, and this time she sounds pained.

"Am I hurting you?" I whisper, worried I might be smothering her with my weight.

"No, you feel perfect." Her fingers leave warm trails up my spine, around my sides, then she cups my face. She reaches for a stray bit of my hair, coils it around her fingertip. She traces the back of her fingers down the side of my face.

That alone has more intimacy and caring than the other girls I've been with. I feel shitty thinking of other girls when I'm in between the sexiest fucking legs I've never touched. But I can't help it. She doesn't look at me like I'm something to use and throw away. She looks at me like she's committing me to memory, and the power of that renders me weak under her touch, even though I'm the one on top.

And suddenly I realize, I know how this ends.

We'll have incredible sex, and then tomorrow she'll be awkward and we won't know what to say to each other. I'll make up excuses and avoid her because I'm a fucking punk, and then she'll move on. I'll regret letting this feeling slip right through my fingers.

I take a shaky breath, rest my face in the hollow of her neck, because I'm about to cockblock myself.

"Don't stop," she says, her voice small and delicate. There's a haziness there, and I know it's the wine she's been drinking before I got here. She lifts up her hips and grinds them against my dick. I could pass out from the heat of her against me.

I press a kiss on the apple of her cheek. "We should stop."

"Why?" She sighs and rests her hand on my cheek. "What do you want from me?"

She's not angry when she asks me this. In a way, she echoes the same thing I want to ask. *What do you want from me?* The real, hard truth would be that I want to slip inside of her and never come out. I want to finish pulling off her T-shirt and bite her until she screams with pleasure. I want to make her feel like she's never felt before. I want to walk down the street holding her hand. I want to pretend like her words never bothered me, like she didn't watch me get buck-ass naked for her best friend. I want to start over. But I can't bring myself to say any of that.

"I don't know," I say. Fucking chicken-shit. I sit back, a chill filling the space between us. I look around for my shirt, but it's on the other side of the room.

"You don't know?" She pulls her shirt down. Her brown eyes look down at my lap. "Doesn't feel that way. I think I know just what you want right now, Fallon."

I clear my throat and put a pillow over my crotch. My balls are tight and ache with the need to release. She sits up, crouches toward me like a mountain lion. Her hair falls over her shoulder and tickles my skin as she settles in beside me, her body long and languid.

The last time I was this nervous around a girl, I was fourteen and about to lose my virginity to the sixteen-year-old babysitter. My heart was a loose screw ratcheting against my ribs, and I pressed the pillow against my erection. How is it that some moments in life seem to parallel each other?

There's something inexplicably sweet about Robyn right now. The rumpled hair, the sleepy squint of her eyes, the swollen pink of her lips.

"I want more than I deserve to have," I say.

I don't know where the words come from. Something deep within me has taken over. It's like looking at her, being near her, I can't lie, not even to myself.

"Why would you say that?" She reaches out for me with delicate fingers. Hesitates. Then, rests her hand on my chest. I press my hand on top of hers, like trying to create an imprint of her touch right over my heart.

"Have dinner with me," I say.

She looks away for a second, breaking our eye contact for the first time in minutes. I wonder what she's thinking.

"Dinner?" She repeats the word, like giving herself time to answer. It's her turn to be nervous.

"I figure, if neither of us knows what we want," I say, brushing her full bottom lip with my thumb, "then we might as well eat while we figure it out. Though I can think of something else I'd rather eat."

"What's stopping you from doing it now?" She looks at me defiantly.

"Because I said I wanted more."

"Fallon—I'm not in a place where I can give you more. Neither are you. You said it yourself."

I laugh. "I never thought I'd have to *talk* someone into having dinner first."

"Yup. I'm a floozy like that," she says sarcastically.

I grab hold of her chin. This girl. This woman. This magnanimous, messy, gorgeous woman is anything but a floozy. I should know. I am one. And maybe I just recognize something broken in her.

"I want to put all my cards on the table," I tell her.

"That's a terrible way to play poker," she says.

"I'm reckless like that, I guess."

"So, what are your cards?" She brushes her hair over the side of her shoulder and it falls in waves, the clean, flowery scent filling every breath I take.

"I'm leaving in a few months. Our show's going down to Reno in the fall. And I want to get to know you in as much time as I have left here."

She grins with her straight white teeth. "There's a room full of women in your apartment. Why not choose one of them?"

"None of them have stolen my thong," I say honestly. "Besides, they want the spectacle. I want someone who might see more in me."

"More than your *Magic Mike* life?" She traces a circle on my right pec. "I have my best friend's wedding. And I'm applying to a second master's program that begins in the fall."

"So, we're both leaving in the fall," I say. "There's an idea."

"A summer fling?"

"A summer something," I say. "Why the frown?"

"I've just never had an arrangement like this before. What, we date for the summer and then good-bye? Aren't we setting ourselves up for disaster?"

I shrug. "Not if we agree that it'll be over when it's supposed to be over. You just have to promise not to fall in love with me."

She slaps my chest. "You are so full of yourself."

"Yeah, but I think you like that about me." I wrap my arm around her waist and pull her completely onto my lap. She wriggles playfully, and I lean my head back at the way my body reacts to her. She's a hundred percent right. We're setting ourselves up for disaster, but I don't care. It's better than having her for only one night.

"Okay, we date exclusively until the end of summer, and then leave with no strings attached," she says. "How do you want to seal the deal?"

In her thin T-shirt, with her skin prickling into goose bumps under my touch, I have a few ideas in mind. But I remind myself to slow down. I want to do this right. I want more, and I want us both to remember it.

"Deal," I whisper, and kiss her.

There's a knock on the door, and the creak of rusted hinges. Ricky stands at Robyn's threshold, a stupid grin on his face.

"Apologies. Door was open," he says, winking at Robyn. "You must be the neighbor I've heard so much about."

"I'm Robyn." She gets up to shake his hand. I want to tell her she shouldn't shake his hand because she doesn't know where it's been in the last couple of hours. But Ricky ignores her hand and grips her into a bear hug that sends her into a fit of giggles. "Nice to meet you, I guess."

"I was looking for you to ask where you keep your TP, and to ask whether or not you were attached to that lamp in the living room."

I groan and look back at Robyn. "I'll call you tomorrow."

My heart gives a pleasant squeeze when she winks. "Try to keep it down. I have work in the morning."

Then I grab Yaz, and follow Ricky down to my apartment, where nothing—not the empty bottles or shattered lamps or feathers drifting in the air or naked bodies in my living room—can put a damper on the memory of Robyn's lips on mine.

8

Slide

ROBYN

"You're in a good mood," Lily tells me Monday afternoon. "Is that the Goo Goo Dolls?"

Too late, I realize I've been cleaning my chalkboard and humming at the same time. I dust my hands together, white powder clinging to my black dress.

"Hey!" I say, my voice breaking. It's the first time I've seen her all day. I don't want to say she's avoiding me, but she didn't wait for me in the teachers' lounge for our morning coffee. Then again, it was her bachelorette party weekend. After getting a handful of hours of sleep Saturday night, I drank a pot of coffee, raised $300 at the bake sale, and barely stayed awake for brunch with Lily and the bachelorettes. I was the first one to leave, and even though Lily was disappointed, she didn't say a word. "I didn't think you'd be here today. Didn't Sophia take everyone out for dinner?"

"No rest for the wicked," she says, offering me one of the two lattes in her hands. I grimace at myself. Monday is my day to get our lunchtime lattes.

"I'm so sorry, I slept, like, thirteen hours last night," I say. "Why are you friends with me?"

"Do you really want to pull at that thread, babe?" she asks, a tiny laugh at the edge of her words.

I shake my head and close the door to my classroom. We

have half an hour left on lunch before our students run back here for the second half of the day. If this were a football game, I'd be losing to them. My lesson plans this week are so half-assed, I should hand in my resignation. It's a wonder that my students all love reading. I can just assign them my favorite books. Right now, I have them reading *The Witch of Blackbird Pond* and tying that to the Puritan part of American history.

Lily pulls up a seat beside my desk. She thumbs through the book at the top of the stack. "You've always loved this book."

"Yeah," I say. "I lost the copy I had when I was little. But these new covers are great. Lily, I'm sorry I ran out Saturday night. And then yesterday, between the sale and not sleeping, I was just not my usual self."

"I'm not even sure what your usual self is these days, to be honest," she says. "I've seen you drink half a bottle of whiskey without blowing chunks, so what really happened on Saturday?"

"Do you remember the first guy who started dancing for you?" I hold the latte between my hands. Blow on the steam to cool it before taking a sip.

"Yeah?" She looks at me with a side-eye, unable to stop a bright blush from creeping up her cheeks.

"That was my mystery neighbor."

She slaps her hand over her mouth. "*Shut* up."

So I tell her everything. Retracing the moment Fallon and I met to our deal later Saturday night. When I woke up this morning, I wasn't completely sure if this weekend was all a dream until I woke to a sweet text from Fallon wishing me a good day at work.

I watch Lily's face shift from shock to awe to sheer amusement.

"So, basically, a temporary arrangement?" she says.

"Basically." I take a drink from my latte, still too hot, and scald my tongue.

Lily is trying her hardest to keep a straight face. I can tell when she's holding something back. She puckers her lips, like she's sucking on a sour candy. Like now.

"What?" I ask.

She looks over her shoulder at the door. The halls are still clear, but Principal Lukas walks past and waves at us, and we wave back.

"It's just—are you sure that's what you want?"

This is what I need. Real talk from my best friend. Then why does it make me feel like I might throw up?

"Look," I say, "I like him. He likes me. We're both consenting adults. I don't know what I want from my life. You of all people must see how much of a mess I've been lately."

"But you can change that," Lily says. "You can put yourself out there again. Dave has a ton of single college friends coming in for the wedding. You have options."

"Wait, this isn't an options issue. I didn't agree to this with Fallon because I'm out of options."

"I didn't mean it like that," she says, rolling her eyes. "It's just that if the two of you are so unsure of what you want from the future, maybe you're actually enabling each other."

"Or," I say, trying not to get angry, "maybe we just both need something that's no-strings-attached."

"You're both going to be exclusive for, what, a handful of months and then walk away from each other?"

Your best friend is supposed to be a mirror to yourself. They're there to be a sounding board, to listen and tell you when you're being an ass. So why is Lily's tone bothering me so much?

"How is it different from a regular relationship that ends after a week or a month or a year?" I ask. "This way, we're setting a timeline. It's like organized dating. I've never been the clingy one."

"What's that supposed to mean?" she asks.

"It means that I've never been the clingy one in any of my relationships. Remember Jake? I had to change my number because he couldn't let it go. And we were together for *five* months. That's like *so much* open-mouth chewing."

Lily sits back and studies the steam rising out of her latte. "It just seems like a setup for heartbreak for you. I mean, is he going to be your plus one for the wedding? Wouldn't that be weird?"

The judgment in her words bothers me more than it should, and I regret the hurt I caused Fallon with mine.

"If you're worried about me bringing my stripper boyfriend to your wedding, you can rest assured. I'm going stag as planned."

"Now he's your boyfriend? Robyn, that's not what I meant and you know it!"

"I don't want to fight. I want you to be happy for me. Who knows, it might end sooner. It might burn out. I just don't see anything wrong with it right now."

Lily watches me for a long time. Her jaw ripples when she bites down on her teeth. She wants to say more, but she isn't letting herself. "Fine. It still doesn't excuse you from leaving my bachelorette party like that."

I breathe a little easier. "I know and I'm sorry. But Sophia's doing a great job."

Lily chuckles. "She's special. Easily the most high-maintenance person I've ever met. But she loves this stuff."

"I'm sorry I'm letting you down."

"As long as you're there, I'll be happy. I know you're going through a lot. I wish there was something I could do."

"Don't worry about me."

"Okay. I'll wait for you in the parking lot for the last dress fitting. Though I should've waited before having all that champagne this weekend." She pats her stomach on her way out.

The bell finally rings, and I let go of a relieved sigh.

My phone buzzes. Fallon's name brings a flutter to the pit of my stomach. *Tomorrow night, 8PM?*

And I type back: *Yes.*

FALLON

Practice is a disaster. Vinny and Wonderboy Suave can't keep time, and I can't stop the annoyance from my voice when I blow the whistle and yell, "Again."

"Come on, Fal," Ricky says, squeezing water onto his face. We're in a rented dance studio in Long Island City close to our venue. Ricky likes to block everything out in a studio before moving onto the main stage. It's smaller than what we're used to, but it's newly renovated, and we also share it with a local theater company and a ballerina school. Though we have to book the latest hours.

I grab hold of the barre and stretch out my quads. I can see all their irritated glares in the mirror.

"I know everyone's tired, but we're only on our first week of the show," I say.

Ricky's choreographed every set we've ever done. He's been training for Broadway since he was in diapers. He had a run on *Rent* when he was eighteen, and was on the *Rock of Ages* tour in the UK for a season, but left it all to start Mayhem City and has been doing it ever since.

"Honeys don't give a flying fuck if I miss a mark," Vinny says.

"I hope that's true considering you and Frank aren't even trying," I say.

"Yeah," Wonderboy echoes. They're identical twins, so when they're quiet, it's like seeing the most annoying double. But Frank, aka Wonderboy, has a slightly higher pitch in his voice than Vinny. "They just want to see a bunch of dudes get naked."

"Yo, Zac, chill," Ricky tells me. He's the only person, other than my father, to call me by my first name. "We've been rehearsing nonstop. I think we've done pretty good so far. Sold out twice a day. We've got that reviewer from *Stars Night Out* coming this weekend and everything."

Vinny goes over to the iPhone plugged in and searches through the songs. "Whose old-man music is this?"

The other guys laugh or try to hide their smiles behind closed fists.

I walk over to Vinny and snatch my phone from his hand. "Funny."

"Come on, lads," Lucky Kris says, shoving his clothes into his pack. "It's been a long-ass day and I'm ready to hit the showers. If you guys want to have it out, then come with me to the ring."

Ricky walks up and down the studio with his fingers tented in that way of his when he gets a new idea. "Or, it could be a new set we can work on. Robes and gloves are easy enough to put together. Yes. I see it. Darla, get over here."

Darla, our publicist and basically our housemother, looks up from her phone. She has nonstop coverage of "behind the scenes" photos and clips for all our social media pages. Honestly, I expect the woman to have eight hands with all the work she manages to get done. Her walk is the tick-tock of a clock running an hour ahead of schedule, sculpted by the finest surgeons in California. She's beautiful in a carefully crafted way. When she talks, we listen. When she asks us to act natural, we do it. When she puts us in ridiculous outfits for promotional photo shoots, we say yes. She's the best parts of Kim Kardashian with a Jersey attitude.

"Fallon, baby, look at me." She presses her hands on my shoulders. In six-inch heels, she's almost my height. "I want you to go to yoga with me. You're more wound up than my first husband on our wedding night, and you know what happened to him?"

I look around the room, slightly terrified.

"You killed him?" Wonderboy whispers.

Darla turns her sharp cat eyes on him. "I divorced him a week later. Just promise. It's around the corner from your new place. Saturday nine a.m."

Ricky scoffs. "I think he'll be less *uptight* after his date with 6A."

Darla pouts, then pinches my chin, and one of her clawlike nails digs into it. But I don't dare wriggle out of her grip. "You waste no time, do you, baby?"

"Don't start, all right?" I mutter to Ricky, once Darla slaps my ass and struts away.

"Is this the same girl that had you weepy last week?" Aiden asks, bending forward to stretch his calves.

"Oh, shit," Vinny jokes, "are you finally losing your virginity?"

"Please," I say. "I've been pounding pussy since you were in diapers."

Wonderboy points a finger at his brother and hollers. "Ohh-hhh, he got you, boyyy."

"You're the same age," Lucky Kris says, rolling his eyes.

Vinny plugs in his own phone, changing the song to trap rap. "Whatever. I got a hot date tonight."

"Tell your mom I said hi," I say, and dump the rest of my water over my sweaty head.

Vinny's eyes light up, and he turns to me like I'm a big red cape and he's going to run at me with his horns out.

"Yooo, chill," Aiden says, ringing his arms around Vinny's to hold him back.

"I'll see you ladies later." I swing my pack over my shoulder. I wink at the twins and that makes them angrier.

"Save it for the boxing set," Ricky shouts at them.

When I walk out, Aiden runs out and catches me before I cross the street. "Yo, Fal. Wait up."

I turn and look at him. His hair somehow manages to stay in that David Beckham puff that he always wears. I swear he puts industrial-strength glue in that thing.

"What's up with you?" he asks.

"I told you guys. We need to be tighter. The sets are off."

"I mean, you're riding the new guys too hard. If they quit, we can't replace them like that."

"Please. There's tons of them."

"But we voted. Just— You never treated me like that. You don't even *talk* like that."

I sigh because he's right. Something about them just brings out the worst in me. "You were never a dick when you started."

Aiden, ever the peacemaker, smiles in that charming and unassuming way of his. "I'll talk to Vinny and Frank, too. He riles up his brother. Just cool it, okay?"

"I'll try." I switch the weight on my pack. Hold out my hand.

He returns my fist bump. "Good luck on your date tonight, bro."

"I was born lucky."

I go home to walk my dog, shower, and shave. It's the first time I've been truly alone all weekend, and my apartment still has traces of the party we had. Try as they will, my boys are not good at cleaning up after themselves. I tie the last of the bottles in a recycling bag and leave it at the entrance.

I have a missed call from my sister, but when I try to call her back, she doesn't pick up. Mary never calls me, unless she's out of allowance money. I send her a text asking if she's okay, but I don't get anything back. *Little sisters.*

I cue up some of my *old-man* music and get ready for my date with Robyn.

I fish out a pair of jeans and iron a button-down. My father was a lousy drunk most of the time, but he always looked sharp. "*Listen, here boys,*" he used to say. "*You only get one shot for someone to size you up. Looking the part is almost as important as the work you put in.*" Sure, he was talking to my brother and me about how he was going to get a job. Dad was a bastard, and half the shit out of his mouth was toxic, but he managed to get hired. Even if he didn't manage to keep the job a month later.

I button up my shirt in front of the mirror, mouthing the lyrics to Stone Temple Pilots' "Interstate Love Song." Then, I hear a louder sound. I can't make out the melody, but it's sweet. I look up where the floorboards creak the most. I turn off my music and hear her. Robyn, singing a song in Spanish.

My Spanish is shit, and I can't make out what she says, but the pitch of her voice makes my guts twist. I'm half inclined to get a ladder so I can bring my ear closer to the ceiling and listen to her, if she didn't stop abruptly to answer her phone. I wonder who she's talking to. I wonder if she's got this same knot in the pit of her stomach. I wonder if we're doing the right thing.

I get back up and spray on some of the cologne Darla gave me for Christmas. She told me I needed to stop wearing the same shit as a college frat boy trying to cover up his stink. I said, "I've never been a frat boy a day in my life." Still, it's some French stuff that isn't half bad, and women seem to dig it.

Yaz runs into the room and sits at my feet. I've walked her, fed her, and played with her. But still, she rubs her head on my legs and walks in a circle. I pet her head, and she barks a few times before jumping onto my bed and making herself a comfortable pad.

"Okay, Yaz, but if I bring a girl back, your ass gets kicked to the living room."

As if she understands me, she growls in response.

My phone beeps at three minutes to eight. I slip into my brown leather jacket and stuff my money clip into the inside zipper pocket. When I take another step, my boot crunches down on something.

I look down and see a crushed white pill. I pick some up and bring it to my nose, and it's odorless. I didn't see anyone taking pills Saturday night, but then again, I was gone for half of it with Robyn.

There's a knock on my door, and I don't have time to clean it up, so I dust my hands and grab the door.

When I see her, I'm breathless. In fact, I have to remind myself to breathe because the air is literally knocked out of my lungs. Her hair is done up in full black waves. I could drown in that hair. Her warm, light-brown skin shimmers, gold at her shoulders. Her lashes are darker than usual, the corners of her eyes lined with makeup so black, it makes her midnight eyes brighter. Her lips are the red of roses blooming, and they match the flowers printed on the dress that hugs every inch of her. From her thin waist to the full curves that make my dick twitch.

"I was going to pick you up," I say.

She quirks her full mouth to one side. "I'm just full of surprises."

9

You Are My Kind

ROBYN

What Fallon doesn't know is that the biggest surprise of all is that for the first time in maybe two months, I'm on time.

Granted, I was on time for the bridal fitting, but that was because Lily picked me up for what would be the most painful hour of my life (I might still be bleeding from the pins the seamstress poked me with a dozen times). The morning wasn't much better, because Principal Lukas chose today of all days to sit in on my class. He's been nothing but friendly to me, but there's something about him that doesn't quite sit right with me. The entire time I was talking to my kids my unease at having him there increased. At the end of it, he congratulated me on a great lesson plan and asked me for restaurant recommendations.

After I ran home, I showered and put on one of my dad's old CDs. It's the kind of music I only listen to when I'm alone, boleros and baladas sung by glamorous singers from decades ago. The old Spanish guitar and songs about all kinds of love calm me the most.

Plus, I was nervous as hell. When was the last time I went out with someone as beautiful as Fallon? Because Fallon isn't just hot. He's got muscles that scream of workouts I avoid like the plague. His jawline could shave a chunk of crystal into diamonds. And where most guys I've dated had thin lips that disappeared when they were upset or worried, Fallon has a mouth that was made for doing sinful things.

But his eyes, the blue of warm seas. The long lashes that frame them. The smatter of freckles on the broken bridge of his nose. Why is it that some men just look better when their noses have been broken like that? Is it because it speaks to a rough-and-tumble nature? Because it breaks the otherwise too-perfect symmetry of his face, and makes him unbearably sexy?

I realize I'm staring, and take the arm he holds out to me, his leather jacket cool on my skin.

"Where are we going?" I ask. "I feel like I left you to fend for yourself with trying to pick a restaurant when you're new in town."

"I'm only good at a handful of things," he says, "but finding good food is one of them."

He holds the parking lot door for me, and leads me to his car. My black heels make a sharp click on the concrete, echoing off the walls around us. My skin warms under his gaze, and I feel a pleasant thrill knowing that he wants me. He opens the door to his car, and waits for me to get in before closing it.

I feel like we never stop looking at each other. Not when he puts the car in drive, which, you know, is probably dangerous. But I find it hard to look away. When he drives, he stares straight ahead, keeping one hand on top of mine. I study the angle of his smooth cheekbones, breathe in his cologne, a scent that brings to mind pinewood and burning fires. When he stops at each red light he turns to me. Every time. His face is bathed in the bright lights of the city.

We don't talk much, and I don't mind it. It's like we're settling into each other's presence. There isn't the *need* to fill the silence with mindless chatter about the weather. We were both out in the world; we know that it was sunny with a high of seventy. We can talk about our days while we're eating. For now, we're just together, and this sensation is so strange and new that it sends me into a nervous flutter.

"Can you give me a hint about what kind of food it is?" I ask.

He gives my hand a squeeze and says, "Delicious. I promise."

"Well, good, because I'm so hungry I could probably eat you."

His laugh is husky, and when he bares his teeth like that I can see his slightly crooked canine. "I was hoping that was third-date stuff."

"Oh, there's a third date?"

"There's a bunch of dates. I thought I had you for three whole months."

I can't help it. I lean over and kiss his cheek. "Let's just see how tonight goes. It's more like an audition."

"God, I haven't had to audition for anything in years."

"Do tell."

"Patience, young Padawan." He lets go of my hand briefly to change gears, and enters the restaurant parking lot.

"I don't know about you, but I'm full Jedi."

"God, you're sexy when you're nerdy." He licks his bottom lip, and I want to follow his tongue with my own. "We're here."

La Isla is a hot new restaurant that specializes in Puerto Rican food and claims to have the best mojitos outside of the island itself. Lily and I have been trying to get reservations for a month.

"This place is harder to get into than Area 51," I say.

He looks amused and takes my hand, making our way to the front of the restaurant where there's a line around the block. I'm glad I wore sensible four-hour heels instead of the just-for-show six-inch ones.

"How many attempts have you actually made to get into Area 51?" he asks, then tugs on my hand. "Come."

Fallon leads me down to the front door, where people who've been waiting for probably over an hour give us dirty looks. As a lifelong New Yorker, I hate being that person. But as a person who hasn't eaten since breakfast, I willingly put pep in my step all the way to the hostess stand. Instantly, my senses are distracted with the scent of roasted meats and savory dishes, the loud chatter and laughter of dozens of tables, the bright neon lights that remind me of the South Beach strip that faces the ocean, the rhythm of the live salsa band playing at the end of the room.

A gorgeous Puerto Rican woman, a little younger than me, greets Fallon with a bright smile.

"Fal!" she shouts over the live music.

"Daya, this is Robyn," he tells the hostess. "Robyn, Daya's brother Sebastian is one of the New York additions in my crew."

"So *you're* the reason he finally leaves his apartment after three weeks." She takes my hand and winks at me before picking up some menus and saying, "Follow me."

Fallon lowers his lips to my ear, and his cool breath makes my skin tickle. "Like?"

Like doesn't even begin to cover it. I want to say that I love it, but the salsa band's horns are too loud for me to try to talk over. Instead, I squeeze his hand and smile. In the dimly lit restaurant with neon greens and blues highlighting his features, I'm positive Fallon is the best accidental thing to ever have happened to me.

Daya sets menus on our table and Fallon gives her a kiss on the cheek. We sit side by side at a table for two facing the band. In their white suits and Panama hats, they're every bit old-Latin glamour.

A waitress comes over and takes our drink orders. She never looks at me, not really. I've never been the jealous type, and I'm not going to start now. If I were in her shoes, I'd want to stare at him, too. His smile is radiant, his eyes are happy and honest. Fallon is the perfect mix of sweet and sexy, the kind that is so rare to find, he might as well be a fucking unicorn.

The band's song comes to a crescendo and takes a break.

"If you're trying to impress me," I say, looking up from my menu, "it's working."

He chuckles and leans back, reaching an arm across the back of my chair. "Good. I want to start fresh."

"What did Daya mean when she said you haven't left your apartment in three weeks?"

He rolls his eyes playfully, his thumb right on my spine. A food runner sets our drinks down. The glasses are slender and tall, mint and ice practically glowing in the black light. We clink the edges of our glasses, and I drink the sweet rum as he talks.

"Her brother is on our crew. Likes to make fun of me for being old."

"How old are you?"

He chuckles. "Old enough that I can't hang anymore. Thirty."

"Well, I'm twenty-eight and I've basically been an old man my whole life."

"Hot," he says, laughing his beautiful laugh. "So we can skip all the dating and sex and go right into reading the paper at six in the morning and yelling at kids in the park?"

I ball my hand and shake it in the air. "Damn youths!"

But as he thumbs the sensitive skin of my spine, I've never felt more alive. I see the lust spark in his eyes as he tries not to be so obvious about looking at my cleavage.

"But seriously?" he says. "I've been so focused on the group that I don't make time for anything else."

"Then thank you for making time for me." I tuck my hair behind my ear.

"Please," he says, as if it's no big deal. "I want to be here. Not just because I've spent the entire day in a studio with a bunch of other sweaty dudes."

"Sexy," I say in turn, and edge a little closer to him. I take another sip of my Best Mojito Outside of Puerto Rico™ and ask, "Am I allowed to know about the elephant in the room?"

He smirks. "I've been *waiting* for it. Come on. I'm an open book. What do you want to know?"

"How—what—" I stop and try again. I have a million questions I can ask, but nothing seems right. I feel like I'm invading his space. Intruding in a life that he chose long before we met. Plus, I'm still embarrassed about having called his profession trashy.

"It's okay, Robyn. You're not going to ask anything others haven't. Let me make it easy. I started when I was nineteen. Before that I was working at a bar back home. I was a little bit of an attention whore when I was younger."

"And you aren't now?"

"Burn," he says, and takes a long swallow from his straw. "I mean, I loved being in the spotlight."

There's something strange about the way he says that. The obvious deduction is that he doesn't love being in the spotlight anymore.

"What's changed?"

"I'm not sure," he says. "It's been a good living. We travel the world. I get whole months off at a time to do whatever I want. I have some of the best friends I can ask for. Sometimes my crew feels more like my family than my real family."

There's something wonderful and sad about that. "Family's important. I used to feel that way about my friend Lily."

"The one getting married?"

"Yeah. Things are just different now. She has the life I wanted for myself when I was in college. I was different then, too."

"Let me guess. You had a five-year plan. Perfect office-working husband. Kids and a white picket fence?"

I poke him in his stomach, which doesn't do much because it hurts me more than it does him. "No, actually. I mean, yes, in a way. I didn't want to be a teacher. I love the kids I teach, I do. I went to school for literature because I love books. I wanted to be a writer. I've actually never told anyone that."

"What's stopping you?" He asks it as if it's the easiest thing to just follow some dream. As if I haven't considered it every waking moment that I'm putting together a lesson plan and grading papers.

"Because it's not practical, and I have always been practical." I rest my hand on his thigh because it feels natural and I want to touch him. "I was raised by parents who always did the right thing. Go to college, get a job, have a family. Somewhere along the line I turned into the person I wasn't supposed to be."

Fallon takes a deep breath and studies my face. The hand draped around my shoulder plays with my hair.

"You mean you weren't supposed to be having dinner with a male stripper?" He smiles when he says it, but he's self-deprecating.

"No, that part is actually pretty amazing. I mean it. What I was trying to say is, I wasn't supposed to hate my profession so soon."

"Then quit," he says, pulling at his straw until the liquid is all gone.

"Now why didn't I think of that?" I say. "Thanks, Fallon, you've solved *all* my problems. Why don't *you* quit, too?"

"Okay, okay. Smartass." He leans in as if he's going to take a bite out of my neck, but instead, he breathes in my scent. "The difference is that I don't hate what I do."

I quirk my eyebrow, unable to stop the vision of him taking off his clothes from entering my mind's eye. "What do you love about it?"

"I'm starving," he says, trying to change the subject. He fidgets and looks around the restaurant. He holds up two fingers as the waitress makes her way back to us.

"Do you want to put in your food order?"

Fallon picks up the menu, but I can tell he doesn't know where to start.

"Actually," I say, "can we have the sample platter for two?"

"What the lady wants," Fallon says, quirking his mouth into a brilliant smile.

"It'll be right out." The waitress winks at me and walks away.

I turn back to Fallon. He's not going to get out of answering that question. "You were saying?"

He looks up and rubs his lips together, deep in thought. He pulls me closer with the hand that's around me. He brushes my hair away from my ear, and I remind myself that we are in public, and I can't rip his shirt off here and now.

"You want the truth?" he asks.

I nod, unable to move my mouth to form coherent words.

"There is no better sensation than making a woman feel sexy." He places a hand on my knee, his thick, long fingers edge under the hem of my dress, and I feel every part of me stir with longing. "When I'm onstage, I can be anyone. I take my clothes off. I dance around. But to that woman, I'm there for her, and only her, pleasure."

I smirk. "How do you stop yourself from—"

"Right now? I'm not," he says, and as gently as I can, I move my hand to the left and graze the bulge that strains against his pants.

He shuts his eyes and sighs, then puts some distance between us. He takes his napkin and drapes it across his lap, but it doesn't help with covering it up. When he takes his hand off my leg, my body screams for him to put it back.

"*Anyway.* The shows are raunchy, but they aren't as scandalous as what you might be thinking. You—you should come see one night."

I'd be lying if I hadn't considered it since the moment I found out. It would help me to understand his life. This life I've only ever seen on Vegas show ads and in Channing Tatum movies. It's different when the idea of male strippers is outside of a sorority or bachelorette party. It's different when it's the man you're planning on dating for a summer.

"Yeah," I say. "I want to."

He's going to kiss me. His entire body turns to me. His hand is pressed on the small of my back, lightly pushing me toward him, his eyes fluttering as they look down at my mouth. I breathe short and fast because I don't know how I'll tear myself away from his lips once they touch mine. They brush against mine, cool and minty from the mojito. Then they're gone too soon. He clears his throat and looks over my shoulder.

"I think he knows you," Fallon tells me, his voice deeper and gruff.

I'm too dazed to understand what he means. He who? I turn around and realize someone has been calling my name.

"Robyn?"

I nearly jump out of my skin. "Principal Lukas!"

Nothing kills a date like your boss sitting at the table right beside you.

FALLON

I don't have good memories of principals. When I was in school, I was habitually sent to their office. So when Robyn's entire body language shifts from comfortable to being caught under the bleachers, I leave principals in the same column I reserve for things I hate. Right up there with clowns and hipster douche bags.

But the real clincher is the way he looks at her. This guy, Principal Lukas or whatever, is on a date. She's young, but looks legal, and she's in a dress that sparkles under the neon lights and hugs her body like paint. Her smile is lovely, and her hair is teased and arranged to frame her assets, a beautiful face and breasts that I'm trying so hard not to look at. Like I said, I'm not a saint, and the nuns at every Catholic school I ever went to reminded me of the fact.

"Hey, man," I say, holding out my hand to save Robyn the introduction. "Zac."

"Lukas Papadopoulos." He squeezes hard, but I don't let go of his grip. "This is Melodie."

"Hi." The girl shakes Robyn's hand. "Isn't this place amazing? We didn't even have to wait in line that long."

"I know the owner," Lukas says, even though we didn't ask. "You should let me know next time."

He's talking to Robyn, who looks like she's either going to have a heart attack or throw up. I'm rooting for throwing up, honestly. She hasn't said anything since she shouted "Principal Lukas!"

"You guys work together?" I ask, trying to fill the awkward need to speak.

"Actually, Principal is my real name," this dick bag says, but smiles the whole time. He brushes a hand in the air, like we're old friends. "And yes, I'm the principal over at P.S. 85, but we have friends in common."

I'm more than happy to ignore this guy, but having confirmed he's her boss, I'm pretty certain she isn't going to want to dive back into our kiss with him three feet away. Then again, it's better that we're being supervised because my dick was throbbing from that kiss. Fuck, it's like being in detention all over again.

"That is so weird," Melodie says, trying not to be left out. "What a small world."

"That's one way of putting it," Robyn says. She's been smiling since she realized they were seated beside us, and it looks painful. "And here you were asking *me* for restaurant recommendations. I should've been the one asking you."

Lukas chuckles, but doesn't respond.

"You should try the mojitos," I say, and raise my glass. I hope that's enough of a lead into *"Get back to your own date, buddy."* The waitress comes over to their table to take their order.

"Can I have a margarita?" Melodie asks. She cocks her face to the side, and a mischievous pitch in her voice says she's trying to get away with it.

"I need your ID."

"She's okay," Lukas tells the waitress. "We're with Reggie."

The waitress looks a little flustered, but writes down the order. I'd bet every cent in my pocket that Melodie's barely nineteen.

I squeeze Robyn's knee and she jumps a bit. *Come back to me, Robyn,* I think. She's distracted now. Whatever moment we had going on is over.

Robyn looks at me apologetically, and sits up and away from me. She takes her drink in her hands and sips, stabbing the ice with a stick of sugarcane for something to do with her hands.

"Tell me about the dress fitting," I say, trying to lure her attention back.

I recognize the chaos in her eyes, as if her mind is trying to be in two places at once. She even rubs her hand over her arm, as if she feels naked. I take my jacket and rest it over her shoulders. She looks up at me, those long eyelashes bat at me, and I swear something inside of me aches from that stare. I want her to look at me like that always.

"Aww, that's so *cute,*" Melodie says, turning to Principal Dickbag. "Isn't that cute?"

"What do you do, Zac?" Lukas asks. His hazel eyes look me up and down as he leans back into his chair. When I was in school, my principals were either priests or men pushing sixty. Lukas's taste is impeccable. He reminds me of Ricky in that way, their slacks pressed so there's a line right down the center. I never understood the appeal of that. His build is large so he's confident enough to wear a shirt so brightly pink. Gold cuffs catch the light as he runs his hand through the side of his dark hair and waits for my answer.

Great, now we're on a double date. Honestly, I'm surprised Captain Principal didn't ask me right off the bat. I know guys like this. *What do you do?* As if my work or how much money I make is the only thing that defines me. He wants to play that game. See who makes more money. See if I'm good enough, or what I'm guessing by the way he looks at Robyn, if I'm good enough for her.

"I'm in the entertainment industry," I say, a tight smile on my face.

Robyn looks between us nervously, drinking her mojito as if it's going to make everything better. I try to give her a reassuring smile, like a promise that I'll be on my best behavior. But something about this guy pisses me off.

"Oh, yeah?" Lukas says. "Bartender? I have a couple of buddies who own some clubs in Astoria and the city if you're looking for work."

Robyn sets her empty drink down. I push mine over to her side and she takes it with a slight nod of her head.

"Thanks for the offer," I say, "but I run my own gig."

"Nice, what is it?"

"I choreograph a show."

"Like on Broadway?" Melodie asks, her voice high-pitched. "I love musicals. *Wicked* changed my life."

I don't know why I'm dancing around the question. I never lie about who I am and what I do. But when I look at Robyn, her body stiff and nervous, I know why I'm lying. I don't want to embarrass her.

I turn to Melodie, her smile honest and sweet. I can't help but smile back. "More of an off-Broadway thing."

"That's cool," Lukas says. "Where'd you go to school?"

"Me?" I'm at the end of my fuse. "I went to Hogwarts. Gryffindor, class of '03."

Melodie rips into a cute laugh, all *ohmigod you're so funny,* which makes Lukas frown.

And Robyn smiles at me. There's that smile. All of this bullshit third degree from her boss is worth it for that smile.

"I knew I liked you for a reason," she tells me.

Thankfully, the food runner brings Melodie's underage margarita and Lukas's red wine.

"I'll be right back," I tell Robyn and press a kiss on her cheek. "Bathroom."

Melodie stands up. "I have to go, too."

I nod at Lukas, but there is no longer a smile between us. Why am I letting a douche like that get to me? I know his type. I'll bet anything he's hit on Robyn a dozen times. He looks at her like she's a juicy steak he can't wait to cut into.

I head to the bathroom area, a unisex strip with this weird water fountain to wash your hands. Melodie runs into a stall. I splash water on my face and dry my hands. I put a couple of bucks in the bathroom attendant's jar and grab a toothpick and some hand lotion.

"Date not going well?" Daya asks. She comes out of a stall and washes her hands beside me.

"It was going great until the other hostess sat Robyn's *boss* next to us."

Daya's eyes widen. "Reggie's friend? He's *fine.*"

"Not helping."

She pats my back. "He's got nothing on you, baby. Since when have you ever felt threatened by someone else?"

"I'm not," I say, and I know part of it is a lie. "We're just from two separate worlds. I think it matters to her, even if she's trying not to let it."

I walk with her back into the dining room.

"Don't let it get to you," Daya says. "If anything, just call it off. But just from the way you look at her, I know you'd regret it."

With a smile, we part ways. When I get back to our table, Lukas is sitting in front of Robyn. I wonder if her cheeks hurt from the pained smile on her face.

"Is this musical chairs?" I ask dryly as I slide back into my seat.

Robyn looks around. "Where's Melodie?"

I shrug. "What am I, babysitting?"

I meant for it to come off as a joke, but I see my mistake when I see the anger flash across Lukas's eyes. Robyn looks down at her lap and smooths out her napkin. But I can't stop now. Something dark and twisted has snaked its way around my thoughts. It's in the way Lukas tries to size me up, as if he doesn't understand what a woman like Robyn is doing with someone like me. It's in the way Robyn is so nervous she has completely shut down.

"Dude," I say, unable to stop myself. I chuckle and lean forward to face him. "Is she even old enough to have that margarita?"

Lukas's face hardens with anger. If he were any other guy, if he thought he could take me, he'd ask me to meet him outside.

Instead, he leans forward, his body bordering on a threat. "That's none of your business, *Brad*."

"*Zac*," I say, sitting up. "What's your problem?"

Robyn sits up and holds her hands up between us. "Whoa, guys. Calm down. Everyone's having a nice time."

"Clearly, you're the one with the problem," Lukas tells me.

I try to rein it in, but he stands and I rise to meet him. "Why don't you go sit back at your own table?"

Lukas gives me a shit-eating smirk and takes a chip from the bowl in front of us. "We were just having a nice chat between colleagues, *Zac*. You're the one getting all *riled* up."

Robyn's dark eyes beg me to sit. Be the bigger man. When she places her hand on my arm, I flinch a bit, too strung up to do anything else.

"Oh *look*, our food is here," Robyn says, pulling at my shirt to settle me. The food runner brings over a wooden board loaded with roasted pork, steaming things wrapped in leaves, sausages, sweet and savory plantains, and heaping bowls of rice and beans. He smiles, brandishing his hand.

"Thank you," I tell him, pressing a hand on my chest. My heart beats right through the layer of my shirt.

"You know what?" Robyn says, standing up so quickly she rattles the table. "I'm not hungry. Have a nice date, the two of you."

"Robyn," Lukas and I say at the same time as the band starts up again.

The singer counts off into the mic, the horns come to life, and the congas beat as rapidly as Robyn's footsteps out of the restaurant.

Melodie chooses this precise moment to walk back and block my path to Robyn. Melodie's pupils are like pinpricks and there's a wide smile on her face. She looks up at her date and me, and at Robyn's empty chair. "What'd I miss?"

"Last call, amigo," a familiar voice tells me.

I look up at the hazy face beside me. Aiden. Daya must've called Sebastian and Sebastian must've called Aiden. His light-brown skin is covered in glitter. I look back down at my mojito. I've lost count of how many I've had, but my bartender is just smiling because I'm tipping in cash.

"Why do you look like a fucking disco ball?"

He peers at the mirror that lines the bar, turning his face this way and that. "Sorry, I had a gig."

"Yeah?" I ask, sitting up. I've been at La Isla for hours. Right after Robyn left, I was too much of a coward to chase after her because she was right to be angry with me. I settled in the far end corner of the bar with my dinner for two and have watched the dinner crowd clear and the dancing crowd thin.

He whistles and grins. "Park Avenue, baby. This bar called The Pleiades. She had me try this tequila that was $200 a shot." He knocks on the bar and Lucho walks right over. They speak back and forth in Spanish. The only part I understand is "tequila."

"Well?" I ask, my voice hoarse.

"Well, what?"

"Do they have the $200 tequila?"

Aiden makes a scoffing sound. "Hell nah."

I shrug and drain my mojito. "That's fine. I think I drank a whole bottle of rum."

"How are you not plastered on the floor?"

"I've been training my liver since I was thirteen. Though after all these drinks, I might go into diabetic shock."

Lucho lines up three shots and pours amber liquid from a shaker. We each take one.

"To terrible dates," I say.

"To wealthy older women," Aiden says.

"To drunk cojudos who are paying for my daughter's tuition," Lucho says.

We each tap the bottom of our glasses on the bar top and then drink. After the sugary cocktails I've been pounding since Robyn walked out on me, the tequila burns so good.

Lucho walks away and Aiden pulls out a money clip from his pocket. He flips through twenties until he finds a hundred and leaves it under one of the empty glasses.

"You want to talk about it?" he asks, taking a napkin from behind the bar to dab at his sparkly-ass face.

"I want to talk about why you went out with a woman who leaves behind that much glitter."

Aiden looks at me, and his face spreads wide with a smile that speaks to dirty, dirty deeds. "It was the edible kind."

And I'm left in a tequila daze trying to imagine all the places one can eat glitter from. "Damn. I guess there is a flavor for everyone."

"I'm serious, man. You want to talk about it?"

I don't but I do. Ever since Florida, I don't talk about women with the guys. Maybe I'm too embarrassed. Maybe I still feel like a goddamn dick.

I wave Lucho over, but he's already got the bottle in hand.

I spin on my bar stool, which is decidedly the worst idea to have when you've practically drunk a whole bar. I shut my eyes, but nothing can get rid of the image of Robyn walking out.

"It's just—" I gulp the tequila in a single shot. The warmth spreads deeper and deeper, like I'm sitting out in the sun. "I'm in fucking Hogwarts."

"Wait, what?" Aiden asks.

"You know, Harry Potter?"

"I know what Harry Potter is. I just didn't know you read, like, books."

I punch him on the shoulder, and he laughs. "You have to be straight with me, Fal, because right now you're not making sense. And my third language is Drunk, okay?"

So I tell him. About my unbelievably sexy lady and how perfect everything was going. About Lukas and how every question he asked me chipped away at the dark parts of my soul I don't let people see. About how she walked out and the only reason I didn't punch the principal in his face was because I didn't want to get Daya in trouble.

"Then I sat at the bar."

"What happened to the food?" Aiden asks.

"What?"

"This place has an hour wait line and the kitchen's closed, bro. Are you telling me you wasted a sample platter for two?"

"I'm pouring my soul out to you and you want to know about *food?*"

Aiden grins. "You wouldn't have me any other way."

I reach for the brown takeout bag I set off to the side and slam it in front of the worst friend in the world. "Here. Someone should eat."

Behind us, the busboys and barbacks are picking up and sweeping and turning chairs on top of tables. The band is long gone, but the house speakers still pump music. It isn't the first time I've closed a place down, but it is one of the few I can think of when I'm this pathetic and not going home with a woman.

No, my beautiful woman is gone. Because I was a dick. Because I couldn't be the bigger man.

"I told you she was trouble," Aiden says, unpacking the food and going to town.

"That's not really what I want to hear. It's not her fault. It's mine and Principal Dickface's."

"Do you want the truth or do you want to hear bullshit?"

"Is there a place between the truth and bullshit?"

"Denial, maybe." Aiden drinks another shot and rolls out his neck. Why can't I be like Aiden? Girls throw themselves at him and he never gets attached. The longest relationship he's ever had was with a carton of milk that expired in his fridge. He's happy. Fucking glowing. Sparkling, even. He's got his side gig taking out filthy rich women who want to shower him with gifts. He sleeps well at night, even if he doesn't have someone to go home to. He's complete.

"I texted her," I confess.

"Bro, come on." Aiden smacks his hand on the table. "You are making every rookie mistake in the book."

"There isn't a book, Aiden."

"*Of course* there's a book. I'm finding out all this stuff about you. First you read, now you let some girl you don't even know stomp all over your dick. What's happening to you, man?"

"This is the worst pep talk I've ever had," I tell him. "And that includes the time my dad convinced me to quit Little League."

"You're the worst baseball player in the world."

"What good are you?" I yell at him.

Lucho walks over with more drinks. "Last call, boys. For really real this time. The guys are almost done packing up the kitchen. Want some leftovers since this bastardo over here ate your dinner?"

I look down and Aiden has almost cleaned off the whole plate. "Yeah, Lucho, that'd be great."

"You're disgusting," I tell Aiden.

Aiden burps, and punches his chest. "I am what I am. But listen to me, Zachary Francis Fallon."

I hold on to the bar and hang my head for a second. As much shit as he's giving me, being ragged on by my best friend puts things into perspective. "Do not middle-name me."

"Zachary Francis Fallon," he says louder, holding his last shot in his hand. "You're too good to be this pathetic. You want to go after her? Do it. Nothing will stop you, and I am positive she won't turn you down. But don't let some douche bag, Principal Pervert, make you feel this way. There is nothing wrong with you. You got this, you hear me?"

We drink, and this time, the tequila and salt wash away the dregs of my anger. The problem is now I'm left with fear and regret. Regret that I acted like a dick. Fear because she might not forgive me.

"Besides, you might not have to worry all that much." Aiden examines the bottom of his glass, like he expects to find a diamond in it. Instead, he finds a few drops of tequila.

"What do you mean?" I grab the takeout bag Lucho gives me, and leave him one last tip for hooking me up and letting me leave my car in the parking lot until I can sober up to drive.

Aiden pats me on the back and leads me out of the restaurant down 30th Avenue. "Ricky got a call from Vegas."

"Vegas?" We cross the busy street, the sun beginning to rise as people are heading to work.

"We got an offer from The Royal. Call came in today. They want to make us a bigger offer than Reno."

"What? That's crazy."

"It's not official, so don't tell the other boys."

That's huge. A spot in Vegas is everything Ricky—we've—wanted. "When do we find out?"

"They're negotiating with the lawyers now, but it looks good. It's short notice because they want us to start before September, so we'd have to leave soon. But the money's good."

"Before September?"

"That's right. We're going to Vegas, baby!"

10

3 A.M.

ROBYN

I can't imagine what's worse: your boss sitting at the table beside you on your date, or discovering that your boss is a complete and utter tool.

How am I supposed to go to work in five hours? How am I supposed to face him after he put me in that position? I type and retype texts to Lily. Lily, who seems to be the only person I know with a life that is put together, will know what to do.

But I can't wake her at three in the morning.

I scream into my pillow, and it comes away with traces of the industrial-strength mascara that needs at least three showers before it completely comes off. Everything was going so great. I can pinpoint the moment everything went to hell.

It wasn't when Lukas sat down. If I were any other kind of person, I would've moved tables. But I sat there and I tried to be the peacemaker. I hate that, because I'm a woman, I'm supposed to watch these two men act like fools over, what? Me? But leaving that behind, it was when Lukas started asking questions of Fallon. It was when I was embarrassed that Fallon would answer with the truth. I shouldn't blame myself, but I do. Social programming is a bitch. I judged Fallon. And at the end of it, he felt the need to lie because he thinks titles and degrees and appearances mean more to him than *his* comfort.

I'm mad at myself for leaving. I'm mad at Lukas for crossing a line. I'm mad at Fallon for not keeping his cool.

I shouldn't have left him, but I couldn't help it. I try to sleep with his leather jacket on top of me, and when sleep evades me, I type, retype, and then delete every message I want to send him.

Finally, I do drift off.

I wake with a start because I know I'm late. I know it.

When I check my phone, it's seven thirty a.m. I brush my teeth and throw on a yellow knee-length skirt, a white shirt, and a white cardigan. I pull my hair into a ponytail as I run out the door and into a cab.

In the cab, I want to cry. Okay, so maybe I shouldn't have gone out on a date on a school night. But if the night had gone according to plan, my morning would look completely different. I could've woken up *with* Fallon instead of with his jacket. All the jacket did was fill me with an ache I didn't think I was capable of feeling. Is that what longing feels like? Like there's a hollow chunk inside of your heart and the only thing that can mend it is this one person.

No, I think. I've felt that way for a long time, and I don't know if Fallon is the solution. Maybe there isn't a solution.

I push those thoughts aside as I arrive at school determined to file a UFT complaint against Principal Lukas. I'm going to call Fallon and right things. I'm going to get myself together, because whatever I've been doing isn't working.

At some point during the day, I lose the nerve. I start to think about how I would file a complaint to begin with. "Principal Lukas and his date sat next to us and asked my date questions!" That's the problem with feeling threatened. How do you explain a *feeling?* Who would believe me, the perpetually late teacher who is lucky to be employed? Or the handsome young principal who volunteers on Sundays at school?

I get to my classroom and set up for the day, but I feel like I've already lost a battle I never had a chance of winning. When I check my phone, I see his name. *Fallon.* A text I missed.

Fallon: *I'm sorry. You up?*

And maybe, things aren't as lost as I thought.

*   *   *

I run down the steps of the school when I hear my name called out.

My stomach constricts with nerves when I look up to see Fallon sitting on the hood of his jet-black Camaro looking absolutely adorable and rumpled. His brown hair curls at the edges of his Red Sox cap. He hasn't shaved, and the closer I get, the more I want to run my hand along his jaw to see what it feels like. But I keep my hands tightly clasped on my briefcase.

A few of the parents picking up their kids do a double take as I walk up to this man who does not belong at an elementary school with his worn-in jeans and sports car and aviators that reflect the afternoon sun. Other than texting, I haven't seen him since our failed first date Tuesday night since he's been busy with practice and shows, and so I savor the sight of him.

"Hey," I say.

"How was school?" he asks.

"Can we not?" I say. "No talking around the pleasantries. Let's just put it out there."

He shoves his hands in his pockets and looks up at me. I hate looking at people when they wear sunglasses. I want to be able to look into his eyes. I reach for them, and he doesn't even budge as I gently pull them off. His blue-green eyes never leave my face.

"Okay," he says. "I shouldn't have started in on your boss. I'm sorry."

I want to laugh. "I'm sorry I left you with him. Do I even want to know what happened afterward?"

Fallon quirks his eyebrow. "You haven't seen him?"

"There was a lot of avoiding being done, I think, by both parties."

He bites down on his teeth, making his jaw ripple. I see the tightness in his body, like a feline ready to pounce. His eyes flick over my shoulder, and I automatically turn to see what he sees. Lukas and Lily are talking at the top of the steps.

"Did you drive here to apologize or do you want to give me a ride?"

"Actually," he says, "both. Are you hungry?"

I know he means if I'm hungry for food. But I feel a different kind of hunger when I'm around him. I'm hungry for his kiss, his touch, his everything. I'm hungry for him.

He opens the door to his car, and I get in.

"You still have my jacket," he says, arms stretched out toward the wheel.

"It's a little big on me," I say jokingly. "But I can be convinced to return it."

"Convinced how?" He's trying to keep his eyes on me while paying attention to the road.

"I'll figure something out." When he turns onto the BQE, I realize we're leaving Queens. "Where are we going?"

"It's Friday and I think we both need to do something fun."

"I can think of something fun we can do back at my apartment," I say. Who am I?

He chuckles. "What happened to not knowing what you want and taking things slow?"

I shrug. "Well, now that we got over the Worst Date Ever, there isn't anything that can beat that. It's all up from here. Plus, we've got a little over three months before you go off to Reno and I go off to whatever MFA program takes me."

Fallon gets quiet and brooding for a long while after that. I wonder if the reminder that this is temporary upset him. It shouldn't. We both decided this. Still, I wouldn't want to be reminded that this, whatever this feeling is, comes with an expiration date.

"There's one thing I've always wanted to do." He winks at me, his sexy smile returning as if whatever was upsetting him is long forgotten.

I tell myself to ignore it. Enjoy the here and now.

Forty-five minutes later we're parking in a lot in Coney Island.

"You've always wanted to go to Coney Island?" I ask skeptically.

"Corn dogs. Beach. Ferris wheels," he states, ticking things off with his fingers. "Men are like children, except we get to drink beer."

"Clearly," I laugh, and follow him out of the car.

I haven't been to Coney Island since I was in high school. When we were little, my cousins and I would run around the boardwalk with our allowances tucked in our shorts, and try to win stuffed animals off the clearly rigged carnival games.

"It isn't season yet," Fallon tells me. As he walks around the car, I can't help but watch his every move. His body is a thing of beauty. Shoulders and arms that frame hard-earned muscles. Jeans that hug an ass that begs to be bitten into.

I think I'm hyperventilating when he closes the six paces to get to me. He takes my hand and leads me down the boardwalk. We pick up corn dogs and two beers, walking and eating as we make it down toward the Wonder Wheel.

It might not be season, but Coney Island is never empty. Neighborhood kids gather in groups on the sand, backpacks on and everything. Hipsters in skinny shorts and waxed mustaches take photos of the garbage, the grit, and the locals that make Coney Island unique to New York shores.

I shut my eyes against the sea breeze that wraps around us, and for the first time today, I feel at peace.

"It doesn't make sense," I say.

Fallon looks over at me. He takes our meatless sticks and throws them in the nearest garbage can. With a touch, he guides me toward the metal railings that separate the beach and the boardwalk.

"What doesn't make sense?"

"You. This."

He stands in front of me with his amber beer in a plastic cup. Drinks from it. It doesn't hide the corners of his smile. When he lowers his drink, he has a foamy mustache, and without thinking, I stand on my toes and lick it, softly sucking his top lip. He answers by wrapping an arm tightly around my waist, bringing us so close so quickly, we slosh beer everywhere. I don't care about the beer. I don't care that this is the most PDA I've ever done. I care that he kisses me back, meeting his tongue with mine, searching and searching. I grip his shirt with my free hand, but the only way to be closer is to be naked.

His hand roams my back, until he reaches my neck. His nails rake hot marks up my skin, and with one pull, he undoes my ponytail, and my hair falls wildly into the breeze. Fallon kisses my ear, my neck. His tongue tugs at my earlobe, tracing circles that send fireworks through my body.

"You're right," he says, pulling away abruptly. "It doesn't make sense. But I'm not trying to force it to."

The sun sets lazily toward the horizon. The lights along the Luna Park carnival start to come alive, empty rides spinning and spinning, waiting for people to hop on.

"Come." I pull his hand. We dump our empty cups. Every step we take is accompanied by touching. He holds on to my waist and I dig my hand in his jeans pocket, as if this is the most normal thing in the world. As if there were no yesterday and there is no tomorrow. As if this entire playground is for us entirely. We get two tickets to the Wonder Wheel, and hop on.

The operator gives me a knowing wink as he slides the grate closed. "Keep hands and legs inside the car at all times. No standing. No—"

His advisory is drowned out by the sound of cranks turning, and the car swinging as we climb higher and higher.

"What are you doing?" he asks, a nervous blush creeping up his cheeks.

I grab hold of the front grates that enclose our car and push my weight forward. "Hang on."

And he does. He grabs the side of the car and keeps one hand on my hips. The car swings outward, and for a brief moment, it feels as if the whole car will fly off the hinges and right into the sea.

"I don't know if that's more fun or terrifying," he says, pulling me back against him.

I turn to him easily, draping my legs across his lap. "That's the point. Cheap thrills."

"You are wonderful, you know that?"

I've been called lots of things by lots of men. *Pretty. Hot. Gorgeous. Sexy.* Words lose their meaning after a while. But *wonderful* is new. *Wonderful* has a certain magic that starts to fill that hole in my chest. But something inside of me won't let me acknowledge it completely, and I do what words can't. I kiss him instead.

His mouth fits perfectly on mine. I wrap my arms around his neck to hold on to him, to this feeling he brings out in me. His hand finds its way beneath my skirt, and I gasp when it grips my thigh hard.

"Sorry," he whispers.

"Don't be." I tug on the collar of his shirt.

The car climbs higher and higher until we reach the top, jostling us closer together. In this moment, I realize a few things: We are high in the sky and I want Zac Fallon more than I can say. I want to do unspeakable things with him, right here with the whole city beneath our feet.

FALLON

I might die in this metallic contraption of doom. But I'll die happy, with the most beautiful woman kissing me senseless. When the Wonder Wheel stops to let on more passengers, we're at the very top. I look up for a moment at the seascape, deep and dark-blue waves crashing against the shoreline. The wind is hard and chilly up here, and Robyn's skin is covered in goose bumps. I rub her thigh until I feel her skin relax and warm to me.

When she moans, I feel the vibration deep in my throat. I pull on her leg to sit her completely on my thigh. I want her to know what she does to me. I want her to feel my dick reacting to every inch of her.

But my pleasure doesn't end with her rubbing her palm on the bulge that (painfully) strains against my jeans. My pleasure starts with her. I trace my middle finger across her thigh, pull away to watch her face change. Her eyelids flutter the closer I get to the magic spot between her legs. I press a kiss on each of her cheeks, never letting my finger stop from roaming.

"God, you're so wet," I say. The breath in my chest might shatter me. Her panties are soaked through.

She whispers too low for me to make out what she's said, but her hands say otherwise. Her clever fingers undo my button and pull down my fly. I shut my eyes. She pulls down my boxers and my dick springs into her hand. Her thumb traces a wet bubble that beads at the head of my shaft.

I want nothing more than to bury myself inside of her, feel her walls close in all around me. Lose myself in her. But the car jostles. Robyn yelps as the rocking motion threatens to topple her off.

"I got you," I assure her, and pull her back up on top of me. "Where were we?"

She takes my hand and guides it back between her legs, and when I push her panties to the side and slide my finger in, I lose all of my breath. I feel her squeeze against my finger as I pull out and slide two fingers in and stroke. With my thumb, I rub wet circles around her clit. Robyn falls into me, rocking her pelvis against my hand, and suddenly we're slowly moving and falling back to the ground. I stroke my fingers faster, deeper. Bite the sensitive spot between her neck and shoulder, until she moans a kiss that lingers and she relaxes wet and slack against my chest.

I slip my hand out of her and bring it to my lips. She watches with wide eyes as I taste her, sweet and slick.

We tear apart from each other just in time for the ride to reach the bottom. I drape my jacket over my dick, stiff and aching with want. While we wait for the Wonder Wheel to ascend, she climbs up on top of me, her knees on either side of my thighs. Her hands cupped around my neck while she kisses me senseless, and we've reached the top of the ride again.

Robyn's sweet laugh makes me even harder, and my dick stands up at attention as she pulls my jacket off and she takes me into her hands. When she gets on her knees and looks up at me, I could break apart and come in a second. But I try to hold back. I shut my eyes and hiss as her warm tongue slides all along the wet tip of my dick. She takes me into her plump, hot mouth and sucks until the friction makes a popping sound, like the smack of a lollipop.

"God," I hear myself say. "Do that again."

My vision is so dazed from how good it feels to be inside her mouth that I can't even see straight. There are, like, four of her. Four Robyns, on her knees, pumping her hands up and down my shaft while she sucks the essence out of me. I buckle when the car swings outward toward the open air. This time, we're bracing for it, and I grab hold of her.

She takes me in deeper and deeper, and I think I might faint when I feel myself against the back of her throat.

"I'm going to come," I manage to say.

I'm not sure I've even spoken, because she doesn't let up, and keeps her mouth around my head, sucking and licking, and I say her name over and over. Robyn. Robyn. Her eyes are dark pools, and I reach over and tug on her hair, breathing hard as I come in her full, raw mouth.

Her mouth is a perfect O and glossy with my come. Her eyes bright as the carnival lights below and the stars above. I might just come again when she sticks her tongue out and licks her top lip and smiles a sinful smile.

"You are so fucking sexy," I tell her, and take off my shirt and offer it to her.

She smirks, and cleans all traces of me off her lips. She tucks her hair behind her ear and hands the shirt back to me. Other guys would be grossed out over putting the shirt back on, but I'd do anything for this woman right about now. A soiled shirt is the least of my worries.

I stretch my hand back over her shoulders, her head resting on my chest.

"You're shaking," I whisper, tracing my hands up and down her arms.

She looks up at me. "I've never done or felt anything like that before."

"Me neither," I say. Though I've done plenty of things like that, the feeling of Robyn touching me—that—that was completely new.

I wish we could roll around in bed right about now, but all we're left with is a view of the loud and glittering Coney Island strip and the ocean as we descend one last time. There could be worse views.

STRIPPED   119

"What are you thinking?" I whisper in her ear.

She leans her head on my shoulder, rests her hands over mine so we're completely entwined.

"I'm thinking I could get used to this arrangement."

And then it hits me.

I'm leaving. Before the time we agreed on.

I haven't told her. And as the silence draws on, and we get off the ride, and get back in my car, and back on the BQE, and into our building, and then I'm kissing her good night—I can't bring myself to tell her the truth.

The next day at rehearsals, there's a buzz of excitement among the guys as we wait for Ricky.

"Do you think things went well?" Vin asks, stretching his quads two spaces away from me.

"Dunno," I say.

"Don't be nervous," he tells me.

"I'm not nervous."

"Well, you look nervous."

"Will you two quiet down?" Gary says, rubbing his temples. Gary's been with Mayhem City since Ricky found him passed out on his front lawn. They were neighbors and Gary's pro baseball career ended with what should've been a life-ruining knee injury. Some dance and water therapy later, he was better, but he'd never play baseball again. In some way, Ricky has rescued all of us but each in a different way. Gary wanted to join Ricky's crazy endeavor and it took off. Though the only batting he does now is with props during his dance routine. "I swear, you guys are going to give me gray hair, and I didn't have kids for a reason."

"You already dye that shit," I point out, and Gary opens one eye to shoot me a death glare.

I spread my legs to stretch my hamstrings and calves. I don't want to be here. I want to be with Robyn. Just the thought of her sweet, sweet face sends a thrill down to my bones. I should say, boner.

I grab my bottle of water and squeeze some over my head. The cold hits my skin, and I feel myself calm down again.

"What is wrong with you?" Wonderboy asks. I've come to realize that I don't mind Wonderboy when he's alone. But when he's with his brother, they set each other off. Still, he's got potential as a dancer, and I can see him taking charge of the group years down the road. "You're like—off."

"I'm fine," I say, and resume stretching.

"Naw, man. You're like—" Wonderboy lets the phrase dangle, and his brother finishes.

"Giddy," Vin says.

"I am not *giddy*," I say.

"Is it that teacher?" Gary asks.

"I had a *mad* crush on my teacher when I was in high school," Vin reminisces, leaning back on his hands.

"Please, Mrs. Benitez was in love with me. She never failed me," Wonderboy says.

"That's cuz she thought you was me," Vin tells his brother.

"You should do a naughty teacher routine," Gary says. "It would spice things up when we get to *Vegas.*"

It has been impossible to just say "Vegas." One word. Simple. All of a sudden, it's been VEGAS! *Vegaaaaas! VE-GAS!* Every which way they can say it, they do. The last time I was there I was on our first tour with the boys, and I was in Vinny and Wonderboy's spot. I was so green, still figuring out my routine. The women out there would've eaten me alive if Ricky hadn't knocked some sense into me. There were rules. No kissing. No putting money in your mouth. No taking drugs. No drinking their drinks. No going home with the clientele. Commonsense stuff that when you're nineteen and showered with tits, ass, and more money than god, you don't know how to act.

Ricky finally walks in, and all the guys get to their feet and surround him. Ricky is dressed in his office finest, if his office were in Milan. His blazer is a sharp blue and tailored to his every muscle. He wears a bright turquoise tie that makes his tanned skin look darker. His hair is freshly cropped at the sides, his beard has every hair meticulously in place, and a dreamy smile is playing on his lips.

"Well?"

"What's the word?"

"You're killing me, Smalls."

The guys jump around, bouncing off one another's excitement. I swear I could set off explosives if I lit a match in the room. Me, on the other hand—I always thought that when I got the news about Vegas I'd feel different. It's everything we've been working toward for eleven years. Longer, for Ricky and Gary. I was happy with the way things have always been. I've never complained about this life, because I chose it. But as I look at my brothers, I can't help but feel apart from them because my first reaction to waiting for Ricky's word is fear. I'm scared as fuck because I don't want to leave just yet.

And I know—the smarter part of me is telling me that I'd be leaving in September anyway. What's the difference? The smarter part of me is telling me that I can't throw everything away for a woman, no matter who she is.

Ricky walks up to me, and rests his hands on my shoulders. He's shorter than me, but I've always looked up to him. He's the definition of someone who built himself up from nothing. I know I can't let him down. So, I put on a smile and I ask, "What's the word?"

Ricky looks down at the ground before meeting our eyes, and in that smile I know the answer. "It's done and done, baby!"

Our studio erupts with a bunch of grown-ass men cheering and screaming. Everyone jumps on Ricky, who tries to act like he doesn't want the hugs and punches we throw at him. It's a pregame huddle that lasts for a long time.

"Okay, fellas," Ricky says, breaking free of the circle. He holds out his hands. I've known Ricky for eleven years. I've seen him at his lowest and highest, but I've never seen him this happy. "They want us as soon as possible. We have a lot of work to do in four weeks."

"Four weeks?" I say, and I'm surprised at my own voice.

Ricky looks like he's doing calculus in his head, and says, "You're right. Closer to three since we want to be there for a week before the show starts."

No matter what doubts I'm feeling, I push them down. I owe everything to Ricky and I'm not going to be the one to ruin this for him. I can't.

He holds out his hand to me. "You ready for the big-time, partner?"

Partner. I've unofficially been his second in command so long, and he's never, not once, called me partner. This crew has my blood, sweat, and tears. This crew is everything I've put my soul into. This crew is my family. What is wrong with me that I couldn't see that right away?

I take Ricky's hand and we embrace, slapping each other's backs. "I'm proud of you, brother."

"I couldn't have done this without you," he tells me, and the sincerity in his voice wrecks me. I can't let them down. "Without all of you."

I look at everyone. The guys who've been with us for a decade, the guys who've joined this season, and everyone in between.

"You know what this means?" I tell them. They trade glances and wait for my response. "No more bitching at rehearsals."

It's their turn to jump on me, jabbing my arms and ribs with playful punches. We wait for Ricky to change out of his business attire, and then we line up for our first group routine. I don't know if it's the news or the excitement, or if all our practicing is finally paying off, but we've never been so in sync, our bodies moving in one tight formation.

At the end of the day, when I'm in my car and on my way home, I realize that it isn't the other guys who have been out of sync. It's me. That has to change, because we're leaving in three weeks, and I know the right thing is to break things off with Robyn. But when her name pops up on my phone, I don't think I'm strong enough to go through with it.

"Hey," I say. "I was just thinking about you."

11

Need You Now

"I can't believe it," I say.

I stare at Fallon, the Central Park greenery blooming around him. Early summer in New York has never been more pristine. He wears a light hoodie and jeans. Even though I try to pay attention to his words, I always end up staring at him. His mouth is hypnotizing, more so than the pretty shade of his blue-green eyes.

"Are you serious?" I repeat, unable to process what he's telling me.

He leans on his side of our picnic blanket and takes a bite out of the sandwich I made.

"I swear. This is my first picnic."

I bring the straw to my lips and look at him skeptically. "How?"

"We were never the picnic kind of family." He smiles, but there's a hint of sadness there. In his big hands, the champagne-in-a-can looks like a miniature toy.

"What kind of family were you?" I wonder if I should ask. But I want to know everything about him in the time we have left. It's been a day and a half since our night at Coney Island and every waking (and sleeping) moment I have is consumed with one thought: *When are we going to do that again?*

"Okay." He sits cross-legged. He rubs his hands together and takes a deep breath. "Honesty moment. I'll tell you about my family and you tell me about yours. Deal?"

"Deal."

"My dad worked at a printing company. Books, magazines, flyers, etc. When I was a kid, the one thing I remember about my dad is that when he came home, his fingers were always black with ink. It got deep in his nails, and no matter how much he cleaned, he could never wash it off. He got laid off when I was thirteen. I remember the exact moment because it was the day he told me I had to quit Little League. Back then I thought it was because he thought I sucked."

"Did you?"

"What?"

"Suck?"

He breaks off a piece of bread and throws it at me. "That's beside the point. I hated him for so long. I wanted to play in a league. I wanted to pitch for the Red Sox. I had plans.

"Instead, I ended up babysitting my little brother because my mom was pregnant again with my sister. My older brother was fifteen and already getting in trouble. Four kids was a lot for them to handle. My dad didn't know how to deal with not working. He was unemployed for a year. It was the longest year of our lives. He drank more in that year than in his whole life, probably."

"I'm sorry," I say, because I think it's the right thing to say and nothing else seems right.

"Not your fault. Anyway, he wasn't a violent drunk. Just a drunk. He never hit us or my mom. Didn't really yell, either. He was just consumed in this sadness. I think—I think he wanted to die. Almost did. His liver is shot now. He was sick for a long time after that. My mom was a maid at a hotel, but when that wasn't enough, she started cleaning apartments on the weekend.

"When she died, my dad fell off the wagon. I was sixteen and flunking out of school. My sister was three and there was no one to look out for her, so I'd stay home instead of going to school most days. My dad always fought with me the most, though. I think it's because I look like him. If you see pictures of when my pop was my age, I look like a carbon copy. I used to think he hated me because I flunked out and then started stripping. But I think he just hated himself."

"Fallon—" I say his name, reach for his arm. He flinches slightly, but then relaxes when I touch him.

"So you see." He takes my hand in his. "We never had time for picnics. Thank you for doing this."

I lean forward and kiss him gingerly. His lips part for me and his hands comb through the sides of my hair. There's a softness to his touch that makes my body melt into his.

I pull away first because I want to look at his face. I will never be tired of looking at his face.

"Your turn," he tells me.

I chuckle. "It hardly seems fair. My family is boring."

"How about this?" he says. "Let's pack this up and walk toward that castle. I want to get all of my New York sights in bef—before the tourists descend like locusts."

We pack up, and he shoulders the backpack. We take a winding path north. No matter how many times I walk through Central Park, I always have the sense of being lost in its enclosed patches of trees and sprawling green. I love watching the rowboats on the pond.

Fallon watches me watch them. "Do you want to do that instead?"

I shake my head. "Another time. Let's keep going toward the castle."

There's a strange frown on his face, but I tell myself to ignore it. "As you wish, Princess."

"You know when I was little my cousin convinced me that we were descended from an Inca princess?"

"Wait a minute," he says, completely serious. "You're not? Dammit. There goes my plan to marry into royalty."

I nearly choke on my own spit at the marriage comment. I think he is shocked too because his face goes slack, as if he can't believe he said that. We ignore it, and I keep talking.

"My dad's from Peru. He lived in a tiny city outside of Lima. He was studying to become a pediatrician and was volunteering at a town that didn't have any doctors. That's where he met my mom. She was volunteering, too, with an American company. She was born in New York, but her family's from Ecuador."

"They fell in love and moved here? There's nothing boring about that, Robyn."

I laugh. "Oh, they hated each other. Dad had to get over his Peruvian machismo because my mom wanted none of it after being raised here. They were both alphas marking their territory. Both wanting to be right. I always tell my dad he was the original mansplainer. You know, I have no idea how he landed my mom sometimes. But she loves him even still."

"You sound surprised."

He threads his fingers with mine and we walk up a hill. From here, Belvedere Castle is visible. Flanked by tall trees and the skyscrapers, it looks like the last remnant of a fairy tale.

"I just mean that I'm surprised they've lasted this long. All of my friends in high school had parents that were getting divorced. I used to think my parents were cyborgs."

"Princess Cyborg," he says. "I like that. You should write that."

I roll my eyes. Ever since I told him that I had wanted to be a writer, he won't stop putting ideas together and telling me to write them.

"When did your parents come here?" he asks.

"They were apart for two years. They wrote letters. Real, honest-to-god love letters. My mom never used to let me read them. I think it's because she was afraid that I'd see her as a *human*."

"She a tough one?" he asks. "Your mom?"

"Tough as diamonds. My mom was one of ten kids in a Catholic family and she was like a mom to her siblings."

"Did you ever get to read the letters?" He looks at me with a mischievous arch of his brow. "I bet you did. You look like trouble."

"Please," I say, scoffing. "Up until a few years ago, I was a model adult. I didn't even have my first drink until I was twenty-one. I waited to be legal because I always followed the rules. I was top of my class. Most Likely to Succeed."

"In addition to Most Likely to Stick a Foot in Her Mouth? Nice."

I swat his arm with my palm, but end up running my hand over the delicious muscles of his biceps. Shameless, I know.

"Reading those letters was the most scandalous thing I ever did. My mom still doesn't know."

"Did you find any juicy secrets?"

"How did you know?"

"Makes sense. Two people during that time. You either called on a real landline or you wrote. No e-mails or texts. They wouldn't be able to see each other, so the only way to talk about their feelings was through those letters."

"My mom was pregnant with me before they got married," I tell him. He gasps, feigning scandal. "I know. It was easier for her to travel to Peru because the visas came in faster through her side. Then, she got herself pregnant before she left back to the States. I'm pretty sure it was on purpose. Two doctors with means of contraception?"

"Baby trap," Fallon says, and we've finally reached the entrance to the castle.

Tourists walk in and out with massive cameras trying to get just the right angles. Kids run around near the water's edge.

"Total baby trap," I say. "She found out after a month or so. Flew back down to Peru and they got married by the priest in the tiny town. My Gran on my mom's side still doesn't know that. No one does, except my parents and me. And that's only because I read the letters."

"Holy shit," Fallon says. "You're crazy if you think that isn't interesting. You should—"

"Do not tell me to write it."

"Okay, I won't tell you. But I will suggest it. Why are you so hesitant to write?"

I grab him by the collar of his T-shirt and pull him down to me. "Because that's a story for another day."

I shut him up with a kiss, and pretty soon we have an audience giggling as we make out. I pull away, my face red from dozens of strangers hooting and whistling our praise.

"Come," I tell him, tugging on his hand.

But he stops at the sound of a ringtone. He reaches into his back pocket for his phone.

"You go up, I have to take this call."

For a moment, my mind goes to a dark place. There's a woman's name on the caller ID. Who is she? How does he know her? Will he tell me about her? Then again, I have to keep reminding myself that this is temporary, and that I have no right to be jealous. It's part of his lifestyle, and I've agreed to be part of that life. I have to be more guarded. At the end of the day, Fallon is not my boyfriend. He's Mr. Right Now.

I climb the spiral steps up to the top of the castle by myself. Each step echoes in my thoughts. Mr. Right. Now. Mr. Right. Now. Mr. Right Now.

When I get to the top, a June wind carries the scent of new flowers and burnt sugar from nearby peanut stands. I turn my face up to the sun and wish that every day could be as good as this one.

"Robyn!" My name is called out, but it sounds far away. I look around and notice some of the other people on the deck are pointing over the ledge at the ground.

I walk over and see what they're looking at.

Fallon.

"Sweet Princess Cyborg," he shouts. "Let down your hair."

And I sit on the ledge, unable to stop my heart from fluttering like petals in the wind. I press a kiss to my fingertips and blow it down to him. Then, I curl my finger and bring it toward me. He disappears into the castle, and I know he's running up here.

"Ugh, you guys are so adorable," a woman tells me, half grimacing and half smiling.

"He's a keeper, darling," an elderly woman adds.

Before I can acknowledge them, Fallon comes onto the deck, slightly panting. I don't know what's gotten into him, but I like it. I want it. I don't want it to stop. He picks me up in his arms and lifts me in the air, slowly, so our bodies slide against each other and our lips are so close there is no other choice but to kiss.

FALLON

By the time I get to the club, I'm walking on air. It's been two days since our kiss at the castle. Then, I remember every opportunity I had to tell Robyn that I'm leaving sooner than we'd discussed. Every single time I made an excuse. I didn't want to interrupt her while she was eating. I didn't want to stop her from telling the story of her parents. Then we were going home, and she got busy with work.

As much as she doesn't want to admit it, she's a romantic. She acts like she isn't, like it's her fault that all of her relationships have failed. But what she hasn't met is the right person. She wants that fairy-tale romance. As much as I want to be the guy who gives it to her, I know I can't be. I know that soon, I'm going to have to come clean, and then I'll be gone and long distance doesn't last. Not in this day and age.

I open the door to the office and hear someone whispering. When I get closer, I recognize Vinny's voice. Something stops me from making myself heard. I stand in the hallway, right by the door of the back office. The buzz of the fluorescent light is the only thing I can hear aside from Vinny's voice.

"Yeah, I got them," he says. I can hear him pacing back and forth. "I told you I would. Nah, the party's going to be lit. I can promise you that. Let's go with forty a pop."

Forty a pop? I have a terrible feeling that I know what he's talking about. I think about the crushed white pill on my floor after the bachelorette party.

Footsteps sound from down the hall, and Ricky appears.

"Fallon!" he shouts.

"I gotta go," Vinny whispers, and I'm forced to make myself known. Vinny sticks his head out the door and sees me standing there with my gear bag on my shoulder. His brown eyes look at me suspiciously, and he's got some fucking nerve smiling. "'Sup, Fallon?"

I shrug and then lie. "Looking for you. We should go over the boxing routine."

"Yeah, about that," Vinny says. "I don't think that's going to fly. See, my brother and I thought it'd be better if we do the set together. Play up the twin thing, you know what I'm saying."

I wish I could act disappointed, but I just let it go.

"Great idea," Ricky says, and gives Vinny a high five. "But rehearsal is cancelled today."

"Why?" I ask.

"The Royal scheduled a last-minute promo shoot. The photographer's coming here. I just called the other boys to have them meet us here."

I don't want to be the one to rain on his parade, so I smile, and head to the lockers to change. I can't shake the feeling that Vinny is shady. But I've never accused one of my crew members of doing anything illegal. I can't now, not without concrete proof.

"You okay, man?" Vinny asks, walking into the lockers behind me. "You seem on edge. Even more than usual."

I look him up and down but don't say anything. "I'm good. Did Ricky say if we were supposed to wear anything specific?"

Vinny shakes his head. I forget how young he is. I wonder if he gets under my skin because he reminds me of what I used to be like. Messy. Loud. Stupid.

"Nah, I think he has everything set up on the main."

"Cool, thanks." I pull off my T-shirt and look at him. "You going to stand there all day, kid?"

"Look, Fallon. I just wanted to say that I know you and I got off on the wrong foot. My brother says you're cool, and I dunno, I guess I just act out. I figure we can start over for Vegas and all."

Be the bigger man. That's what I should be. That's what I *will* be. But I have to admit this is an opportunity in itself. With Vinny trying to be my friend, I can find the proof that I need.

I hold out my hand. "Sure. Clean slate."

The lights on the main stage are kicked up a notch. Mark, our sound master and DJ, is trying to find the right angle with the photographer The Royal Hotel and Casino sent over.

Ricky selected the guys who are going to go on the promo shots. It's Ricky, the twins, Gary, Aiden, Sebastian, and myself.

I pull Ricky to the side. "Can I talk to you later on?"

Ricky's eyes can't focus on me long enough. "Sure, mate. Let's get this shoot down and then I'm all yours."

Ricky has three outfit changes. The first is navy-blue jeans and big silver belt buckles that look like we're on our way to the rodeo. We look ridiculous, but I tell myself that I need to be a team player. If no one else is complaining, then neither am I.

Silvia, the photographer, is an older woman with long frizzy hair piled up on the top of her head. She holds her camera like it allows her to see into another world. She's focused and shouts out directions like a pro.

"You," she says, pointing at me. "Relax your jaw muscles. We want inviting for sexy times, not inviting for murder."

The other guys laugh at my expense and I stretch out my jaw.

"You," she says, pointing at Sebastian. "This is not the WWE. Lower your arms."

"I didn't realize we were going to get roasted," I mutter. Aiden elbows me to get me to shut up, but instead it incites a round of jabs.

"Okay, change," Silvia shouts.

Darla tick-tocks over from the backstage and fusses with Ricky's hair. "Let me get hair and makeup over here. We need you boys to look your best. Lots of competition in Vegas."

"Thanks for the tenth reminder today," I say, sitting on one of the vanity chairs they've lined up. A couple of makeup people appear from backstage with sponges and trays full of powders.

"Aw, honey, I'm sorry," Darla says, leaving Ricky's side and walking over to me. She grabs my chin, getting in the way of Clint, the makeup artist. "Don't do anything to those cheek-bones, Clint."

"He's in good hands," he says. When Darla walks away, Clint sucks his teeth and rolls his eyes. "You think I haven't been doing this for half my life."

"She means well," I say.

"You're just defending her because she's in love with you."

"What?" I shake my head.

"That she-lion wants to eat you alive. And if you're not look-ing, honey, she's going to do it."

With that warning, I sit in my chair and let myself be used as a human Ken doll.

We change our outfits again. This time into white silk shorts that leave absolutely nothing to the imagination. Clint and the makeup artists line us up to reapply body oil.

"Ricky," I say warningly. I hold out my arms so one of the makeup artists, I think I heard someone call him Will, can use a cloth to spread oil down my sides. "Really? Please tell me you didn't choose these outfits."

"Sure," Ricky says unconvincingly. "I didn't choose them. But come on. It's going up smack in the middle of summer."

"Imagine how huge our junk is going to be on the side of the hotel," Vinny says, a cheesy grin on his eager face.

"Yeah," his brother jokes. "It'll be a change of pace for you."

"You know we're twins," Vinny says.

Wonderboy winks at the young makeup artist spreading oil across his thighs. "We're not identical where it counts."

"Okay, enough," I say. I walk to the front of the stage and thank Will before I get ready to line up.

Silvia's waiting with two of her assistants, both of whom haven't been able to look us in the eye.

"You," Silvia says, and walks up to me. She holds out a stick of gum. "Chew this. It'll relax whatever's got you more wound up than a jack-in-the-box."

I take it, unwrap it, and shove the stick of gum in my mouth. The chewing does nothing to calm my nerves. I wasn't even aware I *had* nerves to calm until she kept pointing out how stiff I am. I jump around onstage and do some stretches while I wait for the others. One of the assistants has long dark hair. When she tucks it behind her ear, something in my chest tightens because the gesture reminds me so much of Robyn.

Is this what it's like to miss someone?

An oily hand smacks against my back, and when I turn around, it's Vinny. I remember the conversation I overhead while he was on the phone. I can't return the smile he gives me. I shrug him off and keep stretching.

"Fallon, your phone keeps ringing," Ricky says. "It's Robyn."

I spin around, nearly slipping on the smooth floor. "Give me that."

Ricky has my phone against his ear. I walk behind him across the stage, but he evades me. "Good day, pretty lady. This is Rick Rocket, how may I assist you today? Oh, so you *do* remember me. Well, you've got a lovely voice, you know. Sure, sure, Zac's right here. We're a little busy at the moment. Prepping for—"

"Give me the fucking phone, Ricky," I shout.

Aiden gets in my way, and all of a sudden, all the boys are in on keeping me away from Ricky.

"We've got a show tonight. Yes, I realize it's a school night. First show's in two hours. I'll put your name at the door. See you then!"

I break through the wall of arms that hold me back. Ricky hands my phone back to me.

"It's about time we met her, Zac." Ricky winks at me. Then he steps closer. "You know, maybe you'd feel better if you came clean. She doesn't seem to know you're leaving."

"That's my business," I say, sounding more petulant than I want. I turn my phone off and go to the lockers. I lock my phone in there. But I know Ricky's right. I hate it when he's right.

But now I've got another thing to worry about. Robyn is coming here, and she's going to watch me strip.

12

Tempted to Touch

ROBYN

I check and recheck my lipstick in the back of the cab. Yes, it's still on. Yes, it's still red. Yes, I'm still nervous. I'm nervous about going to watch Fallon. I'm nervous I'm going to like it more than I want to admit. The one time I did see him, I didn't stick around for the whole spectacle.

The cabbie drops me off in front of the club and gives me a surprised look when he sees where we are. I pay, and get out at the curb. The club is unmarked except for a door with the building numbers in red lights and a long black awning that wraps around the building. Dozens and dozens of women are lined up against the wall. They're in groups easily distinguishable by what they're celebrating. Most of the groups are made up of bachelorettes, the brides wearing tiny crowns with white veils and sashes. Then there are the birthday girls, also in glittering crowns. The younger they are, the prouder they are to display the age they're turning. It's mostly the twenty-one-year-olds who let you know that they're finally legal enough to drink. Then there are a few sorority girls. Some women just out about town. Two groups of divorce parties.

I do as Ricky said and go to the door. I hate being *that* girl. I hate cutting in line.

I look at the tall man guarding the entrance. He looks uninterested, typing with one fat thumb on the screen of his phone.

I clear my throat. "Uhm, excuse me."

It takes him a moment to look up. He moves as if in slow motion, taking in my black three-inch heels, my bare legs, and the black velvet dress I chose for tonight. Compared to all the red, pink, and white dresses down the line, I feel like I chose the wrong outfit.

It's a stupid thing to be self-conscious about, but I've also never dated a stripper, and I've never shown up at his place of employment with an invitation from his boss. I realize that I'm about to enter Fallon's world. It's as easy as walking through a door. I think of how out of place Fallon looked standing in front of my school with his black sports car and his rumpled-and-out-of-bed attitude. Did he feel as nervous as I do now?

When the bouncer's eyes reach mine, his face spreads with a smile. "Robyn."

"How did you know?"

"I know things," he says, and opens the door for me. "There's a table with your name on it."

As he lets me in, people on the line start to complain. *Why does she get to go in first? My feet are already killing me! What the hell? Who is she?*

Who is she?

Who am I, really?

I'm a woman going to see the man she's dating.

I'm a terrible teacher and a wannabe writer. I'm early. I'm overexposed. I walk inside the club as if I'm walking into a cave full of treasures I'm not supposed to touch. The lights are dim, but neon strips line the floor between the aisles. They're like yellow-lit roads that take you anywhere you want to go—the bar, the bathroom, the main stage area.

The stage itself is interesting. I can't help but think it looks phallic in the way there's a short catwalk that ends in a round tip. Against either side of the walls, there are two small stages. I was expecting poles, but I suppose those are reserved for female strip clubs.

Waiters and waitresses put little notecards on tabletops. The women are beautiful. They all wear simple black tank tops and shorts with back pockets for notepads and pens. The men are blinding to look at. Each one prettier than the next. They straddle the line between masculine and feminine with expertly done eyebrows and hair. One of them sees me standing at the back of the club.

"You must be Robyn," he tells me.

"That's me," I say, trying to go for "relaxed" when really, I look like I've been holding in my pee for six hours.

"I'm Jax," he says. His dark hair and sandy-brown skin have a certain gleam, like he's the new spokesman for coconut oil. "I've got your table ready."

Up at the side of the stage there's a table with a rose on it. "B—by—by myself?"

Some of the waitstaff look up and chuckle at me. "Cute," I hear someone say.

"First time?"

"How can you tell?" My voice is climbing octaves by the second. "I can just sit at the bar, if that's okay?"

"Sure thing." He puts his hand on the small of my back and guides me to a seat.

The bar is long, with dozens of mirrors and a light that changes gradually into different colors. There's a woman behind the bar. Her hair is bright red, and she has a splatter of freckles.

"What's your poison?" she asks, dry but friendly.

"Jack and ginger," I say, fishing out my credit card.

She grabs a glass, makes sure it's clean, and sets it on the counter. She pours without taking her eyes off me, and I think it's a wonder that she doesn't spill a drop.

"Put your money away, darling," she says, and pushes the drink toward me with a smile and a wink.

I leave her a cash tip, and accept the drink. "It's a little weird seeing the place before the show starts."

She laughs and leans on the bar. "Yeah, it's like seeing the wizard behind the curtain. Does it disappoint?"

I think on that. "I actually wasn't sure of what I was expecting, so no. Do you get tired of the same show?"

She shakes her head. "It's a good gig. Beats the other clubs I worked at."

"I'm Robyn," I say and hold out my hand.

"Rachel. Get comfortable, because we're about to let in the crowd."

My stomach flutters. "Any way I can see Fallon before he gets onstage?"

"Believe me, you don't want to go back there. They do their preshow bro-bonding or whatever. Just sit, relax. Let me know when I can get you a refill."

I realize I've been sucking my drink like it's a smoothie, but Rachel only laughs and gives me another one.

The lights dim even more. At the far corner, past one of the side stages, is an enclosed area where a DJ puts on his big head-phones and taps on the mic.

"Too, two, and to, mic check." The sound is clean, and a background track comes on.

The front doors open and women come pouring in. Each table is numbered, but the waitstaff is there to usher them to their reserved tables.

Rachel refills my drink, and I sit with my entire body as tight as an overtuned guitar string.

Some women sit behind me at the bar. They whisper. "I'm so glad I could get tickets. I hear the show's going to Vegas soon."

Hm. I thought they were going to Reno.

Everything happens quickly after that. The DJ comes on through the speakers, a low rumbling voice that reminds me of warm butter spread on toast. "Welcome, sexy ladies of New York Cityyyyy! The Deluxe Astoria proudly presents Mayhem City, the hottest men from around the world. Remember, no photography is allowed until after the show, but tonight you can look and certainly, most certainly, you *can* touch."

The women in the audience holler excitedly. Each table is de-signed to face the stage with easy access for the waitstaff to take down drink orders. Two more bartenders appear to help Rachel out, and then the overhead lights come alive. Brilliant strobes that crisscross on a floor-to-ceiling white screen.

"Ladies—are you ready for the show tonight?" I recognize the voice as Ricky's. Over a hundred women answer with whistling screams. I vaguely remember feeling this way the first and only time I saw NSYNC in concert.

A blaring bass and light show thunders across the stage as Ricky comes out. He's a little bit older than I imagined from his voice, but stunning all the same. Even from the bar, I can see his light eyes sparkle. His black-and-plum suit is tailored to a tightly sculpted body. His blond beard is closely trimmed to killer bone structure, and when he walks across the stage, he commands attention.

"I said, are you ready for the show tonight?"

The crowd goes wild, and I feel a contact thrill right through my center.

"We've got a special show for you. As some of you might know, we're new to the city, but New York is one of our favorite places." He hypes up the crowd, shouting out Brooklyn and the Bronx. He's got a way of moving his body and making it feel like he's there just for the girl he singles out. "I'll be here to make sure you're entertained, but most importantly, we're all here for your pleasure. Now, allow me to introduce the men of Mayhem City."

It's a fine moment for my phone to light up. I silence it as quickly as I can, and Rachel loads me up with a Jack and ginger refill. It's Lily. If she only knew what I am doing right now.

I nod along to the sexy roll of hip-hop beats as six silhouettes appear behind the white screen. They stand tall, shoulders back. My heart thrums because even though I can't see their faces, I recognize Fallon's build. The shape of his body. I can find him even in the darkness.

The screen rises, revealing every part of the boys. They look down, waiting for the song to come to the right beat and then they sway from side to side. They're in button-down shirts open down to their chests and tight trousers that highlight their asses just so. Fallon is on the far right, closest to the empty table where I was supposed to be sitting. I catch the slightest moment of when he looks and realizes that I'm not there.

I should've said something. I should've sent word. But now

it's too late. I think I prefer looking at him from back here where he can't see me. I can concentrate on watching them, all six of them. They glide across the stage, each one of them show-casing a different specialty. Twin brothers whose names I don't catch because of the screams are mirror images of each other. Another guy break-dances his way onto the floor and spins on his head. Two more guys are expert at acrobatics, spinning across the stage in somersaults that could win them gold. And then there's Fallon.

It's a side of him that leaves me completely perplexed. There's the funny, charming, *sweet* man I've been around. He's always sexy. When I met him he was sexy. He's never stopped *being* sexy.

But on the stage, his smile speaks of things only whispered in the cover of darkness—or at the top of a Ferris wheel. His face is smoothly shaved, his hair styled back. He stands center stage and points at a girl. She looks up at him as if god himself were asking her to stand. Then he twists his torso and flips one handed in the air, lowering his body slowly, like the ripple of honey along skin.

I scream.

I can't help but scream. I cup my hands around my mouth and holler. He looks up, and I don't know if he can see me through the bevy of lights that rake across the audience, but he still smiles into the crowd.

My head is pleasantly dizzy, and when I turn around to Rachel, she refills my drink and leaves a water bottle. But I don't feel drunk. I feel so much more.

The boys return to a line formation and, in one fluid move-ment, rip off their shirts. They toss them off into the dark where they disappear behind the stage. Every movement is followed by high-pitched screams, and I wonder if the whole city can hear it.

Each guy smiles as they turn, bend over, and pull their pants off. I blink and it happens. The lights beam on their rock-solid asses covered by skin-hugging briefs.

Then the stage goes pitch black and I can't hear myself think over the screams. Ricky comes back out onstage. He's changed blazers to a sharp red number that makes him look like a sexy devil.

"Okay, ladies," he says, "we're going to kick it into high gear. I'm going to need a volunteer." He picks a middle-aged woman wearing a DIVORCED AND FREE sash across her tight hot-pink dress.

"What's your name, baby?" Ricky asks her. He holds her hand and walks her all the way upstage, as if she's a princess being escorted to a ball. He's so delicate, I forget what he's bringing her up there for.

"Nanette," she says, a nervous quiver in her voice. The white lights flood her face, and I bet she can't see the audience at all. She stands at the center of the stage, completely exposed, with Ricky still holding her hand.

"Well, Nanette, I see you've got your freedom stamp," he says. "Should I offer you congratulations?"

"You should offer me a drink!" she says, and then hoots into the mic. Everyone cheers her on with whistles and praise.

"Have I got a drink for you," Ricky says, his voice a bedroom growl into the mic. "Two of them, actually. They're going to fight for your affections, is that all right with you, baby?"

She raises her hands and howls like he's the full moon.

"Perfect! That's what I love to hear!" Ricky turns and winks at the audience.

I've finished my water and Rachel leaves another drink at my side. I fish more singles out of my purse. I thought I'd be needing them, but so far, it isn't the kind of stage where you make it proverbially rain.

While Nanette is being taken center stage where a makeshift boxing ring is set up around her, I study the faces of the women near me. They come alight. They scream and smile so hard their cheeks are pink. They cheer for her. They clap for her. This entire place is designed for *them* and them only.

Then, the twins appear. Their bodies are slick with some sort of oil, every muscle defined to perfection. They're younger than the other guys, and I wonder if these are the new kids that Fallon was talking about.

They wear boxing gloves, silk robes with names emblazoned on the back. Vinny Suave in red and Wonderboy in blue. The spitfire reggaeton beats blast through the house, lights flashing in tune to the heavy thud of the song. They stand on either side of Nanette. She keeps her legs crossed on a wooden stool, turning her head back and forth like she can't decide who she wants to keep looking at. They're both all-consuming, swiveling their hips toward her, closing into her space. She rakes a hand down each of their torsos, and pulls at the tie that holds their robes together. There's another holler as the gloves come off. Then the robes. Without the robes, I can't tell them apart. Twin #1 takes her hand and trails it down and across his abs. Nanette bounces up and down, as if her adrenaline is taking over her every movement. Then, Twin #2 pushes #1 away, play-fighting for her attention. He lifts her from her seat and starts to carry her away. But #1 comes back, takes hold of her waist. She looks back and forth between them, and makes a decision. She pulls them both against her, and the Sauve twins grind and dance, sandwiching Nanette, the divorcée, like jelly between two generous slices of toast.

The song comes to an end, and both of them hold her arms up, and lead her into a bow. When she comes back up her hair is in disarray but the smile on her face is unstoppable.

"Yeah, baby!" Ricky shouts. His blazer is a bright white number now. "I like the way you think, Nanette. Why pick one when you can have both?"

Ricky moves on to a bondage set. A beautiful black guy picks a birthday girl and sits her on a chair. He dances on her, taking her hand down his body, but he doesn't stop there. He keeps going into the waistband, and the birthday girl lets out an excited scream.

Each set is different from the other, from solos to group numbers. There's a baseball number that involves a lot of phallic symbolism with a bat but the crowd is undeniably into it. Next up is firefighters doing a set to "It's Getting Hot in Here." They jump off the stage and dance on tables, stripping down to their underwear, dozens of women's hands reaching up their legs and abs. They tease and pull and pump their bodies, and all I can think is *Where is he?*

But then Ricky comes back out, all in black this time, and introduces Fallon.

"Now, we shipped this guy all the way from Boston," Ricky says. There's a smattering of laughter, and he goes, "I never get tired of that joke. Now, I need a very special lady." He scans the audience.

Rachel appears beside me. "You're up."

I shake my head. "Me? No, no, no."

"Why do you think they set up the front for you?"

"To watch?" I say.

"Is there a Robyn here?"

Two women in the audience stand up. "I'll be Robyn!" another shouts.

Rachel grabs my hand. "Come on. Time to bite the bullet."

I've never wanted to bite any kind of bullet before. But now, my legs are betraying me, and I'm walking down the yellow-lit floor, a soft blue spotlight shining over my head. My heart thunders in my ears and my hands are so sweaty I slip out of Rachel's grip.

She gives me a friendly slap on my butt, and Ricky takes my hand.

"You are looking lovely tonight," he tells me.

"Thank you," I say, and my voice is louder than I wanted it to be.

"Robyn," Ricky says. When he says my name, I get a chill up my spine. I can't see the audience at all because the lights are so bright but I can hear them cheering for me, their breaths bated as they wait for Ricky to put me on blast. "I didn't tell you when I was on the phone with you earlier today, but I wanted to surprise you with being part of our world. Tell me, love. What's your fantasy?"

I can feel my mouth open up but my words won't come out. I shake my head.

"Can I surprise you?" he asks, quickly picking up the silence.

"I think it's safe to say I'm already pretty surprised."

Ricky turns to the audience. "To give you all a little back-story, this is Robyn's first time at our club. Give it up for her. Now, we pride ourselves here on making fantasies come true and inventing new fantasies along the way. Give it up for our boy pumped with Boston cream *filling*."

The curtains open and a plush rectangular white bed is brought out on one end of the stage. Ricky sits me right in the center of the silky sheets so the audience can see my profile.

I try not to move. I hardly even breathe. I can feel hundreds of eyes on me, the heat of the spotlight, the brush of a hand down my arm.

The music drums, the lights dim, and Fallon, dressed in white from head to toe, appears right in front of me.

FALLON

Robyn isn't sitting at the table I reserved for her. It was a stu-pid idea. But I can't let that affect my performance. Still, my eyes drift toward the red rose that has a table to itself.

When the song ends and we turn around to leave the audi-ence with a look at our asses, I feel like I'm going through the motions.

She didn't come.

I go backstage with the others, as the twins' routine is next. The backstage room is a mess of clothes and costumes draped over leather couches. Each one of us has a vanity mirror with exposed lightbulbs. The two makeup artists that we hired for our stay in New York get busy touching up anything that needs to be touched up. I don't wear makeup. It isn't a macho thing. It's more of a "it looks terrible when it's dripping off my face after sweating" thing. But two of the guys have futuristic sets, and they do a wild routine to "Alien Sex."

I start to stretch when Rachel, one of the bartenders, pops her head around the door.

"Fal?" she says, her long red hair tumbling down her back like a curtain. "There's someone here to see you."

I don't say anything. My heart is too busy doing the mambo.

I hate this feeling. This stupid lovesick feeling that shouldn't make sense. Because it's not love. It's hard infatuation. I can't fall in love. Not when I'm leaving so soon, and not with a girl who'd probably be embarrassed to be seen in public with me.

But my heart, the Epic Fool, will do what it wants. I follow Rachel through the yellow-lit hallway that leads to the main floor. We step into the dark room. Women stand up from their seats and scream. Ricky is at the top of his game. It's like he lives off the chorus of voices and the air teeming with hormones and lust.

The music is too loud to hear Rachel speak, so she points to her bar, then gives me a smile that says, "You're in trouble."

Robyn.

Her posture tells me that she's not comfortable sitting there by herself in a den of male strippers. It's cute, the way her dark eyes flit to every corner of the room. The way she clutches her cocktail and takes long sips. Her eyes are trained on the stage now, watching as Greg takes it off for this one woman. I don't want her to look at anyone like that except me.

Rachel's right. I am in trouble. I can't stop staring at Robyn. My heart, which moments ago felt useless and defeated, is back to beating a song I've never heard before. She adjusts herself on the barstool, and as she does, she arcs her back a bit. Her small round breasts are pushing against the black dress she wears. That dress looks like it was painted on. She's wearing shorter heels than she wore when we went on what should've been our first date, but they're still black and leather and all kinds of sinful.

I head backstage.

"You're smiling like my date on prom night," Gary tells me. "Your girl here?"

"She's at the bar."

"Why don't you switch with me?" Gary says. "That cool, Rick?"

"Fine with me. I'll call her up. Robyn, yeah?"

"Robyn."

Ricky slaps me on the back. "Go get changed, lover boy. This might just be the biggest performance of your miserable life."

I laugh, and they keep on ragging on me. It's not that the guys are all anti-love. Gary's been married for five years, and Benny had sworn off serious relationships until he met his now-boyfriend when we were in Miami. The other guys love the lifestyle too much. Sex, booze, and music. I loved it, too. But none of them have danced for their wives or girlfriends or dates like this before.

I get dressed in an all-white suit and look in the mirror. Why am I nervous? I've done this number hundreds of times.

Because it's her, the Epic Fool in my chest says.

"You're up," Ricky tells me, and he goes ahead.

I wade through my own nervous fog, hands slapping against my back, and whistles trailing behind me.

I can do this. I've done this a hundred times.

I enter stage right, and stand in the dark. I get in position with my hands clasped in front of me, and my head tilted down. When the spotlight hits me, and a boom of voices cheer, I look up at her.

Robyn sits on a stark white bed with satin sheets. She's a sensual dark shadow at the center of it all. I want her. I've never wanted something so badly.

As the music cues on, the sultry R&B vocals fill the room. My heart beats in tune to the heavy bass. The spotlight tracks me as I walk across the stage to reach her. It's the longest walk. Like I'm wading through miles of sea to get to her. She doesn't seem to know what to do with her hands. Crosses them on her bare thighs, rests them on the bed.

I stand in front of her, our profiles to the audience.

"Hi," she says, her voice a sigh, looking up at me because sitting like this has her eye level with my abs.

I give her a smile that she returns easily. That smile, full of amazement and curiosity, turns into a perfect circle when I take her right hand and guide it to my chest. I turn to the audience and wink. Even the subtlest move drives them wild because they keep anticipating the next one.

I pull off my belt. Fold it. Crack it. The snap echoes across the stage and makes Robyn jump. Her chest heaves, and a jolt of excitement runs through me as the half-moons of her cleavage rise and fall.

I've trained myself how to not get wood when I'm onstage. It's not that hard, really. Most of the time, they're women I can have fun with, but the attraction isn't there. It's all a show. But with Robyn it isn't a show. I want her. I need to have her. And getting naked for her isn't an act. It's everything I've wanted to do since I met her.

"Hold your hands out," I say, my voice deep and commanding.

She does it. I tie her wrists with the belt. Gently pull her up with the strap so she's standing, and swaying, and I spin her around so her back is pressed against me.

I want her to feel me. Feel the way my body reacts to her.

She lets out a startled gasp, her mane of hair intoxicating my senses as she gives in to me and leans her head back a bit. I run my hand from the base of her neck, down her shoulder, her arms. She starts to put distance between us. It's only a few inches, but I grip her hips and slam her back against me, and when she feels my erection, I can practically feel her heart race against my own.

There are sharp whistles and we're egged on by thrilled screams and hollers.

I spin her, and for a moment, her wide brown eyes settle their lust on me. I give her a light push onto the bed, but I stay just out of reach. She bounces a couple of times, and then the bed starts to move. The audience loves this, and suddenly, their cheer is louder than the blood bubbling in my ears.

She turns her head to find me.

I rip my shirt open; the buttons unsnap easily. I press my hand on my chest and move it down my abs.

When the song lyric signals my cue, I turn around and bend forward. I can feel heat radiating from her as the bed comes to a standstill in front of me. I grab the waist of my pants and pull them off in one movement.

She looks down at my bulge. I can feel my heart beat at the base of my throat, in my wrists, inside my ears. But she isn't the only one who notices. The audience is losing their shit.

I wind to the rhythm of the song, but for the first time in any performance I've ever done, I'm not motivated by the thrills and screams of the women watching me. I'm motivated by the way Robyn looks at me. No one has ever looked at me like that. Her thick dark lashes are heavy, giving her a dreamy look.

I rest a knee on the edge of the bed. Then another. I box her in with my legs. Without having to tell her, she raises her hands in the air, and then we fall down and against the bed. She pulls her knees apart to make room for me, and I thrust to the beat of the song, dry-humping her. Everything about her welcomes me. The way she sinks into the bed, the way she raises her pelvis to rub against me.

Atta girl, I think. Because she isn't running from me. She's coming undone in my arms. And if we weren't in front of hundreds of people, I'd rip off what's left of my clothes and let her have her way with me.

The bed spins with both of us at the center. The strobe lights come on, creating a freeze frame effect that makes the audience wild with scandal, and everything happens too fast.

I untie the belt around her wrists. I pull her on top of me, so she straddles me. Her wild hair cascades when she leans back, nails raking down my naked chest.

And as the song comes to a crescendo, Robyn leans forward and kisses me.

13

Bed

ROBYN

"That was *some* show," a woman named Darla says to me, with a voice so syrupy my teeth ache. Her blond hair is perfectly done to frame her contoured face.

"I think I'm ready to make my Broadway debut." My cheeks burn under her blue cat-lined stare. What else do I say? "Thanks!" It doesn't seem like the right response, and neither does, "I've never done anything like that before."

By the way she looks at my shoes, my dress, and probably even the acne scar on my chin, she's sizing me up. Fallon introduced her as their publicist and unofficial house mom. I always thought a house mom was for sororities, but I guess it's a stripper thing as well.

The staff and crew linger at the bar for post-show drinks but they let me stay, and it's like getting an insight into Fallon's day-to-day. After I was escorted back to my seat, the show continued. My skin hummed as I walked to my seat at the bar. Women high-fived me down the aisles of their tables. I've never, not once in my life, been on such display. It's a strange feeling, and not entirely terrible. Not when I felt the way Fallon wanted me. I wasn't the only one who noticed his dick straining against the white fabric of his thong. It was a thing of beauty, hard and huge. When I sat down, Rachel hooked me up with another drink, and I watched them finish their set. They did a SWAT

team one that made me think of Lily's bachelorette night, a cow-
boy number, and finished off with a lifeguard performance that
involved all of them getting wet.

Speaking of wet.

Fallon walks over to me. His smile is bright, and his eyes lock
on me and never move. Not as he wades through the group of
guys from his crew, not when a group of waitresses try to grab
his arms, not when Darla starts talking about ticket sales.

He takes my hand, surprisingly shy. How can he be shy? We
just dry-humped in front of hundreds of people. I pull him
closer to me, and he leans into the crook of my neck and inhales
my scent.

"I have the closing paperwork right here."

"Huh?" he says, like he's coming out of a daze. His eyes turn
to Darla, who's holding a clipboard. "Oh, can we go over it in
the morning? I'll come in first thing."

Darla looks at me, then back at Fallon. I can't quite place the
way she looks at him, but suddenly, I feel uncomfortable under
her stare. "Okay, but you better bring me my coffee."

"I know how you take it."

Darla saunters over to the bar and gets a rundown from one
of the bartenders. It must be stressful having to do all of this
work.

Fallon and I don't have a moment alone. His teammates
come over to meet me. So far, my favorite is Aiden.

"Hey, mi reina," he says, his voice flirty and his Colombian
accent so adorable I let him get away with the pet name. He's
got killer cheekbones and a body that's sculpted to perfection.
His eyes are a light brown and his hair is still damp from the
beach finale. "It's nice to finally meet the famous laundry thief."

He takes my hand and kisses it, then gives me a smile that has
Fallon stepping in.

"Okay, enough, Suavemente," Fallon says, batting his friend
away.

"I can't help it. Beautiful women should be worshiped,"
Aiden says.

"I don't disagree. Just go worship another one." He keeps a

hand around my waist, and I can't help but feel a spark of thrill at the way he holds me. Claims me.

Ricky comes over. Up close, he's even more striking, even in casual clothes. He puts a hand on my shoulder and levels his eyes with mine. "Pleasure, luv. I really loved your hair flip at the end there."

"Did you have a favorite set?" Aiden asks me.

"Other than mine," Fallon adds.

"I don't know," I say playfully, "the twin thing was really sexy, but there's something about men in uniform."

"If we find one of the firemen outfits missing," Ricky says, "we know to blame Fallon."

And on they go. They're so welcoming. It's the most charming group of men I've ever been around. They're attentive, and affectionate, but not in a creepy way. I can tell how close they all are by the way everyone always makes body contact. A touch of the shoulder, a playful jab on the chest, a slap of the hand. There's a bond there, and I love that Fallon is letting me witness it. I don't have anything like that in my workplace, and I wonder if part of that is because I never made an effort to get to know anyone other than Lily.

Beers are passed around. One of the twins flirts with a fan that doesn't look like she wants to go anywhere. Some of the guys jump around, and I wonder if they ever come down from the adrenaline they rack up onstage.

"So, Robyn," Ricky says. "You're a teacher?"

"Shit, if my teachers had looked like you, I would've stayed in school," Aiden says.

"I do hope you didn't drop out of fifth grade," I tell him.

Fallon lowers himself to nip at my earlobe. Everything about him is distracting. I love that he doesn't act differently toward me when he's in front of his friends. Even though they rag on him, he doesn't look like he's going to let go.

"I'm glad you enjoyed the show," Darla says, finally sitting down. She kicks off her heels and massages the arch of her foot. "Better get in a few more before we're off to Vegas."

"I thought you guys were going to Reno," I point out.

"We're actually going to Vegas instead, luv," Ricky says.

There's an awkward pause, and the background music fills the space. Some of the guys look down at their beers, and I don't miss the look that Ricky shoots Fallon. Like they're sharing a secret message that I can't decode.

"Hey." Fallon turns to me. "Do you want to get out of here?"

I set my beer on the bar and run my hands along his muscular arms. "I thought you'd never ask."

Fallon drives down the dark avenue. The train rumbles above us. I don't want to think about the inevitable fact that Fallon isn't going to be here after our summer together. I don't want to think that I'm already falling for him and that it's going to hurt. I don't want to think about Darla and how calculated it was to drop that reminder.

No. I don't want to think of any of that. What I do want is to enjoy the moments I have with Fallon. I want to re-create the way I felt when I was on that stage. I want to feel every part of him.

"What are you doing?" he asks playfully.

I rake my fingers across his thigh. He stares out the window, but glances at me. I lean forward, inching my hand little by little.

"What does it look like I'm doing?" My heart races when I reach his crotch. He's already hard and waiting for me. I pull on the string of his sweatpants. His breath is ragged as I reach my hand inside and I gasp a little. "Commando."

He threads his fingers into my hair and brings me close. He sucks on my bottom lip, then pushes me away and looks back at the road. "Robyn."

I lean into his neck and dot kisses along the vein that throbs against his skin. I move my hand up and down his shaft, turning my thumb in circles under the head of his cock. At the red light he brakes hard, and holds me so I don't get thrown forward.

I lower my lips to his dick and coat the tip with my tongue. He moans, and I take him in deeper. He rests his palm on top of my head, brushing my hair back with nimble fingers. There's a honk behind us, and he hits the gas, cursing as I pick up speed with my tongue, slurping and licking my way up and down his hardness.

He tugs on my hair, guiding me off his dick. He kisses me at the red light, his teeth biting down hard, his tongue wanting.

"I need you," he tells me. We go on green and at the next right we're home. He parks haphazardly in the garage. We kiss across the parking lot. We kiss in the stairwell. We kiss up the steps. We kiss at the door to my apartment.

I fumble for my keys and unlock the door.

"Wait," he says, his voice hoarse and needy.

He picks me up and I wrap my legs around his waist. The door slams.

He squeezes my ass all the way into my bedroom. For the second time tonight, we're on a bed. My dress has already ridden up over my hips, exposing the black lace thong I picked out for myself.

He stands at the side of my bed watching me. "You're so fucking hot."

He takes off his shirt and tosses it on the floor. Drops to his knees and runs his hands along my hips, my thighs. He grabs my knees and spreads them apart. For a moment, I look at my ceiling and let the insecurities wash over me. Better get them over with now because I want to, need to, enjoy this. I haven't had sex with anyone in six months. I'm afraid that I won't be able to let go. I'm afraid that I'm my worst enemy. *That's right, Robyn, get all those thoughts out of your system,* I think.

Because when I look, Fallon is kissing my hip bones. His mouth presses hot, wet kisses all across my belly. He loops his arms under my thighs and I yelp when he pulls me inches from his mouth. I can feel his breath on the thin silk material of my thong. His tongue draws a line up and down my wetness, and I squirm in his solid grasp.

I can't handle it. I need him now. I start to pull at the sides of my underwear but his hands hold mine down.

He climbs on top of me. "I want you to enjoy this."

"Believe me," I say. "I am."

He looks at me for a long time. The blue of his eyes is so bright, I don't ever want to look away.

"Fallon?"

He answers me with a kiss. A kiss so deep, I could fall right through the mattress and through the floors of our building. I dig my toes into the elastic waistband of his sweats and push them down. His dick slaps against my wet center and I moan loud enough to wake the neighbors.

He rests his forehead on my breasts and grunts. "You're so fucking wet."

He freezes. Doesn't move for three whole breaths. I can feel myself tighten in anticipation of him.

"Top drawer," I whisper in his ear.

He gets off me, the absence of him like a deep loss I can't begin to put into words. I watch him walk around my bed. His body is a wonder. His body belongs on top of mine. His body is everything I could have ever wished for.

He grabs a condom from the box and kneels back in front of me.

"Where was I?" He takes my thong in his fists and rips it into threads.

I gasp as his mouth closes over my pussy. He drags a tongue down the center, twisting delicious rings around my clit. He cups his hands under my ass and pushes me up, like he can't get enough of me. My body feels like it belongs to someone else. It writhes under his touch. A spark of heat blooms in my belly, and a warmth floods my entire body. His tongue, his tongue deserves gold medals. But when he slides his fingers inside me, I decide every part of Fallon is better than the next.

I grab hold of his hair and tug. The vibration of his moans rides up my body, and my breath hitches because I come hard and fast on his mouth.

He kisses the sensitive skin between my legs. My breath is heavy and my face hurts from the smile on my face. I grab the condom beside me and throw it at him. I move myself up higher on the bed. I curl my finger, and drag it toward me.

"Come."

FALLON

Robyn grinding her pussy against my face is my new favorite feeling in the world. Robyn moaning my name is my new favorite sound in the world. Robyn. Just Robyn is my everything.

I rip open the condom foil and slide the latex down my dick. She sits on her bed, her legs angling to the side. She pulls off that slinky black dress and throws it off to the side. She reaches behind her back to unhook her bra.

My dick twitches. If I were any harder, I would bust through this condom.

She holds the fabric of her bra against her. Pulls one strap down. Then the other. I smirk, because she's stripping for me.

"Let me see you," I tell her.

Her black wavy hair falls around golden shoulders. She lets go of one hand. Then another.

Her tits are small. Full and perfectly round. Her nipples are like drops of chocolate kisses. I follow the curl of her finger as she begs me to come forward. I feel possessed by her beauty. Effortless and seductive and downright sexy.

"Come," she says, and I fully intend on it.

I climb on top of her and line up my dick to her wet pussy. I kiss her mouth, wrap my hand around her neck, and feel her moan against me, into me.

"Tell me what you want."

"I want you inside me."

That's all I want to hear. To give her what she asks of me. I slide inside of her, a knife through melting butter. When I close my eyes, I can see stars. I can see the swirl of the galaxy and the makeup of entire heavens. She presses the heels of her feet on my ass cheeks to push me deeper.

"You're so fucking eager." I chuckle against her ear. "I want to take my time with you, Robyn."

She answers by biting at my neck. Pushing her tongue in circles that drive me so wild, I slam all of me inside of her. She cries out loud and needy, wrapping her arms around my neck.

"You feel so good," she pants in whispers.

I slide back out all the way, then slip back in, my breath caught in my throat. I grab her hips and lift them up; the pressure of my dick tightens and if I move I will come in seconds. So, I let myself breathe. I wet my finger in her mouth and rub her clit in slow circles, the walls inside her contracting around me.

She wriggles and winds and pulls me closer. "Fuck me, Fallon."

And that. The hitch in her voice. The way she calls for me, needs me. It breaks me apart. I dig my fingers into her soft hips and slide in and out. She grabs hold of the mattress and pulls. When she lets go, she runs her fingers through her hair. That hair that drives me out of my skin because it is so lush and gorgeous. Her tits bounce to the rhythm of my dick coming in and out of her, and I lower myself and take one nipple into my mouth. It hardens against my tongue.

I fucking love this girl. "I fuc—"

I feel myself start to say it out loud but I stop. No I love you's. None of that.

Instead, I sink deeper and deeper into her wetness, until she cries out my name, and I come hard inside of her.

Later while Robyn sleeps naked, I take a quick shower. I use her body wash, something called "Sea Spray," which smells of her. I hold the soapy loofah to my nose and inhale.

This is trouble.

I know this is trouble.

I knew she was trouble the moment I couldn't drag myself away from her very presence.

Sex complicates things. Especially when it's good. So fucking good.

I'm reminded of Darla bringing up Vegas. When I found out Robyn was coming to the show, I asked the boys to not mention anything about when we're leaving. Ricky gave me a concerned eye and said, "Careful, Zacky. That's not going to end well." I called him the nickname he hates the most. "Thanks, *Dad*." But

Darla wasn't there, so I can't blame her for bringing it up. I should tell Robyn that I'm leaving in three weeks. No, not three anymore.

Eighteen days.

The countdown clock starts in my head. I know it shouldn't affect anything. What's the difference if something ends in four months or three weeks? I wash under my pits, the tepid water falling over my head.

I'll tell her in the morning.

And hopefully, she'll still be game to keep this going for two weeks because that was the hardest orgasm I've ever had. And I haven't exactly been a saint.

"Hey." Robyn's sleepy voice announces her.

She rubs her hand on the glass shower door. Through the steam, I make out her sweet swollen mouth, her rumpled dark hair, and her nakedness.

My dick is at attention at once.

She opens the door, something metallic in her hand and a wicked smile on her face.

Seeing her like this, ready and searching for me, makes me lose myself. I grab her around the waist and press her against the cool, wet tiles. She groans against my mouth, her tongue searching for mine. I grab the condom from her, rip it open, and slide it on.

"Fallon," she sighs against my ear. "I want you so much. I've never wanted anyone like this before."

My heart, the Epic Fool, thunders in my chest. *I feel the same way.* But I can't say it. I won't. Even if it's the hardest thing to keep myself from letting the words spill out of my mouth. I'm going to show her instead. I bite down on her bottom lip. I pick her up, using the wall to steady us. I cup her thick ass with my palms and press my cock into her pussy, already wet and waiting for me.

She shuts her eyes and cries out.

"Does it hurt?"

She nods, and digs her nails into my skin. "But don't stop. Please don't stop."

So I don't. I fuck her against the slick bathroom wall until I'm trembling and shaking and coming. I set her down and pull the condom off. I get on my knees and drape one of her legs over my shoulder. She tugs on my wet hair and guides me to her swollen, sensitive pussy. I grab the leg draped over me with one hand and her waist with the other and lock her in place against my mouth. I close my lips over her clit and lick until she can't stop herself from trembling and screaming my name. *Fallon.* Over and over again until she shakes and sighs and her voice is a high-pitched cry of, "I'm coming."

We towel off together. She smiles as she brushes her teeth. She has an extra toothbrush because she buys things in bulk. We stare at each other in the mirror. She spits into the sink first, and I follow.

"I don't have any pajamas that fit you," she says. Her voice is sexy and gruff, tired from all that screaming. I'd give myself a pat on the back if she wasn't watching.

"Oh, am I spending the night?" I ask, playful. "I thought you'd kick me to the curb."

She stands on her tiptoes and turns her lips up to me. It's as if we've done this a thousand times because I instinctively bend down to meet her puckered mouth.

"You could go back downstairs," she says. "Or you could spoon me to sleep."

"Tempting. But what if I want to be the little spoon?"

She looks as if she's seriously considering this. "We'll flip a coin."

I kiss her, this time harder. God, I want her so much. Her mouth is minty fresh, and her skin glows with the lotion she slathered on after she got out of the shower.

"I'll be right back," I say, and when I start to walk out she tugs me back to her.

"Don't go." Her voice is so soft it aches in my gut.

"I'll go get a change of clothes and Yaz needs a walk." I kiss her forehead, grab nothing but my keys and a towel.

One of my neighbors chooses this moment to take out her garbage. An older lady I've never met gasps at the sight of me. I mutter apologies and quickly change into a shirt, sweats, and sandals. I try to carry a barking and wriggling Yaz downstairs and wait while she does her business. When I take her back upstairs, I freshen her water bowl. I consider bringing her upstairs. The thought of falling asleep with Robyn, Yaz curled up between us, comes to mind.

I shake the thought from my head and tell myself to stop. I don't get to fantasize about happy endings like that.

"I'm sorry, sweetheart," I tell her, scratching between her ears as she barks a few times before stomping around the center of my bed. "You're still my number one girl."

As I run back upstairs to Robyn, I'm not expecting my heart to squeeze the way it does at the sight of her. She's in that ridiculously sexy silk robe, leaning at the doorway to her room. I go to her like she's an oasis and I'm a fool lost in the desert. I kiss her all the way back to her bed, the silk coming undone to reveal her smooth light-brown skin. I pull off my shirt, and her fingers roam my skin.

"Oops," she says, tracing her thumb on my neck.

I look at the wall-length mirror over the dresser. There's a dark bruise on my neck, two on my shoulder, and one right over my right nipple.

"Nothing the makeup girls can't cover up," I say.

She presses a kiss to the bruise on my pec. "I've never lost control like that."

The revelation is soft, her voice sleepy and cute as ever. But I know what she means. There was a wildness to her that I never would have guessed at our first encounter.

"When I'm with you—" she starts to say, pressing her hand on my chest. I rest my hand over hers. She frowns, then smiles, like she's catching herself. She tucks a wet strand behind her head. "I'm sorry, I know we're not supposed to get sentimental."

I bite down on my teeth to stop myself from screaming "GET SENTIMENTAL." Because I want to do it, too. I'm just too chicken-shit to do it first. Instead, I press a kiss on the apple of her cheek.

"Let's go to bed."

*   *   *

This time, we sleep. I am the big spoon. I love being the big spoon. Robyn fits against me like we were carved from the same tree trunk. She falls asleep instantly. I memorize the way she breathes. The way she mumbles whatever she's dreaming about. The way she traps my hand around her body, as if I could even stand to tear myself away.

This isn't going to end well. Ricky's words echo in the back of my thoughts.

And yeah, maybe I know that. We're from two different worlds. Have different lifestyles. We were brought up different. Maybe she's better than me in some ways. Maybe I'm not the kind of guy who can give her what she wants.

But I can make her feel like she's never felt before, and I can make love to her like she deserves.

It's been a long time since I've slept beside someone. Maybe that's why I can't fall asleep. Or maybe it's because I know, in the morning, I won't have any excuse not to tell her that I'm leaving sooner than expected.

It shouldn't be this difficult. We had an agreement. But as she moves in her sleep, her damp hair cool on my skin and her soft body against my own, I know I'm not strong enough to tell the truth.

14

Leave the Night On

ROBYN

"Remember to get your permission slips signed!" I tell my kids at the end of class. They run out of the room like tiny Oreo-filled bats out of hell.

"Ms. Flores! Ms. Flores!" Kendra Wilson stands in front of me. "I have a gift for you. I drew you."

She hands me a piece of paper with her final-hour art project.

"Thank you, Kendra." I rub the top of her head. "See you next week, okay?"

Before I can take a look at the drawing, there's a knock on my door. I fold it and put it in my purse for something to do because it's Lukas. My chest fills with white-hot anxiety, and my body fidgets like I don't know which way is up or down anymore.

"Ms. Flores," he says, when I don't answer. "I wanted to talk to you."

It's been a week and a half since our disastrous accidental double date. I start to put away the things on my desk. Pens, stacks of papers, apples, clock, stapler. Wait. No. I take the clock and stapler back out.

"Yes, Principal Papadopoulos?"

"I wanted to apologize . . . about that night. I should've done it sooner, but the next day I had meetings, and you always run out of school so I can't catch you. Then the days stretched too long, and what can I say? I suppose I'm embarrassed."

He's a striking man. His bright hazel eyes zone in on me. His tight, muscular body is hugged by a fine suit, and he stands casually, one hand in his pocket. If I hadn't gotten to know him, to see what he's really like, I'd be like the other teachers and women in the building fawning over him. Lily was right. All it took was one afternoon in the teachers' lounge and I realized everyone was pining for him.

But when I think of Lukas, I think of the restaurant. The neon lights, the salsa music, the pretty date who he ignored and treated like crap. The way he sat with me while Fallon and Melodie were in the bathroom. I never told Fallon what Lukas said. *You can do better than that, right? I think you and I could make the perfect couple.* Who says that to another person who is clearly on a date? Who says that to their subordinate?

Anger flashes red in my eyes. I turn for something to do. I grab my chalk eraser and get to cleaning off today's vocabulary.

I want to say, *That's not an apology.*

"We don't have to do this," I tell him. "Your apology should be to Fallon."

He frowns, confused. "I thought his name was Zac."

"I call him by his last name."

Lukas raises his thick black eyebrows. "Right. Zac Fallon. Perhaps I'll be able to apologize to him in person at the rehearsal dinner?"

I steel my breath. "Fallon isn't going with me to the rehearsal dinner."

"Why's that?" He sounds friendly, concerned.

"I don't really feel comfortable talking about my personal life with my boss."

He holds his hands up in surrender. "I'm sorry, Robyn. I wanted to clear the air before Lily and Dave's wedding. Dave's an old friend and I know this is the moment he's been waiting for his whole life. I want everything to go right for them."

"You won't have to worry," I say, trying to smile. "The air is clear."

I dust off my hands as he looks down at his shiny leather shoes. I should say more. I should tell him where to shove it. But I don't.

"See you tonight," he says.

Back in my apartment, I dance around my room holding my dress for tonight's wedding party dinner. It's a blue-green dress I found on sale. My grandma Consuelo would be proud of me for finding an $800 dress on sale for $150. It's sleeveless, with a sweetheart top that hugs my breasts and waist, then falls loosely in soft chiffon layers that just brush the floor.

It's the color of Fallon's eyes. The blue of turquoise waters. I slip into it, and search for my earrings. I want to pretend that Lukas's non-apology never happened. I just want to remember the way Fallon felt. His lips, his skin, his dick. The next day at school, I couldn't even sit down the whole day. Not comfortably, and at that memory I smile at myself like a fool.

His name lights up my phone as I put on gold Swarovski crystal earrings. They were a graduation present to myself after finishing my master's. Something pretty, shiny, that would remind me that I have a bright future.

Fallon: *You home?*

Me: *Just getting dressed.*

Fallon: *Don't get dressed on my account.*

There's a knock on my door, and I don't have to look through the peephole to know it's Fallon.

He stands there holding a plastic bag that smells like Chinese food and a six-pack of beer.

I realize that, in this moment, I'm going to hurt his feelings. "Hey. What's all this?"

"Holy fuck. I forgot to wear my tux." He looks me up and down. He doesn't look like he's breathing. "You look—incredible. What—"

"Tonight's the rehearsal dinner," I say, stepping aside to let him in. My heart gives an anxious tug.

In blue track pants with red and white piping down the side and a long-sleeve white shirt with buttons at the collar, he looks like the low-key Han Solo of my dreams.

"My bad. I should've called first. I just wanted to surprise you. I should go."

"I am surprised." I shut the door and press myself against it. *Invite him,* a part of me says. But I'm not sure if that's the best idea. I'm not sure he'd even want to go to a wedding party where he doesn't know anyone there. "I wish I could stay and enjoy it with you."

"I thought the wedding was next weekend." He takes one of the beers, twists off the cap, and drinks.

"It is," I say, taking one of the beers for myself and tapping the bottle to his. "But they moved up the rehearsal dinner because of some of David's family scheduling I won't bore you with."

"I don't think you could ever bore me."

He sounds so honest, it makes something inside my gut twist. Maybe I'm just hungry. Maybe a terrible part of me wants to say, *Fuck it.* And stay here with him.

I set my beer down.

I close the distance between us and take his face in my hands. I take his full bottom lip between mine and suck it softly. His tongue flicks inside my mouth, reaching for mine. I loop my arms around his neck. The hickeys I gave him are fading, and my body is thrilled in thinking I can give him new ones.

He slams me against him, pulls up the sides of my gown. My fingers pull down the front of his pants, releasing his erection. I wrap my hand around it and stroke. "Damn—"

"What?" he whispers against my ear.

"It's just—every time I see you I'm always surprised at how fucking big you are."

"Flattery will get you everywhere." He chuckles softly against my throat. He moans, and slides his fingers between my legs. He pulls away, startled. "Robyn Flores, were you going to leave this house without underwear?"

My breath hitches with the sensation of his fingers stroking me. I smirk. "Maybe I was just waiting for you."

We stumble back and hit the side of my sofa. He pulls out a condom and rolls it on.

"You're so beautiful, Robyn." He slides inside of me. It hurts, still raw from our marathon night. But I ache for him, and I wrap my legs around his waist. "I want to rip this fucking dress right off you."

He grabs my hair and pulls my head back, exposing the tender skin of my throat. He kisses me from my chin, down to the scoop of my clavicle, to the tops of my breasts. Every kiss is matched with a thrust of his cock that reaches deeper and deeper. He touches every part of me with his hands, his mouth, and I can't get enough.

"Come with me," I tell him. "I'm so close."

I hold on firmly, and we fall backward over the armrest and onto the couch. He moans in my ear, holding me so tight I might burst in his arms. When I come, I wriggle against him, the friction against my clit better than any feeling I've ever had.

We lie like that for a long time. He drags lazy kisses across the tops of my breasts, and I twirl his hair around my fingertips.

Then my phone buzzes and I remember that I have to be somewhere.

"Baby, I have to go." I tap Fallon on his shoulder and he climbs off me. He ducks into the bathroom to clean off, and I go to my bedroom mirror to assess the damage. The chiffon of my dress is a little wrinkled, but I can just say it's part of the "look." The "I just got my brains fucked out of my skull" look. The "best sex I've ever had" look. The "I never want this to end" look. The "girl, you're in trouble" look.

I spritz my hair with some spray to tame the flyaways that are a result of rubbing against the couch. I use a Q-tip to clean off the smudges of my eye makeup. I reapply lip gloss. And oh, yeah, I fish out a pair of underwear.

"You look gorgeous," Fallon says. He stands at the doorway to my room, shirtless and breathtaking. Every time I see him I have to remind myself to breathe.

"I'm sorry I have to go," I say, slipping into gold pumps that make me just shy of eye-level with him. "Can we do something tomorrow?"

He walks over to me and presses a sweet kiss on my lips that aches right down to my core. "I'm putting in my request for the whole weekend. We leave tomorrow and come back Sunday night."

"Did you just come up with this? Where are we going? What do I pack?"

He presses a finger to my lips. "Yes. It's a secret. And casual clothes. No, you won't need underwear."

I try not to think that a weekend away is too soon. But with our unconventional timeline, it might just work.

"Okay, but I have homework. Just to let you know ahead of time."

"No problem." He follows me, kissing my neck, my cheeks, as I grab my purse and light jacket. "Hey, can I give you a ride?"

I'm afraid of what I might be tempted to do to him if we're alone any longer. I resist my impulse to say yes. I tell him so, and he just laughs all the way downstairs and as he puts me in a cab, leaving me with a kiss that racks my soul and leaves me wanting more.

"Hey, can I talk to you?" Lily asks as soon as she sees me.

She looks beautiful, a vision in a white dress that harkens to the fifties, with a dazzling white veiled fascinator.

"Of course, what's up?" I follow her down the restaurant hallway, away from the hordes of her family, future in-laws, and friends. A waiter stops us with a tray of white wine, and we each take one.

"I don't know how to say this," she starts.

"Oh my god. You're pregnant," I say, cupping my mouth with my hand.

She widens her eyes. "No! Hello, this is my second glass tonight. Look, Robbie—" She hasn't called me that since high school. Now she reserves it for when she wants to break bad news. Like the time she told me she hated my college boyfriend and he was all kinds of wrong. She was right. Like the time she found out she'd flunked out of her first college semester and we wouldn't be roommates anymore. She got it together after that.

I patiently wait for her to speak.

"I know you're going through a rough patch," she says. "But I thought that maybe it'd make things easier for you if Sophia took over completely as maid of honor."

"Lily—"

"Let me finish—I love you. You're like the sister I never had. But there's still a ton of stuff to do. This whole party happened because of Sophia. This is *my wedding,* and I can't help but feel that you aren't completely happy for me."

I wait for my chest to feel like I can take a breath without crying. It's true, I haven't been on my best friend game. I've been coping. My lateness. My messiness. My aloofness. I've been barely holding it together and I can't fully understand why.

I take a deep breath. "I understand. Sophia deserves it. Hell, she's been there to pick up my mess from the beginning."

"You can still be a bridesmaid. It's just not fair to have you up there while Sophia did everything. It's almost like you don't want to be here."

"If I didn't want to be here," I tell her, "I wouldn't be. I'm here, Lily."

She puckers her lips. "You show up half an hour late looking like you just got fucked in the back of the car."

"You know what, Lil?" I hold up my finger accusingly. "There was once a time when the tables were turned. When you dropped out of college and I let you live in my dorm while you lied to your parents. When I had to fireman-carry you out of a cab and up the stairs because you were *unconscious.* I could go on and on, but I'm not because I didn't think we were keeping score. Did you ever stop to think for a second that maybe I'm finally finding something—someone—that makes me happy?"

"If you would take two seconds to talk to me instead of avoiding me, then maybe I would understand."

"I can't talk to you about this. Don't you get it? I don't want to bring you down."

"I'm supposed to be your best friend, Robbie. I feel like I don't know you anymore."

This is the moment Sophia decides to walk around the corner and notice us. She takes in Lily's red cheeks and my stiff posture. "Everything okay here?"

"Fine," I say curtly.

"Lil?" she asks, ignoring me.

"We're fine. I'll be right in."

Sophia smiles politely. "We have to start the toasts in fifteen, okay? Nice of you to drop by, Robyn."

I shut my eyes and breathe until my desire to smack her subsides.

"I'm sorry you feel like you don't know me anymore, Lily," I say. "But I'm the same person."

"The Robyn I know wouldn't keep secrets from me."

"What secrets?" I'm close to shouting. My wine sloshes over my glass and onto my dress. *Great.*

"That your date threatened Lukas. That you're putting your career in jeopardy."

"Whoa, hold on a minute," I say. "Who told you about Lukas?"

"David did." She smiles and waves at a couple walking into the dining room. "Lukas is one of his groomsmen and he wasn't sure if he should tell me."

"And you just believe that?" I ask.

"I wouldn't. Not if you'd *talk* to me."

"Don't you understand I've put all of my energy into not bringing drama into your wedding?"

"Well, you've done an excellent job so far. Because Lukas was Sophia's escort. I can't even deal with having to rearrange all of this."

"You don't have to," I say. "I can walk down the aisle with him. It's one day. I can be around that lying, two-faced piece of shit for one day."

Lily stares at me like I'm a stranger, and I hate that I've caused her all this stress. I should try harder. I should be better, even if it's just for her. I place my hand on her shoulder.

"I'm sorry, Lily. I really am. You won't have to worry about me. I promise."

And I truly hope it's the one promise that I can keep.

FALLON

Vinny and Wonderboy have a place in Sunnyside, Queens. The bottom half of a two-family house. Its decor is better suited to a suburban housewife, but it's just a rental.

I drink vodka from a red plastic cup and sit on a single recliner watching the others act a fool. There are scantily clad women downing shots of Midori that makes my stomach turn just by thinking of it. Instead, I let my mind wander to Robyn and how amazing she feels in my arms. I rewind our fuckfest in her bed. In her shower. On her couch. How I left her looking rumpled in her fancy evening dress. If I were a better man, I'd feel sorry. But I just can't help but think that I fucked her to claim her. To let the world know what we'd done just moments before.

"What's wrong with you, bro?" Vinny asks, walking over to me. He sits on my armrest. I can barely hear him over the ratchet rap pumping from his sound system.

I shake my head. I've decided to give him a chance. "I'm just tired."

"Did you finally hook up with the teacher?" He takes a drink, the corners of his lips peering from the rim like the Cheshire Cat.

At the thought of Robyn, I smirk. I can't stop myself, no matter what exterior I want to put out. Robyn makes me happy and I have to give her up.

"That's my dude!" he shouts and bumps my fist. "You should've brought her around."

"Nah, it's not her scene. She's at a wedding rehearsal for a friend."

"Oh, one of the girls here's talking about some wedding next week. Her coworker or something."

I look around the room and my eyes meet those of Anise, one of the girls from the bachelorette party. I look away, but it's too late. She's noticed me and raises her glass.

"Here comes trouble," Vinny says, then pulls out a little plastic bag of blow. "Hey, you want to party?"

I shake my head. I don't care if the other guys put that shit in their bodies. There was a time I did, too. I'm not proud of it, but I thought I was invincible. I loved the high. Then one day, I woke up not knowing where I was, buck-naked in a stranger's house. When the owner got home, he nearly fucking shot me, until I explained it was a prank by my friends. "I'm good."

Anise sits on the other armrest of the recliner. She's in a white slip dress that hugs her tiny body. Vinny's in a red shirt. I can't help but think that they're like manifestations of my conscience. An angel and a devil sitting prettily on either side of me. Though neither of them offers any good choices.

"Why are you being antisocial?" Anise asks, her voice as perky as her breasts.

"He's the serious one in the group," Vinny tells her, and winks. "But I'll be social for him."

I laugh at the pair of them. "See? You wouldn't even miss me."

"You could always join," Anise says suggestively, lifting an eyebrow toward me as she takes Vinny's hand.

Vinny is trying not to crack up behind her, but failing.

"You guys have fun," I say, and lift my cup to them.

I should be pissed that Vinny's sleeping with clients. But a part of me just doesn't care because *all of me* would rather be with Robyn right now. I was supposed to tell her that I'm leaving the week after her best friend's wedding. Instead, I invited her on a fucking weekend getaway.

I down my drink and Irish-exit out of the twins' apartment. I take a cab back to my place where there's a girl slumped in front of my door.

"What are you doing here?"

"Hey, loser," my sister says. "Thanks for answering my calls."

*   *   *

"Mary Lee Fallon," I say, sounding more like our dad than I want to. I unlock the door to my apartment and let her in. "What the fuck are you doing here? You're supposed to be in school."

"It's a Friday night," she says matter-of-factly, rolling her eyes as only seventeen-year-olds do. "I don't have anywhere to be tomorrow."

She drops her backpack on my couch, and Yaz runs into my sister's arms. Mary falls into a fit of unintelligible noises because Yaz is cute as hell. "When did you get a dog?"

Yaz licks my sister's face and barks.

"Since none of your business." I go to the kitchen and grab a beer and a can of soda. Mary tries to grab the beer from me and I slap her hand.

"You're in high school."

"So?" she says. "You dropped out of high school when you were younger than me."

"I did that for a good *reason*." I lick my lips and slump onto my couch. A headache pushes against my temples. "You shouldn't do what I do."

"That's easy for you to say." Mary sits on the couch beside me. Yaz dozes sleepily on my sister's lap. "You're the reason he's so strict with me. My curfew is seven p.m. SEVEN. No one even bothers to try to be my friend because I'm the girl who can't leave her house."

"Good," I say. "Keep the boys away."

"I don't like *boys*, Fallon." She flicks the top of her soda can, and gives me a sheepish smile. "You'd know that if you were home. Even Dad knows. He still just wants me home, studying, and never leaving. I just want to have your life. Traveling and being, I don't know, *free*."

I let go of a long breath. How do I make her understand? "And running away is your answer?"

She lifts one shoulder and drops it. "You're the only person I thought could understand me, but I never see you."

"Let me shower. Take my phone and order food. My passcode is Mom's birthday. There's money on the kitchen counter. Don't spend it all in one place."

This is not how this weekend was supposed to go. My little sister just came out to me, sort of, and I haven't been there to show her my support. Not that she needs my permission, but she's right. I should be there. I should be home more.

And to hear that she wants to be like me, that I'm the person that she thinks of when she thinks of the future. That terrifies me.

I hear the doorbell. I open the shower curtain and shout, "That was fast. What'd you get?"

She doesn't answer for a little while and I wonder if she didn't hear me. I lather, rinse, repeat when the doorbell rings again.

"Zac!" Mary says, suddenly playful and giggly. "*Robyn's* here!"

Oh, fuck.

ROBYN

After the rehearsal dinner, I head back. Instead of going home, I stop at his floor. What I don't expect to find when I knock on Fallon's door is a teenage girl. She has bright green eyes and dark hair pulled back in a high ponytail. She has broad shoulders and wears a Patriots hoodie. She gives me a smile that is achingly familiar to Fallon's.

"Are you Zac's girlfriend?" she asks, grinning and blushing all at once. "Nice."

"Uh—" That I don't know how to answer.

"He's taking a shower, but we're about to order food if you want to stay. I'm Mary Lee."

"I can come back," I stutter, taking her hand.

We didn't cover meeting family in our arrangement. I didn't think it'd have to come up at all. But here I am, shaking hands with his little sister.

"Please stay. I need a girl on my side. Fallon is being lame and telling me that I can't run away from home."

I chuckle. She has zero filter and I love it. "Tell you what. I'm going to put on something less formal, and then come back."

She nods with a smile, and I run up to my apartment to change. Fallon's little sister is here and she's run away from home. We're getting into super-personal territory. And yet, it doesn't feel weird. It feels right. Like I should be there as some sort of support system for him. I rummage through a closet and find some board games. Do teenagers even like board games anymore? I feel about a hundred right now. But it could be a nice icebreaker.

I tuck them under my arm, run down, and ring the bell again. Mary Lee opens the door and shouts after her brother, "Robyn's here!"

I set the board games on the coffee table. Yaz barks and runs onto my lap. The husky pup is everything I need in this moment. She's warm and fluffy. Nothing bad can happen while holding a puppy in one's arms. That's a scientific fact.

"Do you want something to drink?" Mary Lee asks. "Fallon's got a bunch of booze. He'd probably get pissed if I have some, huh?"

"That's a safe assumption," I say. "And I'm okay for right now."

She sits next to me and examines me. "Are you a model or something?"

"Me? No, I'm a schoolteacher."

"I didn't know teachers dressed like that."

"We have personal lives, too! I was at a rehearsal dinner. My best friend's getting married."

Mary Lee throws her head back and laughs. The pitch of it is just like Fallon's. "I hate weddings. I never want to get married."

"Smart. My parents have been saving for my supposed wedding since I was in diapers. It's too much pressure."

"Wow. You're the first person to not say, 'One day you'll change your mind.' I hate that. Like I don't know my mind."

I brush Yaz's head and she makes a tiny growling sound, also kind of like Fallon. I must remember to tell him of this later.

"Well, this whole year since my best friend's engagement,

everyone in our lives has been asking when I'm next. And I hate that question. I hate the assumption. Only you know what you want, and even if you do change your mind, that's up to you."

Mary Lee takes a drink of her soda and stares at me with curious eyes. "How did you and my brother meet?"

I nearly choke on my own spit. "Well—"

"Don't answer any of her questions," Fallon says, running out of his bathroom so quickly he nearly slips on his own wet feet. He's in a Red Sox T-shirt and basketball shorts. He dries his hair with a towel, and I lean toward the scent of his clean, musky soap. "She's a tricky little hobbit."

"Excuse you," Mary Lee says, holding up a finger. "If I'm anyone in Middle Earth, I'm a powerful wizard. And I'd save your ass. You're an ugly dwarf."

"I don't know," I say, tracking Fallon's movements as he goes to his refrigerator and brings out two beers. "The new dwarves are kind of hot."

"Gross," Mary Lee says.

"Do you want me to put you on a bus back home tonight?" Fallon warns her. He hands me a beer and musses up her hair. "Because those are a long five hours."

"*Fine*," she says. "I'll behave. Let's play Scrabble. I don't think Fallon knows how to spell, so we'll kick his ass."

Fallon rolls his eyes. "This is the kind of abuse you get from family."

"It's sweet," I whisper, and he sits on the footstool across the coffee table.

"Okay, so let's establish some rules." Mary cracks her knuckles. "Whoever skips a turn has to answer a question."

"What kind of question?" I ask.

"Any kind. It just has to be the truth. Why is the sky blue? Why did you abandon your family to travel around the world? That kind of thing."

Fallon narrows his eyes at his sister. "Fine. If I win, you go home on the first bus going back to Boston."

"What if I win?" Mary asks, her bright green eyes defiant. "Do I get to stay?"

"Then you still go home. I just tell Dad it was my idea and I bought you a ticket and forgot to mention it to him. I'll even put you on the Amtrak instead."

Mary goes serious. "You'd do that?"

"Do we have a deal?" Fallon asks.

"Wait," I say. "What if I win?"

"Then you get to give your points to one of us. You're tie-breaker."

"That's not fair!" I say.

"Tough shit, Flores." Fallon winks at me. And in that wink, I know exactly what we're playing for.

Mary Lee kicks off the board with BRASH. I have all vowels and end up with BEE. Fallon surprises us with THRIVE. I'm the first to pass.

"How does this work?" I ask Mary, since she's making up her own rules. "Do I have to answer a question from both of you or just one?"

The brother and sister glance at each other. Fallon looks relaxed, comfortable, happy. He looks whole. It's a side of him I haven't seen before, and the intimacy of it all scares me, because there's nowhere else I'd rather be on a Friday night than playing a board game with his little sister and cuddling with his puppy.

Lily's words echo in my mind. *I don't even know who you are anymore.*

I don't know, either, but this Robyn, sitting in this living room. I like her. She's happy, and she's not going to apologize for that.

"Both," Mary says. "Let's see. How did you two meet?"

So I tell her about the laundry incident.

"Ew, you have a sequin thong? Doesn't that itch?"

"It's a specialty show, get over it. My turn." Fallon levels his eyes with mine. "How was the dinner tonight?"

I line up my letters in alphabetical order. I have a lone L, and now I just need somewhere to put it.

"It was good. Actually, I got demoted from maid of honor to a run-of-the-mill bridesmaid. I don't mind, but now I have to be paired up with my boss."

Fallon knocks over his beer. His reflexes are so quick he grabs it just before it hits the floor and brings it to his lips before the foam starts overflowing. Then he keeps drinking until the bottle is empty and sets it down with a light *thud*.

Mary Lee makes a face that says, "Shit's about to get real." It's better telling Fallon this now. Though probably not fair to catch him off guard with his sister in the room.

"Principal Pervert gets to take you out after all," Fallon says, stroking his smooth jaw.

"It's just a couple of hours."

Fallon shrugs. "It's fine." But the subtext is, "It's not fine."

"I take it there's history with this Principal Pervert?" Mary Lee asks, her ponytail swishing with the turn of her head.

I hold up my finger. "I think the rules dictate that you have both asked your questions."

"Dammit!" Mary shouts, then we resume the game.

Fallon comes in with ZEST, and I could throttle him. He pumps his fist in the air and laughs at both of us. I manage a weak EVERY. Mary curses up a storm that even makes Fallon blush.

"I'm about to wash your fucking mouth out with soap."

It sends Mary Lee and me into laughing fits and a round of calling him *Dad*.

Mary Lee smacks her hands on her head. "Why are there so many Rs in this game? Pass."

I sit back and let Fallon ask the first question.

"Why'd you run, Mary?"

She frowns and pulls at the tufts of cotton from the pillow on her lap. "Dad had a relapse."

"What?"

"Rules are rules," Mary says, trying to smile.

"Fuck the rules," Fallon says. "Why wasn't that the first thing out of your mouth when you got here?"

I place my hand on his shoulder. He sits back and tries to calm himself.

"Mary," I say. "What's wrong with your father?"

"I'm not sure. But he's been taking more pain meds. He doesn't complain in front of me, but I know that there's something wrong. He's just so freaking stubborn he won't *talk* to me. No one talks to me."

I give Fallon a look that says, "Talk, you big idiot."

"You can talk to me," he finally tells her, his voice strangled with hurt.

She scrunches up her face and gives us her cheek. "How? You don't pick up. When you have free time you're halfway across the world. It's not like you're going to come home. We're not as cool as some mountain range in India, I guess."

The ache in her voice hits me right in my chest. Fallon looks like he's been sucker punched. Guilt makes his eyes crinkle at the corners.

"I'm sorry, Mary. I'll handle this. I'll talk to Dad, okay? You shouldn't have to be here. I should've gone home."

She nods, then rubs her face with her palms. She's putting on a front so we don't see how much she's hurting, but she is. I know because I recognize the mask she's putting on. I've been doing that all year now.

"Let's play," she says. She manages a ROWS. I put down LOVE, and for a moment, I look up at Zac. He's already staring at me, a sad smile pulling at his mouth.

"Pass," he says.

"When is your next trip?" Mary Lee asks him.

Fallon's face goes blank for a moment, and he fidgets with his tiles. "Vegas. I'll figure something out with Dad, okay?"

That's not what his sister asked him, and he seems to avoid it. Maybe he doesn't want to acknowledge that our arrangement is going to be over soon. But something about the way he avoids my stare bothers me. So I ask him.

"*When* is your Vegas show, Fallon?"

His eyes flick to mine, but he can't hold my gaze, so he stares at the open mouth of his beer.

"June thirty."

My heart twists painfully. That's in two weeks.

"Oh."

Mary looks back and forth between us, sensing something's wrong. "I have to pee."

When she leaves, Fallon tries to speak. "Robyn—"

"Were you always going to leave so soon?"

He shakes his head. He gets up and sits beside me. My senses are accosted with his scent, the warmth of his arm against mine, his eyes glassy and pleading.

"It was a surprise. We were supposed to leave in September. But Vegas wanted us, and it's always been the dream. I wanted to tell you, every day since, but I couldn't bring myself to do it. I was afraid you'd end it."

I have two choices. I can end this, whatever this is, now. I can go upstairs to my apartment and avoid the hell out of Fallon the way I've avoided so many things in the past year. I can cut this string that's wrapped itself around us, keeping us together. Let go.

Or, I can see this through. What's the difference between ending things now or in September? Everything comes to an end, doesn't it? This is no different. This way, I can have my cake and eat it, too. The most amazing sex of my life and what was supposed to be a no-strings-attached romance.

Then why does the idea of him leaving feel like a wrecking ball through my chest?

"Hey, you should've told me sooner," I say, pressing my palm on his chest. He places his hand over mine. Thumbs his finger across my skin. "But I want to see this through."

"Really?"

"Really. I just, I want to break a rule."

He quirks his eyebrow up. "What rule is that?"

"I want to ask another question." I lick my lips, my heart

beating loudly in my ears. "Do you want to be my date to Lily's wedding?"

He looks taken aback. "You want to bring me to your best friend's wedding? Won't that bring up too many questions?"

"It's okay if you don't want to. I just want to spend as much time with you as possible before you go. And I can't miss it, so—"

"Then, yes," he cuts me off. "I'm yours. Whatever you need."

I'm yours. For just a little while longer, Fallon is mine.

And I'm going to make those days count.

15

Take Your Time

ROBYN

In the morning, I go through my mail. When I see the Savannah College stamp on the envelope, I open it quickly. It's my first official rejection to grad school.

You didn't want to go there anyway, I tell myself.

I can't wade into those thoughts, because Fallon texts me. *Mary is on a train back home. Meet me downstairs in five.*

We haven't spoken since last night's Scrabble match. To mine and Mary's surprise, Fallon beat us by forty points using QI. Still, he called his dad and told a white lie for his sister with the provision that if she does it again, things won't go down the same way. He's a good brother.

I pull my weekend bag over my shoulder and head down. Yaz is at Ricky's apartment for the weekend and some of his boys are covering his shifts.

Downstairs, Fallon is waiting for me against his car with two cups of coffee in hand. I take one and inhale the bitter aroma of fresh-brewed coffee. I take a sip, the dark roast coating my tongue. "How'd you know I drink it like this?"

"Well, there's no sugar or milk in your kitchen," he says, opening the door for me. "But the first time we met you had a full pot. You know I read somewhere that people who drink black coffee have the potential to be psychopaths."

I roll my eyes and settle into the front seat. "Maybe I just like the pure taste of caffeine. I've been drinking coffee since as long as I can remember. My dad used to pour me some in one of the little cups from my tea party set. Back then I used to load it up with sugar. But I lost the taste."

"No sweets," he says. "Got it."

Part of me wants to say, "It doesn't matter because you won't have to remember this soon." The other part of me that enjoys that he notices such little details wants to cling to him and not let go.

"Am I allowed to know where we're going?"

He shakes his head. "You'll see. My buddy Aiden suggested it. As much as he tries to deny it, he's a romantic at heart."

"You are, too," I say.

"What?"

"Romantic at heart."

He takes my hand and kisses my knuckles. We drive north, and by the time we pass Sleepy Hollow and drive along the Hudson River, I know where we're going. We park in the North-South Lake Campgrounds of the Catskill Mountains. There's a great big lake with people rowing and kayaking. A small beach is full of early summer people barbecuing. It's too cold to swim, but that doesn't stop the hordes of kids who splash into the cold water.

I remember our date in the park. I wanted to go in the rowboats. When I turn around to face him, Fallon is smiling down at me.

I press my hands against his chest and reach for a kiss. "Thank you."

We rent a tandem kayak, put on the puffy orange life vests, and set off into the dark water. We paddle, our rhythm in sync from the beginning. The day is bright and clear, and we are surrounded on all sides by lush green trees. The tops of the nearby mountains are capped with snow, but the sun is so bright, it feels like the height of summer.

We reach a patch of lily pads, and I think of the wedding. I failed my Lily.

"Where'd you go, Robyn?" Fallon's fingers run down the

length of my ponytail, then settle at the back of my neck. We rest the paddles across our thighs.

"I was just thinking about Lily." I reach out to touch one of the flowers, not yet blooming. "I need to make it up to her, but I don't know where to start. The wedding planning is over. It's not like I can usurp the maid of honor title back from Sophia."

Fallon drags his fingers across the cold surface water. I feel his cool fingers on the back of my neck, droplets trailing down my back. It's a nice reprieve from the heat, and I love that he knows just where to touch me.

"Maybe she was right. Maybe you need to talk. But get through the wedding first. You can't talk about what's bothering you if you can't put it into words. Come, try it out with me. I'll be Lily."

I look over my shoulder. "You're nuts."

He shrugs, but smiles. "I've been called worse. Come on. Use your words. I'm Lily." He coughs and makes his voice more high-pitched. "Robyn, you're the worst maid of honor ever. Why?"

My laugh echoes in the wide-open space. "She doesn't sound like that."

"Work with me, Flores."

"This is dumb." But I go along with it. "I'm sorry. I've been late to every single fitting, dinner, and shower. I try to be there, but I don't know what's wrong with me."

"Why are you late?"

I look up at the green trees, so perfect and serene. No one expects anything from trees but to grow when they're supposed to. I should be a tree.

"Sometimes I have a hard time sleeping. Then I oversleep. Then I'm a mess the next day. It's a domino effect, really. Eventually, there's too much to catch up on. At one point, I realized there was so much to do that it was easier to not do anything at all."

"Sounds like you were depressed," he says.

"I shouldn't be. My life is great. My parents are freakishly happy together. I had a boyfriend who thought he loved me, but I wasn't attracted to him."

"Are you talking about me?" Fallon asks, laughing.

"No, stupid. This was an ex last year. I'd have to be unconscious to not be attracted to you. And even then, I'd be dreaming up ways of how to sex you up."

"Good. Continue."

"I think I've spent my whole life trying to get into the perfect school, to have the perfect career, to meet . . . to meet the perfect man."

"So far you're batting zero?"

"I don't know how to answer to sports references," I say playfully. "But I did the perfect school thing and I burned out. I gave my everything to trying to have a stable career and I'm an elementary school teacher. I love my kids. You know the other day one of my girls drew a picture of me? I was a knight. I told them a story about a lady knight who rescues her best friend from an evil wizard. I made that up. But she saw me that way, and I wonder, what if I saw myself with a fraction of the love that my students see me with? They deserve better."

"So do you, Robyn."

I realize we're moving, and he's carrying both of our weights across the great lake. I shut my eyes against the cool air. *I deserve better.* Now I just need to figure out what that better thing is.

"What about the perfect man?" Fallon asks, his voice a whisper in the wind.

"He's leaving soon." I turn to look at him. My voice hitches, and I feel my lip tremble, so I turn to face the trees again. "But at least I know I found you. Even for a little while."

"Robyn—"

A fish jumps out of the water and startles me. It flops on my lap. I yelp and laugh, trying to get the little guy back in the water.

"Don't move!" Fallon shouts, but it's too late. We're rocking too hard, and then we're plunging into the freezing cold lake. I hold my breath and try to let myself out of the harness. Fallon unhooks himself, but I'm stuck. He grabs me, his hands already freezing from the water, my chest tight from holding my breath.

He pushes me up toward the surface. When I break the water, I gasp for breath.

"Fallon?" I shout his name. I'm still buckled to the kayak, soaked from head to toe. "Fallon?"

A nearby couple in a kayak paddle over to us. Fallon surfaces, and seeing his face is a relief.

"You okay?" the couple asks.

"We're all right," Fallon says. "Lost a paddle. Thank you."

They paddle away, and when they leave, Fallon splashes me with water. I splash him back.

"Can you get back in?" I ask, wiping water from my eyes. My teeth chatter and I hold on to the one paddle we have left.

"I might tip you over again," he says. "Can you paddle back alone? I'll swim."

"You'll *swim?*"

"I was raised on a bay, baby," he says. Then he dives under the water and swims back.

My fingers are numb as I grip the paddle and drag it through the water. The wind picks up, and threatens to push me. But I keep going, trying to stay a safe distance near Fallon.

I reach the beach first. One of the park workers helps me drag the kayak in and I explain that Fallon is swimming over here.

He appears from the shore, water dripping from his light-brown curls, some sort of green plant wrapped around his ankle. Even covered in lake sludge, he's the hottest man I've ever seen.

I cup his cold face with my hands. "Are you okay?"

"Nothing a hot shower won't fix."

The ranger brings out towels and blankets. We pay for the lost paddle, and then we're on our way back to the parking lot. I fuss over him the entire way, even though there's nothing I can do to help. We just have to get somewhere warm. Still, he never lets go of my hand, from the lake to the car to the ride leading into a small town. We park behind the bed-and-breakfast and ring the doorbell.

An older woman greets us.

"Sorry," Fallon says, all charm and smiles. "We fell in the lake."

"Oh dear," she says, leading us in. "Don't worry about the floors. I'll take care of that later. Are you the Fallons?"

Fallon looks taken aback. "The reservation should be under Fallon, yes."

"That's right," she says, flipping open a book. "Mr. and Mrs. Fallon. Well, this is no way to spend your anniversary. I'll take you up to your room. I told the girl on the phone we only had the honeymoon suite. But she said you wouldn't mind."

"Girl?" I ask.

Fallon sighs. "Mary Lee."

"Follow me," the old woman says.

I smirk as he waits for me to go and says, "After you, Mrs. Fallon."

FALLON

Mrs. Fallon.

I like the sound of that, especially when Mrs. Diaz, the bed-and-breakfast owner, keeps referring to Robyn as such. Robyn smirks, and even though we've been had by my little sister, we play along with the ruse. It's a lot easier than explaining the real situation. That in a couple of weeks, we won't be together. That my little sister is getting back at me with what she thinks is humiliation. Being pretend-married to Robyn isn't humiliating.

In fact, it's terrifying that I like the sound of it.

The room is small, with a rustic woodsy feel. Everything is a deep green pine color, and the bed is solid wood. There's a fireplace, and the warmth of the room feels nice as we shiver our way in.

"I'll be right in with towels. You're a bit earlier than I expected, but it's no trouble at all."

The minute Mrs. Diaz leaves, I chuckle. "I'm going to kill Mary."

Robyn grabs a blanket from the love seat near the fireplace.

She shivers as she wraps it around her shoulders. She looks up at me and I close the distance between us. I rub her arms over the blanket, and she leans into my chest.

"It's okay," she says, and winks. "Plus, we're getting top-notch service."

I'm going to kiss her, when Mrs. Diaz knocks and pushes a small food cart into the room. There are towels stacked on the bottom shelf. The top shelf has a bucket with iced champagne, strawberries, and a box of decadent chocolates.

"If you need anything," she says, "my husband and I are on the first floor to the right. Happy anniversary."

There's a cheerful twinkle in her eye, and for a moment, I'm worried we've lied to her. But when she's gone, the guilt vanishes.

Robyn lifts the champagne bottle. "Nice. Want to do the honors?"

I take the bottle from her, suddenly hot despite the goose bumps on my skin. I undo the foil.

"I'll be right back." Robyn darts into the bathroom.

My heart, the Epic Fool, has taken over my senses. Right now, I'm not a guy on a date with a girl. Right now, I'm celebrating an anniversary with the woman I love. Fuck me. How am I supposed to leave her?

No, the Epic Fool scolds me. *None of that. Pop that champagne.*

So, I do as my heart commands. There's a bunch of noise coming from the bathroom, water running and items being moved around. I blow on the bubbles that threaten to rise from the bottle, and pour two glasses in the delicate flutes. They look ridiculous in my calloused hands, but I'll roll with it.

"Fallon, come in here." Robyn's voice is a siren song, and I'm helpless against it, walking toward the bathroom holding two glasses in my hands.

"Fuck me," I sigh.

She's naked.

She's naked and I'm hard as hell and she's standing in the middle of a giant bathtub brimming with bubbles. There are candles. Where did she find candles? Oh, right. Honeymoon suite. Of course, there are candles. But who gives a flying fuck about candles when Robyn Flores is naked.

I nearly drop the champagne, but then I take a breath to steel myself.

"You are perfect," I manage to say. I mean every single word. Her long dark hair is still damp and curls at the ends, covering her breasts. Her waist is so small, with hips that bloom outward like the curves of mountains. Her thighs are muscular, powerful, and I picture them draped over my shoulders, my face nestled between them. Her long calves disappear into the bubbles, water still rising around her. She sits, waiting for me. Just looking at her sends fire alarms going off along my skin.

"What are you waiting for?" she asks, her hand extended to me. That hand is a lifeline to her.

I set the glasses down on the rim of the large bathtub and undress. I take her hand and step into the warm water. It sloshes in small waves with the movement of our bodies finding each other. She faces me, straddling me. Soapy water moves around us as we kiss. My dick rests against her pussy. Just one slip and I'd be inside of her. *Fuck. Fuck. Fuck.*

She bites at my neck, sucking fresh bruises onto my skin. I find my way through the water and search until I find the treasure I'm looking for. I sink my fingers into her silky wetness.

"Ohh, keep doing that," she moans, pulling my hair and pressing her slick body against mine. I pin her against me, fuck her with my fingers until she cries out and is nothing but trembling against me.

We lie back in the bathtub. There's water all over the floor, soaking into the bath mats and our mountain of clothes. She lies down on top of me, her ear right against my heart.

She turns her face up to mine. My heart seizes when I look at her, and this feeling, this feeling of wholeness and calm, is more terrifying than anything else I've experienced.

The champagne has miraculously not fallen over. She picks up one by the stem, and flips around, moving like a clever mermaid into a sitting position between my legs. I brush her hair over one shoulder and press kisses across her back. Her skin is a warm light brown, radiant in the candlelight.

"To us," she says, taking her glass and bending it toward mine.

I drink the whole glass in one shot and when I look at her I know I'll regret not asking.

"Come with me to Vegas," I say, in a rush.

She spits out her champagne. It's a good thing we're in a bathtub surrounded by bubbles. She turns around, her eyes wide open, a smile on her lips that seems to ask "Are you serious?"

Then she does ask, "Are you serious? To Vegas?"

"Like a heart attack." I brush my thumb on her cheek. "Robyn, I'm not sure about a lot of things. Where I'm living every six months, or if I have health insurance, or where my life is headed. I'm not even sure if we're ready for this. But I know that I don't want to be without you. I want to go to sleep with you and wake up beside you and bring you coffee. I want to fuck you every waking moment, and make love to you every other. I know that you feel it, too. I'm not sure how we'll work it all out, but I know I'll regret it if I don't at least ask you."

Robyn takes a drink from her champagne. She swallows half of it in one mouthful, and I envy the champagne that gets to slide down her throat. She sits on her knees facing me, the ends of her hair floating on the surface like the lily pads we passed earlier. Her eyes are wide and dark and I think I might be consumed by her midnight stare.

She rubs her hand along my chest, her palm sliding through water. She lands on my heart, feeling for my pulse there.

I think I might die in the moments it takes her to decide this.

But then she smiles, and I could die a happy man just looking at that smile.

"Yes," she says. "I want to come with you."

16

Follow Your Arrow

ROBYN

The weekend is a daze of sex and kisses and making plans.

I said yes. Fallon asked me to go to Vegas with him and I said yes. Yes to moving across the country with a man I'm falling in love with but have only known for less than a month. In my heart, I know it's the right thing.

We make plans. He's going to go out there first. They have a week to rehearse with their new choreographer and look for places to live. The hotel is putting them up for a week, but he doesn't want me to have to share rooms with all the guys. He's going to find us an apartment off the Strip.

I'll finish the year and put my time in first thing Monday morning. I'll have to tell my parents and Lily. But I'm not sure how that's going to go. I'll wait until after the wedding. He'll meet my parents at the reception, and ask my parents as a formality.

I have enough savings that I can take off half a year, more if I'm savvy. I'll write for a year and see what comes out of that. When we get back to our building on Sunday night, it seems like the easiest thing in the world.

That's right, I'll have to sublet my apartment until my lease is up. My landlord loves me, so I'm sure that won't be a problem.

"Are you sure?" Fallon asks me one more time.

We're in my apartment. I look around at all of my things. I

haven't moved in eight years. My apartment is so *lived* in. But I want a fresh start. I think about what books I want to take. What clothes I'll pack. What do I leave behind?

"I've always wanted to be the kind of person who picks up on the fly," I say, wrapping my arms around him. He leads me into the bedroom. I lie down on my stomach and he crawls on top of me, buries his face in my neck. He tugs at my pants and I turn my face to kiss him. I'm sore down there, but wet in an instant as he pulls my pants down to my knees.

"Ow, baby. Be gentle."

And so he kisses and licks my pain away.

I knock on Lily's door at school on Monday morning. Her eyes flit to the clock on the door, and I'm a little offended that she has to do that. "Hey."

"I need to tell you something," I say.

"Oh my god. You're pregnant?" she asks dryly, throwing the question back at me from her engagement night.

"Har, har, har," I fake-laugh. I take a deep breath and decide to come clean. The sooner, the better. Besides, no matter what's happening between us, Lily is still my best friend. "I'm putting my notice in."

I wave the official envelope in my hand.

"What?" She walks over to me and feels my forehead. "Are you okay?"

I grab her hand and smile. "I've never been better. Fallon's leaving the week after your wedding. His show got a headlining gig in Vegas and he asked me to go with him. I said yes."

"Robyn, have you thought this through?" she asks, and her disbelief hurts a bit. "Where are you going to live?"

"He's getting us an apartment."

"And you're just going to—let him take care of you?"

"Hey, don't say it like that. I have my own savings. He's encouraging me to write for a little while until I get into grad school. I've got one rejection so far, but I can have my cousin Sky pick up my mail and if something changes I can figure it out then! And if I don't get in anywhere, I think I'm okay with that.

J. K. Rowling didn't go to grad school for writing. I just—I need a fresh start and I've got the opportunity to take it. Why aren't you happier for me?"

"Because, Robbie!" She presses her hand to her forehead, like she can't believe what she's hearing. "This isn't like you. You don't just *pick up* and go."

"I know that. And maybe that's the reason I've been so fucking miserable this past year. I'm not happy, Lil. I haven't been happy in a long time. When I'm with Fallon, I'm happy. He brings out something inside of me that's always been there, but now it has room to shine. I'm not afraid to be myself. I'm not afraid to try something new. Who knows? Something good can come of this."

Lily paces across her room. There's still half an hour until the bell. The last couple of nights I've gotten the best sleep of my life. True, I still don't want to get out of bed, but Fallon waking me up by pressing his morning erection against my ass is an incentive.

"What did your parents say?"

"I haven't told them yet. I was going to wait until after the wedding. I want them to meet him."

"You're bringing him?"

"That's what I wanted to ask," I say. "I still have that plus one."

"Robbie, I'm worried."

"Don't be." I try to keep my optimism, but she's dragging me down. "I've thought this through."

"How long? This weekend? You're ready to make a life-changing decision on a weekend?"

I rest my hands on her shoulders and look her dead in the eye. "I'm sure. I don't think I've ever been this sure, not even when I said yes to Columbia."

"Thank you for telling me." She pulls me into a hug and holds me tight. "Well, if you're sure, bring him. I'll be happy for you. I just want you to be careful. I don't want you to get hurt."

I kiss her cheek. "Don't worry about me. I got this."

After school, I stop by Lukas's office. The staff is mostly gone, but his secretary is still packing up. She's young, and her eyes roam around the room until they inevitably return to Lukas's door. Part of me wants to warn her, "You can do better." But then Lukas is at the door and greets me.

"Ms. Flores." His hazel eyes never leave my face. "Isn't this a surprise? Come in."

I walk into his office but don't sit. His diplomas and awards are on full display. There's a baseball, a red marble apple on top of a stack of papers, and a plaque with his name on the desk, in case you forget whose office this is.

"What can I do for you?" He's all smiles, as if we've never had an awkward exchange before.

To make things simple, I hand him the letter. "I'd like to give my notice. I won't be coming back next year."

He stares at the envelope with my letter in his hands. He runs his hand across his tie and sits back. "I see. And what's the cause behind such a rash decision? I hope it wasn't because of me. I've apologized multiple times."

"You apologized once, and not to Fallon. You also lied to Lily's fiancé and said that Fallon attacked you."

Lukas arches an eyebrow and picks up the baseball on his desk. There's an autograph on it, but I wouldn't know which player. He tosses it back and forth. He's probably a Yankees fan on top of everything.

"Technically, that's not a lie. He did challenge me to a fight. That's a verbal attack."

"Look, I didn't come here to talk about that night." I rest my knuckles on his desk. I don't want to sit and make myself comfortable. "I just want to let you know because, despite your inappropriate come-ons to me, you're still my boss."

"Come-ons? To you? Robyn, you flirt with me when you're late so I won't write you up."

"Excuse me?" I stand up straight. "Do you want me to repeat the words you said to me when you hijacked my date with Fallon? Because I haven't told him, to *spare* you the attack you claim happened. I believe your exact words were, *You look good enough to eat.* But it doesn't matter now. I have a week left before the school year ends. Please stay away from me."

"You know I can't," he says, shaking his head. "You're my partner at the wedding. You're honestly blowing this out of proportion."

And in this moment, I am angrier than I've ever been. "Fuck you, Principal Platypus."

I slam the door on my way out, startling the secretary. She grabs her papers and runs out the door. I'm sure she was listening, and I'm glad. Maybe she'll be better prepared. Maybe she'll do what I *didn't* do, should he ever behave the same way.

I grab an incident report from the UFT rep's office, and stuff it in my purse. Then I walk out of the building, and get into Fallon's car because he's waiting for me.

Our future is waiting for us.

FALLON

Ricky's in his office going over a mountain of paperwork.

"After all these years, I still don't know how you get everything done, brother." I sit in the chair in front of his desk.

He looks up and his face quirks into a grin. "Passion keeps me young and thirsty, you know what I mean? What's gotten into you?"

I shrug but am unable to hide the smile on my face. "I asked Robyn to come with me to Vegas."

"Holy shit. I take it, since you're smiling harder than the time you had a threesome with Ms. Colombia and Ms. Australia after the pageant, that she said yes."

I cross my fingers over my stomach and put my feet up on his desk. He hates feet. "How is it that *I* barely remember that, but you do?"

"That's the only time I've been jealous of you, Zacky." He stacks a bunch of papers on their ends and adds them to another pile. "If you're happy, then I'm happy. The boys will welcome her like one of our own. Are you sure she's a hundred percent on all of this? She's not going to go all Crazy Jealous Girlfriend on the clients, is she?"

"The only time that's ever happened was with Aiden, not

me," I say. "And that's because he really was double dipping. I'm not like that. I'm not going to hurt her."

"I'm not saying you're going to hurt her, kid." Ricky looks at me. "I'm just making sure that you're going to be a hundred percent."

"Thanks for looking out for me, brother. What's all this paperwork? I thought everything was going through the lawyers."

Ricky gets up from his desk and closes the door behind him. "It is. But something hasn't been adding up lately."

"What do you mean?"

He sits on his desk and lowers his voice. "I mean the door numbers don't reflect what's on the bank account."

The first thing that comes to mind is Vinny. I remember the time I heard him speaking on his phone near the office. I tell Ricky as much.

"Are you sure?" he asks, his voice hard. Ricky will put up with a lot of things, but fucking with his money will get you close enough to dead when he's through with you. Five years ago, he caught one of the guys skimming from the bar, and nearly beat him senseless. It's the only time I've ever been afraid of him.

"I didn't say anything because I wasn't sure what I heard. But it could be him. I know I never liked the kid, but he's also the newest one among us. His kind of partying ain't cheap."

"Let's see what the cameras say." Ricky opens up the cabinet with six cameras that show different areas of the club. He keeps them running during the day, and Darla's in charge of watching them when Ricky isn't in the office. "There's a pattern. Every other day. Then three days with no action. Then there's about a grand in missing money from either the bar or the door."

"I'd like to think that if any of the guys were in a bind they'd come to us. I have." Back when my dad was sick the first time, Ricky gave me the money to pay for the hospital bills. I swore to pay him back but he wouldn't have it.

Ricky runs his fingers along the hairline of his perfectly trimmed beard. He's tuned out, watching the monitors. He hits pause, then rewind. "The cameras go off."

"Who has access to this room other than you?"

"No one. But then again, anyone can pick a lock, right?"

"I'm sorry, man. Should we call a meeting or something?"

Ricky slaps my back. "Let me worry about this. I'll figure it out. You go get yourself a tux that doesn't come with holes at the bum. Go to my guy in the Village. Best threads in the city."

I take the card that he gives me. "It isn't going to be bright purple or whatever acid trip color he makes for you, is it?"

"Just fucking go. Take Aiden with you. He needs to pick up some of his own blazers. He's going to start emceeing when I'm not around."

"You got it."

"My boy's finally becoming a man," Aiden tells me the next day. We're on the train to Manhattan. I hate the trains here. They're crowded and smell of dead rats and Cheetos.

"I've always been all man, baby." I punch his shoulder.

But Aiden is distracted. He's making eyes at a woman sitting in front of him. She's all class, with a tight pencil skirt and high heels. Her jacket is perfectly tailored to her body. I wonder what a lady like that is doing taking the subway. But I guess that's just New York, full of inexplicable wonders. I guess I'll miss it when I'm gone.

"Have you ever even lived with a girl before?" Aiden says, once the woman exits on Fifth Avenue, and he can bother to give me attention once again. "And not with your sister."

"Not for long periods of time and not officially. But this is new. We both want this. She needs a fresh start and I don't want to be without her."

Aiden nods, and bounces his head to the mariachi band that's entered our car and proceeds to play a tune Aiden seems to know the lyrics to. When they're done with their song, Aiden and I leave them some bills.

"I don't know, man. I don't know how you can settle down with one girl."

"Woman, Aiden. *Woman.*"

"Fine, woman. Doesn't it get tired? The sex with the same person?" Aiden catches the eye of a hipster girl eye-fucking him from the other side of the train.

"No," I say. "She's the best I've ever had. And I've had a lot."

"I've had more."

I roll my eyes. "Sure. Whatever. Doesn't change anything. I fucking l—"

Aiden points a finger in my face. "Don't say you love her. You've known her for three weeks."

"I love being with her. I love the way she smells. I love who I am with her. I love her, bro."

Aiden shakes his head and slumps in his seat. "I've lost you."

I laugh and get up. Our stop is coming next. "I can't wait until it happens to you."

Aiden looks back over his shoulder and smiles at a full-figured beauty with bright red lips and a pinup dress that hugs all her curves. He waves, then we're out onto the platform. "Never going to happen. I'm single for life."

I slap his back and hurry up the steps. "Famous last words."

17

Heart of Glass

I spend the night at Lily's house with some of the bridesmaids. T-minus twelve hours to wedding day madness.

Lily doesn't drink champagne because she wants to be super-fresh in the morning. There's Sophia and three of the bridesmaids who live farther away, plus Yennifer, Xiomara, and Anise, who are staying to avoid morning traffic. They also work at P.S. 85 but teach in different grades. We go over details like signing off for corsage delivery, making sure the emergency kits and clean pens are in everyone's purses, limo coordination, tampon supplies, emergency flasks.

When all is said and done and we're sure (for the fifth time, according to super maid of honor Sophia) that we've crossed all our t's and dotted our i's, I plop down on the couch with a big glass of wine.

"You look different," Anise tells me. She's wearing a Korean face mask that's infused with roses and honey. Her brown skin is glowing with a scrub she made herself and brought in little jars for all of us.

"Yeah," Yenni says. "When you're in school you usually look like one of those memes that hates Mondays. Except every day."

Anise and Xiomara fall over each other laughing at my expense. That's okay. I can take it.

"You're right. I didn't want to say anything until later, but I actually put in my notice earlier this week."

They gasp in sync. "Are you for real?"

"For real real." And my smile is genuine.

Sophia runs around the apartment, still going over the list. Looking at things now, I'm glad Sophia is the maid of honor. She's done an amazing job, and she's happy to be part of Lily's life. They're going to be family, after all. I feel a little bit guilty for being jealous of her.

"Where are you going?" Xiomara asks.

"What are you going to do?" Yenni asks.

"Is it for a *guy?*" Anise asks, getting to the heart of it.

I take a long sip of my wine. Lily sits at my side and leans her head on my shoulder. Things feel a little better between us, but I wonder if my mess-up as her bridesmaid has caused a rift we can't come back from. Just because my life is changing doesn't mean I want to lose her.

"Today is Lily's night," I say. "I won't get into it. But yes. There is a guy. I've wanted to quit for a while. We're going to Vegas for a little while. Then who knows? I've always wanted to travel the world."

Anise looks at me curiously, then sips her wine through a straw so she doesn't mess up her face mask. "Vegas? Do we get to meet the mystery guy?"

"Robyn's bringing him tomorrow," Lily says, and when she takes my hand in hers, I think everything will be all right.

"Can't wait. Then, cheers to you," Anise says. "To Happily Ever Afters for all."

The day starts off without a hitch. For a while.

Everyone gets plenty of sleep and the hair and makeup people arrive bright and early. The limo is clean. Lily looks radiant in her white lace gown, a fairy tale come to life. There isn't even any traffic on the way to the hall. The Astoria Foundry is a building with a brick industrial façade. Half of it is being consumed by thick ivy. Inside, the floors are polished stone. The walls have deep grooves tall enough for glass candles. White flowers wrap around a banister that leads to the ceremony hall. There are two suites for each bridal party.

I'm running around looking for my parents when I hear a quick, loud clicking sound. Sophia's eyes are wide and her hands bat in the air like hummingbird wings.

"Robyn! I need you to talk to her," Sophia says, barreling into me at the entrance. She looks like she can't even, and is talking too fast. "She won't talk to me."

I head into the bride's room. There are unopened champagne bottles everywhere. Lily is a vision in white, standing in front of a full-length mirror.

That's when I get closer and see her face. She's frowning grooves into her makeup.

"What's wrong? Everything is going off perfectly."

Lily takes a deep breath. Her eyes are red and watery.

"Oh, no," I say, fishing through my purse for napkins. Where the hell is that emergency kit? "No, no, no. What's wrong?"

"I'm pregnant."

I look at her, eyes wide. "Oh my god."

She breaks down into tears, and I hold her in my arms. "Lily— forgive me for asking this. But are you crying because you're happy or because it's the milkman's?"

There's that laugh. She laugh-cries, her makeup running down her face. "Only you would make a joke like that at a moment like this."

"I mean," I say, smiling down at her, "I'm trying to figure out this reaction."

"Of course I'm happy. It's just not part of my plan. Our plan. I found out yesterday." She sighs, deflating like a forgotten party balloon. "You were right."

"Well, you're talking to someone who just threw out the playbook and decided to move to Vegas with her beautiful stripper boyfriend."

"I haven't told anyone yet. Not even Dave."

Then, I think of this past year. All of the missed calls and appointments. Lily needed me and I wasn't there. But now, now I can be here. "I'm sorry things have been weird lately. But you're going to be okay."

"What if Dave gets so upset he won't marry me? He wanted to make partner first. I wanted to wait six years, minimum. The ceremony is in fifteen minutes—oh dear god, I'm going to be a pregnant girl left at the altar."

I pull her into a hug. The only thing I can do is be here. "Dave loves you more than life itself. He would never leave you. You told me I had to be honest with you, and now it's your turn. So, it's happening sooner than you expected. You're going to be great parents."

"How do you know?"

"Because when I needed you to take care of me you were there. Because you're a good person. Because you love with all your heart and this kid is going to be so lucky. Just don't tell it about your wild college years. I'll take care of that when the kid is in its teens."

She laughs, and wipes snot from her face. "Is the makeup artist still here?"

"I'll get him. You stay here. I'll send Dave in after." I start to walk away when I remember something. I open up my purse. "Oh. I know Sophia is in charge of the New-Old-Blue things. But I found this while I was packing."

I hold out a hairpin covered in blue crystals. "Remember? We made them when we had matching prom dresses."

Lily holds it in her hands. "You kept these? God, we were such losers."

"The best kind of losers."

When I walk outside, Sophia ambushes me in the hall.

"Is everything okay?" she asks frantically.

"Yeah, she just thought something was wrong. But she's fine now. I need to find the makeup artist to touch her up."

Sophia puts a hand on my shoulder. "Thanks, Robyn. I mean it."

"What are friends for?"

The ceremony hall is straight out of a fairy tale. We line up for the procession. I go right after Sophia. Right until I absolutely *have* to take Lukas's arm, I busy myself with fluffing the tulle of my lavender dress.

Lukas, as promised, doesn't say a word to me except, "You look nice." I answer with a polite "Thank you." And then we're going down the aisle.

I catch my mother's eyes, from where she is sitting beside my father. What are they going to say when I tell them I'm leaving? I want to believe that they'll be happy for me, but then you never know with parents.

They want the best for me, and in the end, I know that Fallon *is* the best thing for me. Maybe it's the wedding, maybe it's the relief of having things between me and Lily be okay, but I feel a well of tears rise in my eyes. I'm afraid if I blink, I'll cry.

I pay attention to the flowers, the young rabbi waiting at the end of the aisle, the chuppah where Lily and David will stand underneath, the men in their suits with matching lavender pocket squares. I catch Dave's blue eyes and they're glassy, but I've never seen him so happy. He holds Lily's hands like a true promise, and when I blink, tears run down my face.

When I was younger, I used to think that I wanted all of this by the time I reached my age. Part of why I've been so hard on myself, why I haven't let myself be happy, has been because I let myself fall under the pressure of what I *should* have instead of enjoying the life that I *do* have.

Lily and David say their vows. The way he looks at her, as if she's the only person in this room of four hundred people, I know that he's going to make her happy. And when David shatters the glass under his foot, I know more than ever that I do want to get married one day. But first, I want to enjoy my life. Now, more than ever, I know that saying yes to Fallon is the right choice. The best choice.

Among the cheers and shouts of mazel tov, I follow the bridesmaids back out of the hall.

Fallon's standing there, waiting for me. I take his hand. We join the crowds moving into the reception area for cocktails.

And because everything that goes up must come down, they do come down, crashing down in epic proportions.

FALLON

The groom crushes a glass under his foot. People stand and cheer and clap. The bride and groom kiss, but I only look at her.

Robyn is in a sweet light-purple dress with a white ribbon that ties around her perfect, tiny waist. I stay in the shadows and watch her. But somehow, out of the massive crowd, she finds me.

Her face breaks into a smile when she sees me. She jumps on me and kisses me, a full-mouth kiss that makes nearby geriatrics either giggle or scoff in shock.

From the corner of my eye I see a familiar face. It actually takes me a moment to place her because I've put her out of my thoughts completely. Anise. The last time I saw her she was offering to have a threesome with me and Vinny Suave.

I nod an acknowledgment, but give my attention back to Robyn.

"You clean up nice," she says, running her hands down the fitted deep-blue jacket.

I run my fingers along the pearl buttons of the white tuxedo shirt. "Thanks. I used Ricky's guy. Are you sure it's not too *blue?* Everyone here seems to be wearing black."

"It's the perfect blue." She runs a finger along the lapel. Suddenly, I feel hot, overdressed, like I'm wearing someone else's skin. "Come, meet my folks."

Don't choke now, Fallon, the Epic Fool of my heart commands me.

In this instance, I'd agree with him. Don't choke. I get that this is a test, and I don't want to fail her. Not now when it matters the most. I'm leaving in two days, and she's going to meet me at the end of the month.

It's cocktail hour. The light filters from the rustic glass ceiling covered in ivy. I take a glass of white wine, figuring it's safe as long as I don't drink anything with colors. My palms are sweating, so I clutch the stem of the glass harder as Robyn weaves through the crowds of people picking hors d'oeuvres from trays and throwing around kisses and greetings as if they haven't seen one another in ten years.

I can't remember the last time I went to a wedding. My circle of friends don't exactly get married at a cutthroat rate. Gary's married, and it was the biggest bash of the year. Best time of my life, and a record number of times I was propositioned by men and women in a single evening.

Still, Robyn is happy, and her smile shows it. That alone was worth the dozen times Ricky's tailor stuck me with needles because he was in a rush.

We home in on an older couple. I instantly recognize them as Robyn's parents. She has her mother's slender hourglass figure and defiant stare. She's got her dad's thick hair and light-brown complexion. Mr. Flores isn't even going gray yet, except for the well-trimmed beard he tugs on when he sees us approaching.

They give me the once-over. I wonder what they see. An expensive suit. A guy who wants to take their daughter away. Or do they see further down? A high school dropout. A stripper. Not good enough for Robyn.

I smile through my doubt and hold out my hand to Mrs. Flores first. "It's a pleasure to meet you." Normally, I'd ham it up. Compliment Mrs. Flores on how beautiful she is, but her bright blue eyes are watchful as a hawk's, and something tells me she's not the kind of woman easily wooed by compliments. "Mr. Flores."

Good grip.

"Mom, Daddy," Robyn says. How fucked up am I that I'm kind of turned on by the way she says *daddy*. "This is Zac Fallon. My boyfriend."

I smile when she says that. I can't help it and I don't care if I look stupid. *My boyfriend*. The words give me a funny feeling I've never felt before. It's not half bad.

Her mom takes my hand again. "It's a pleasure to meet you. Even though our daughter never makes time to call us and give us an update about her life."

"Ma," Robyn groans.

"So, Zac," Mr. Flores says. "Give us the summary. Where

are you from? Where did you meet? How long have you been dating?"

The man is probably a foot shorter than me, but he's no less terrifying.

"I'm from Boston, originally. But I've spent the last ten or so years traveling around the world." I look to Robyn, and she smiles.

"That sounds wonderful," Mrs. Flores says. "Robyn's always wanted to travel, but she never quite got around to it."

"There's still time," I say, and Mrs. Flores seems to like that.

"So, Boston," Mr. Flores says. "Where'd you study? One of my colleagues went to BU."

The feedback of a mic makes everyone in the hall wince. A DJ taps on the mic and calls for our attention. I feel a sigh of relief as Robyn pulls me closer to the dance floor. Now dancing, that's something I can handle.

"Ladies and gentlemen, please welcome Mr. and Mrs. Cohen for their first dance as husband and wife!"

Everyone cheers. I clap and whistle between my index finger and thumb.

Lily and David dance to an acoustic version of Guns N' Roses's "Patience." Then, when the DJ welcomes everyone to the dance floor, I take Robyn by her hand and pull her along with me. I twirl her under my hand, and she's a vision as her dress swirls wide, then falls around her knees.

"Am I doing okay?" I whisper in her ear. I keep her close, a hand on her waist and another in the air, rocking our bodies to the music.

"Please don't feel like you have to lie to my parents," she whispers. "They're going to love you because I love you."

I pull back and stare at her. The way she says it, so easily, without hesitation, renders me silent. *I love you.* It's been on the tip of my tongue for days and I haven't been able to get it out.

Until now.

"I love you, too, Robyn Flores." I lean down and tap a kiss on her lips. Lily's watching us and she gives me a tiny nod, as if she approves of me.

That's it. That's all I cared about: Robyn's parents and Lily. No one else after that matters.

We dance for a while, and couples fill the dance floor. Lily even joins us, and I might be showing off some of my best (family friendly) dance moves. I spin Lily back to her groom, and Robyn is there waiting for me. I'm about to take a step toward her, when I see Lukas walking over to us, with Anise by the hand. Rage clouds my vision, and it takes every ounce of self-control I possess to relax.

She taps Robyn on her shoulder. "Can we cut in?"

Robyn looks from me to Lukas and from Anise to me. I shrug one shoulder, and take Anise's small hand.

"So, you've been dating Flores?" I'm not sure if she means it to be a question or an accusation. "At least I know why you turned me down."

"It wasn't personal, Anise," I tell her, and spin her when the ballad calls for it. "Besides, you had fun with Vinny, right?"

"I get it." She turns her face up and smiles. Her dark eyes slide toward where Lukas and Robyn dance stiffly. "But I'm not the one you should worry about. Maybe you shouldn't be here, not if you're going to fight with him. Be the better man."

Like I should've been that night at the restaurant.

Another bridesmaid saunters over to where Anise and I are dancing. Lukas and Robyn are on the other side of the dance floor.

"Excuse me."

The other bridesmaid grabs my suit jacket, unable to balance on her heels. "Where do I know you from?"

Her eyes are bright and dark brown. They trace my face, my shoulders, and linger at my dick. Subtle.

"I just have one of those faces," I say, and pull out of her grasp.

But as I walk away, I hear her gasp to Anise and say, "I know him. He was—"

I walk faster, and go back for my date. But Robyn isn't with Lukas; she's dancing with her dad now. Mr. Flores winks at me, and twirls Robyn back my way.

"I—I think I should go," I say, taking her hands in mine.

"What? Why?"

I shake my head and pull her out of the dance area and toward a dimly lit brick wall. "Because the bridesmaid recognized me from the shower."

"Which one?" she asks.

"The one walking with Anise," I say. "They're heading this way now."

Anise and the other girl walk arm in arm, nearly dissolving into a fit of giggles. "I'll handle this," Robyn says.

I linger in the hall. A waiter comes by with a tray of wineglasses and I grab one. I'm curious about how Robyn is supposed to "handle" this. I walk around the wall where the three of them are huddled in the corner.

"You're dating the stripper!" Bridesmaid #3 says. "Why didn't you say so before?"

"It's none of our business," Anise says. "Robyn can do what she wants."

"You knew?" Robyn asks.

"No, I just hooked up with one of his friends. He talked about a girl, but I didn't know it was you. If I did I wouldn't have thrown myself at him."

"Anise!" Robyn shouts.

"What? He's fine," Anise says.

"He's totally fine," Bridesmaid #3 says. "Is he for, like, hire? Or are things serious?"

"He's not for fucking hire!" Robyn says. "He's my *date*. What kind of question is that? This is Lily's wedding, not the day Robyn brings a male stripper to the reception, so just keep it to yourself."

"Jeez, Robyn," Bridesmaid #3 says. "Suddenly, you're moving and you become a total bitch."

"Yeah, well, this bitch is about to start telling people about your nose job, so you should probably walk away from me right now."

Heels echo quickly down the hall.

"Damn, girl," Anise says. "I've never seen you stand up for yourself."

"I need a drink," Robyn says.

I walk around the hall. Anise sees me and scatters.

"Hey," I say, and hand Robyn my glass. "I heard you needed a drink."

"You heard that?"

"I don't belong here," I tell her. "I mean, I love attention, but not this kind of attention."

"You belong with me. What Xiomara said doesn't change how I feel about you. It doesn't change that we're moving. Our life doesn't include all of these strangers. My dad took one look at Lukas and shooed him away. He likes you. The tough one is my mom."

She perks up when she hears a song she likes. It has a ballroom salsa flair with loud horns and quick percussion. And just like that, the desire to make her happy trumps every discomfort in my body. I lead her back to the dance floor.

"You can salsa?" she asks with a sly smirk.

"I've danced for ten years, baby." I spin her and grab her around her waist, pressing her against me. I give her a nudge on her shoulder and lead. She matches my rhythm, our feet moving to the one-two-three-one one-two-three-one of the song. She's amazing, her hips moving from side to side, her hair coming undone from her hairpins. I spin her, again and again, until I catch her, and sweep her backward, her hair grazing the floor.

The song ends, and I realize we have an audience. They applaud and someone whistles between their fingers. We take a small bow, and the DJ announces dinner.

I take a seat beside Robyn. "I did not know you have moves like that."

"You never asked. Plus, we never got to do the dancing part of our first date."

"The first thing we're doing when we get to Vegas is going dancing. I don't care if I'm jet-lagged."

"Vegas?" Lukas says, sitting down beside me. A couple of other groomsmen and bridesmaids take their seats. "So you're the one who's taking Robyn away."

"He's not *taking me away*," Robyn says, stabbing her steak

so hard her fork nearly cleaves the plate in half. "I want to leave."

Lukas looks like he's in his cups. He keeps drinking. Other groomsmen shake my hand and compliment my dancing.

"I'm a freelance choreographer," I say, which isn't a lie. I've worked for other crews here and there.

"My girl loves ballroom. She even had me sign up with her."

"It's easy," I tell the guy. His hair is already receding, but his face looks younger than mine. "Practice, like, fifteen minutes at home. Tape your shoes if you have to. After a while, you need to stop thinking that there are people watching you and just enjoy the moment. Listen to the songs on your run."

"Thanks, man," the groomsman says. "You play sports? I heard you tell Mr. Flores you went to Boston."

I shrug. "I played baseball when I was a kid, but I sucked."

"Are you going to teach in Vegas?" a bridesmaid asks Robyn. "I just heard."

"Cat's out of the bag," I whisper in her ear.

"I'm going to write, actually."

"You're giving up your career to become a writer?" Lukas asks her. He slurs the last word. Everyone at the table looks uncomfortable and keeps cutting their meat in silence. "What are you going to write about?"

"I haven't decided. I've always had ideas, I just never took the time," Robyn says, eating a bite of steak. She never loses her smile, not once, and I wonder how she does it. How she doesn't just slam her knife down into his hand spread on the table.

"My cousin's a writer," one of the bridesmaids says. "She writes kids' books. She goes on all these tours. I keep telling her to write the story of our lives and we can split it fifty-fifty. We'd make a fortune."

Robyn laughs amicably. "Thanks, Yenni. But I think I'm going to take time and figure it out. I'm excited. Fallon's the one who's been encouraging me to follow my dreams."

"The Stripper and the Writer," Lukas says, and that brings a snicker and a series of whispers around the table.

Robyn holds my hand as I get up. "What do you want to drink?"

"Whiskey, one ice cube," she says.

I look around the table, tugging at my tux jacket to smooth it out. "Anyone else?"

"I'll take a Manhattan," Yennifer says, smiling.

I walk over to the bar on the other side of the room. Lily and David dance at the center of the room.

Try as I might, Lukas is getting under my skin. I've never been insecure. Not the way he makes me feel. I can't believe I went on and on about *choreography*. Who am I? I tug my tie loose and come up to the bar.

"Woodford, one cube; Manhattan up; and the best, chillest tequila you can manage." I might regret this tequila shot, but a twisted, dark part of my mind tells me I need it.

From here, I watch the wedding crowd. David's in finance and Lily's a teacher. Everyone here went to school, and they're probably the kind of people who enjoy talking about what they majored in or how they still root for their school's team. These are things that matter to some people, but it doesn't make anyone special.

This is not my world. This is Robyn's world. I know who I am. My world involves being offered to have a threesome and do a line of coke off someone's abs. My world involves wrong choices and regret. My world involves someone perfectly kind like Ricky beating the shit out of a thief. How can I bring Robyn into that?

"You okay, buddy?" the bartender asks. He looks like my kind of guy with a full beard and arms covered in tats.

I put down a $20 on the counter. I know it's an open bar, but leaving a heavy tip up front just means he'll take my orders first when he sees me coming toward him.

"I'm five by five," I say, and I down my shot of tequila and it goes down smooth. I bite down on the lime, and the only thing that could make it more bitter is seeing Lukas standing beside me.

"What?" I ask him.

Lukas is drunk and visibly ticked off, which doesn't make for a good combination. I can't make a scene at Lily's wedding. Robyn won't forgive me. I won't forgive myself.

"Dude, just lay off," I say, slightly defeated. "There are hundreds of girls you can get with. What is your obsession with Robyn?"

A cluster of men nearby glance at us. I catch them in my peripheral vision, but turn my back so I'm only facing Lukas. He's wearing a charcoal-gray suit with cuffs that catch the light. I laugh in my mind because, in another world, he and Ricky would get along famously.

"Because she deserves better than you," Lukas says, and turns to the bartender. "Vodka Red Bull. None of that house shit. Top shelf."

The bartender doesn't say anything, just busies himself making drinks. I always, always judge people on the way they treat staff.

"What was I saying?" Lukas asks. "Oh yeah, Robyn. I asked her out, you know, before you. She said no."

"I figured that, what with her moving across the country with me. Take it easy, Luke."

I grab the drinks from the counter and start to walk away, but Lukas tugs on my sleeve. I see the drinks fall in slow motion. One of them crashes at Robyn's mother's feet. The other falls next to Lily, amber liquid soaking into the train of her dress.

"I'm *so* sorry," I say, bending down to pick up the glass. People speak around me, but I'm not listening.

"It's okay," Lily tells me. She rests her arm on my shoulder and smiles. "I saw what happened. I'll get someone to make him leave."

Lily whispers something into the ear of one of the groomsmen and he runs off to get someone else.

"I got you," the bartender tells me and pats me on the back.

So I stand, with all eyes on me. People watch the mess on the floor, and there Lukas is leaning against the bar. In my mind, he's sprouted devil horns and a tail. What an evil motherfucker.

"Let me ask you something, Fallon," Lukas says, this time

loud enough that the curious crowd has started to gather. All I see, though, is Robyn making her way toward us.

I turn to Lukas and face him. "I'm not stopping you."

"You going to give us a show later on, or is that just for Robyn's after hours?"

I clench my fists and then Robyn is there, wrapping her arms around me. Her scent fills my senses. *Think of Robyn,* the Epic Fool in my heart screams, and pushes against my chest as if he can force me to stand back.

People are watching now. Robyn's parents. Everyone around the bar.

"There she is!" Lukas shouts.

"Hey, Lukas, calm down," one of the groomsmen tells him. He tries to grab his arm but Lukas shrugs him off.

"Robyn Flores, who *rejected* me for a stripper! What kind of thong are you wearing under that getup, Zacky?"

Robyn screams my name. I can hear her. It's like she's miles away, because my eyes blur, overcome with rage. I land my fist square on Lukas's jaw.

I'm aware that dozens of eyes are on me. Lukas is out like a light on the floor. The bartender has lined up a tequila shot for me and I drink it.

I set the empty glass on the table.

I've had it.

I leave and I don't look back.

18

Locked Out of Heaven

ROBYN

It takes three groomsmen and David himself to carry Lukas out to the street. I follow them out. Lukas is a messy slump on the side of the building. One of guys is in charge of getting him into a cab.

I keep walking to the corner. My shoes click on the cement, and my heart thunders in my chest.

Fallon is gone.

He reached his breaking point.

And he doesn't even realize that he didn't do anything wrong. I try to call him but it goes to voice mail. I send him text after text, but nothing.

I walk back into the reception and show my face. I keep my chin up and walk through the throng of people to where my parents chat with Lily and David.

"Is Fallon okay?" Lily asks.

"Oh, he'll be fine," I say, trying to keep myself together. I don't think it's fine. I have a very, very bad feeling about this. "You guys enjoy your night. I'm sorry Lukas is such a tool."

"Don't apologize for him," David says, as he takes my hands in his. "I think we've done that enough. I owe you an apology, Robyn. I'm sorry."

"I'll be fine," I say, though my voice wavers. "Today is about you guys! You're married. You're going to be parents!"

There's a series of gasps, followed by Lily folding in half with laughter. Their family and friends come over for a new wave of congratulations. Dave wraps his arms around Lily, keeping his palm over her belly. She isn't showing, not by far, but they've never looked happier. They go back to their celebration, moving from table to table. Their happiness radiates through the halls.

I'm not sure what to do with myself, so I post myself at the scene of the crime. They've cleaned up all the glass, and when the bartender sees me, he pours me a whiskey on the rocks.

"Robyn Helena Flores," my father says, his voice stern.

I face my parents. "Yes, Papi." He's always softer on me when I speak Spanish.

"Why didn't you tell us that principal was such a pendejo?" Dad asks. "I'm surprised Fallon stayed so calm after everything Lukas said to him. I would've clocked him as soon as I saw him."

"Benjamin," my mom says. But she gives me a secret smile. "We don't encourage our daughter to act out on violent impulses."

"I guess you heard about the move," I say. "I wanted to tell you, but Lily's wedding didn't seem like the right place."

"Robyn, you've always been so uptight," my mom says.

"Excuse me?"

"All of this pressure you put on yourself to be perfect. It was about time you broke. At least you've found yourself a—cómo se dice these days?—un super-fly honey?"

"No one says that, Mom. In English or Spanish." Still, I hug her, because I need my mother. Now more than ever. Dad wraps his arms around us, and our little trinity is complete.

"I don't know if I can fix things with Fallon. He kept telling me that he didn't belong here. From the very beginning. I made him feel like this. I don't know if I can fix it."

"Well, like when I won over your father," my mother says, "you have to make a big gesture."

"Your big gesture was getting pregnant."

My mother raises her hands up in defeat. "It's about time I had some grandkids."

"Gross," I say. I don't know what's worse. Getting romantic

advice, or my mother telling me to get knocked up as a grand gesture. "I'm sure there's a middle ground. I just have to find it."

The bartender smiles at me. "You're Robyn, right?"

"That'd be me." I raise my finger in the air. The bartender sets an envelope on the counter.

"The guy who punched the other guy dropped this."

He slides it over to me, and my heart races. It's a letter from Fallon.

FALLON

I walk into the club toward the end of the set. Hicks, the bouncer on Saturday nights, nods at me as I walk in.

"Lookin' sharp, Fallon," he says.

Right. Sharp. My tie is undone and my shirt is splashed with bourbon. I undo the suffocating buttons as I make my way toward the bar. The boys are doing their closing number. All twelve of them rush to the stage, shirtless and in nothing but thongs. They wind and thrust and pump and do all kinds of suggestive things to the air. Women get up from their seats. This is the set where the boys jump onto tables. Hands rise from below to reach for naked legs, ass cheeks, abs. There's always the occasional hand that goes for the jewels.

I love this world. I love the rush of the stage. Yeah, there's terrible things that go along with it. There's an endless supply of drinks and laughter and a party that doesn't end. But there's also family. A family that sticks with you through good and bad.

I hate that a girl made me doubt myself.

Rachel sees me walk up to her bar. One of the waitresses comes up to my right, cutting me off. She's sweet, blond, with winking brown eyes that tell me she hasn't lived a full two decades. She's here to make a buck. She's here for the thrill of the nightlife.

"Can I get you a drink?" she asks.

I shake my head. "I'm okay."

I sit in front of Rachel and she examines the state of me before speaking. "I take it things went well?"

I sigh and take the cold shot of tequila she sets in front of me. I've got a cut on my palm from trying to pick up the glass I dropped, and another gash on my knuckles from when I punched Lukas.

"It's as close to a red wedding as we're getting outside the *Game of Thrones* universe."

She rolls her eyes, but then smirks. "The North remembers, fuckin' nerd. We can always send Hicks to go knock him out."

"I can handle myself."

And I can. In the end, it wasn't Lukas. I mean, yes, it was everything that Lukas said to me. But it was also the way I let myself feel when I was there.

"Tell Ricky I'm going to be in the office." I take my drink and head to the back of the house.

When I get there, someone's already inside. Ricky never keeps it unlocked, and I have his key. I stand against the door and wait for whoever is in there to come out.

She walks out holding a bank bag, the kind we use to deposit money after every shift. Darla. When she sees me, her eyes widen into perfect circles.

"Hey, Darla," I say, sadness seeping into my voice because today has been a day. And now, I know I've caught her. She doesn't have a key to the office. "How'd you get in here? We don't close the registers until after the show."

She brushes her blond hair out of her face. Her voice trembles. "Ricky sent me."

I look down at my feet because the betrayal runs deep. "So, if I ask him after the show, he's going to say he gave you his key to come here?"

"Fallon, I'm sorry."

"You're the one," I say, yanking my arm away as she tries to touch me. "This whole time I thought it was Vinny. Why, Darla?"

"I'm in trouble, Fallon. I owe people money."

"You could've asked!"

Out in the club, there's the final booming cheer from the crowd. Soon enough, Ricky will make his way down this hallway.

"It's the perfect time, isn't it? When Ricky and everyone is focused on finishing the set."

I hold my hand out and wait for her to hand the money back.

"I was going to pay it back."

"When?"

She looks down at her feet. "Are you going to tell Ricky?"

"Yes," I say. "If he wants to find you, he will. Get out of here."

"Fallon—"

"Give me the key."

She has the audacity to look pissed as she slaps the key on my palm. "I never meant to hurt you boys."

"Tell that to Ricky."

Darla's been there before. She's seen what Ricky does to men who've stolen from him. But it's never been a woman, and it's never been someone we've trusted for so long.

Once she's gone, I lock up the safe and the door, then I head back out to the club where the crowds are leaving.

Ricky catches my eye. He's smiling the same brilliant smile he has after a good show. But I can't return it. He knows something is wrong, and he wades through the mass of bodies and comes to me.

In the loud club, I watch the incredulity cross his face as I press the key on his palm and say, "Darla."

He excuses himself, and heads back.

And I take no pleasure in knowing I'm not the only one with a broken spirit tonight.

19

Happy Now?

ROBYN

"Do you have a trunk full of them dresses?" the bouncer asks me as I get to the club's door. His large ringed finger points to my bridesmaid dress.

"Why?" I ask. "You want to borrow one?"

He chuckles, then looks me up and down with a small smile. He glances inside the club then back at me. "You're here for Fallon, right?"

I nod.

"I don't think you want to go in there tonight, sweetheart."

I steel myself. What would I do if I felt defeated and punched someone at a wedding? I'd probably get drunk and feel like the world was against me. I'd surround myself with people who made me forget mistakes. I'd make mistakes. But the letter he wrote to me feels like it's burning a hole through my purse. I think about our conversation in the park. How I told him about my parents writing letters. How no one does that anymore.

I opened it the minute the bartender gave it to me.

> Dear Robyn,
> I've never written a real letter to someone, but you make me do a lot of things I never thought I'd do. Being with you makes me a better person. I don't believe in a lot of things, but I believe in you and

me. I know you're scared of what the future will
bring us. I just want you to know, I want to make
sure that you know, that you aren't alone in any of
it. I want to make all of your dreams come true.
You're my dream. And I love you.
    Fallon

Of course, Lily yanked it right out of my hands and passed it
around to the girls for all of them to read. It made them all turn
to their significant others and ask, "Why don't I get letters like
this?"

I already knew it, but I know deep in my heart that I will
never find someone like Fallon. Whatever is waiting for me inside this club, I have to face it.

"I need to talk to him," I say.

The bouncer opens the door for me. "Suit yourself."

The club has turned into an unofficial after hours, clusters of
bachelorettes and partygoers still lingering at tables. The guys
are in different stages of disarray and undress. I see Aiden surrounded by a party of older women who fawn over him. Vinny
and Wonderboy are at the bar with Fallon. Each one of them
has a girl perching on his knee like a bird on a tree branch and
something sharp forms in my stomach.

I think about how welcoming all these men were when I
showed up here. How comfortable they tried to make me feel
when I was on that stage. They embraced me. Why wouldn't the
people around me have welcomed Fallon in the same way? Why
did they have to wait until he was gone?

Rachel sees me first. I linger at the back of the bar, my dress
too frilly and pastel for this dark club.

"You want me to get him? He walked in here two hours ago
half out of his mind."

"It's okay," I say. "I don't really know what to do."

"You could, you know, talk. Like human adults."

"Really?" I chuckle. "Is that all?"

The bar is still so full of customers that Fallon doesn't even notice me. The girl on his lap is pretty. Her eyes are bright, and she glances at him shyly. Every time she leans into him, he leans away. But he never loses that smile, as if it's plastered to his face, because once it's gone, it's going to be gone for a while.

"What are you drinking, hon?" Rachel asks. "On the house."

"Whiskey."

"Girl after my own heart."

I rest my arms on the bar. "Do you go with everyone? When they go to Vegas?"

"I'm not a Vegas girl. I'm too rooted here in New York. Even when it chews me up and spits me back out. Some people just belong in one place."

"I used to think I was the kind of girl who was rooted somewhere." I take the glass of amber liquid and smell it, bring it to my lips, let the warm spirits coat my throat.

"What kind of girl are you now?" Rachel asks.

I don't know. Even my mother says I'm too wound up. Too scared. Too—jealous.

The girl on Fallon's lap lunges her face at him. He holds her back by her shoulders to avoid her lips. She kisses the sleeve of his tuxedo shirt, leaving a red trail down the arm. Ricky taps him on the shoulder. The girl sitting on Fallon moves to an empty chair, while he follows Ricky through a door near the stage.

"I'm not sure, but I think I'll find out soon enough." I shrug, an idea blooming in my mind. I set my drink down, and wait for another.

FALLON

"Darla," Ricky says. He repeats her name over and over.

"I'm sorry I let her go," I say.

Ricky grips the back of his office chair and nods. His eyes stare out the door as if suddenly she'll manifest. Then he chuckles darkly. "I suppose that's fair. You've seen what I do to those who cross me. I wouldn't hurt her, Zacky. I loved her. Even if she never felt the same way."

"That's a mind blow, brother," I say. "Since when?"

"Since always. But she's too much like me. We were never ready to settle down. I always thought in the end, after Vegas—perhaps. I didn't know the kind of trouble she was getting herself in."

"You should go look for her," I say.

Ricky turns to me. He's still got glitter from one of the audience members who must've rubbed her face on his. "Are you going to take your own advice, or are you here after hours because the wedding went swimmingly?"

"Can't keep anything from you," I say.

Ricky changes his mood in seconds. He's a chameleon, onstage and off.

"What's the word, Zacky?" he asks me.

I tell him about the wedding. The ups and downs and punches.

"Do you remember the first time we met?" he asks.

"Of course," I say.

"You've always had a sort of life about you. Every girl in the room wants you and every guy in the room wants to be you. But you never see that, do you? You lack the right amount of self-esteem. You always have."

"I don't lack self-esteem," I tell him. "What are you, a headshrinker now?"

"I've known you for ten fucking years, brother. I've watched your every move. The way you interact with people. And I have never, not once, seen you doubt yourself the way you do when you're with Robyn."

"I don't belong with her, Ricky. I'm not good enough for her."

"Fuck that noise!" Ricky shouts. "Says who? You? The king of getting his heart broken by the prettiest girl who will bat her fake fucking eyelashes at you? No, Zacky. You're wrong. You're a better man than most of us because you're the only one willing to risk it all for what you're feeling. I've never been able to do that. Never could, never will. Go look for Darla? I'd probably die an old man clinging to the dregs of my glory days before I ever see her again. I've seen you grow up, brother. And I can tell you that you're the best man I know."

I never knew Ricky thought of me this way. He's not wrong. He's not wrong one bit. And deep in my heart I know what I have to do.

The only thing *left* for me to do.

"Ricky—I quit."

ROBYN

Ricky appears from the back of the bar. He's the best dressed out of the lot of them, still in his tailored scarlet-and-black blazer, looking like the devil himself.

"All right, everyone," Ricky says. "I have an announcement. Everyone get a drink, on the house. For ten years I've known Zack Fallon. He's been with me through thick and thin. Now, he's ready to leave the nest and fly on his own. Where is he going? That's between him and the Almighty. But as we head to Vegas, Fallon is going out on his own.

"This is for every night you pulled through. Every show we danced together. Every moment on the road. Cheers, my brother. Godspeed."

Everyone at the bar raises their drinks to the ceiling, and then they drink. I drink, too.

Fallon isn't going to Vegas?

How did we get from leaving together to coming undone? He's only yards away but we're a world apart. I slam my glass on the table, so loud people turn to look at me.

When Fallon sees me, he stands. I can see his body react to me. The way his eyes track my body, the way he fidgets with his clothes. Why is he fighting this?

"When did you get here?" he asks.

"A while ago." I look at the girl who was on his lap, now leaning against the bar.

He walks across the room to get to me. Corners me. "You don't belong in this world, Robyn. And I was selfish to try to bring you into it."

"But you're leaving."

"That's right. I have to figure myself out. I don't—I don't know what I want or what to do. I don't know what comes next."

I look into his eyes and whisper, "I thought you loved me."

His mouth turns into a sad smile, but he won't look at me. "It wasn't love, Robyn. We were just—caught up. Trying to make pieces fit that didn't."

"I chose you, Fallon. Why isn't that enough?"

"Go home, Robyn."

I turn and walk out the door. Rachel asked me what kind of girl I am. I guess we'll just have to see.

FALLON

In the morning, I pack. I cancel my ticket to Vegas, and there is something freeing about the moment I hit "yes" when the website asks if I'm sure. It's time that I go home. At least, that's what Mary says. My younger brother's got a spare room for me until I figure out where I'm going to go next.

Ricky tried once more to get me to stay. He's going to give me another solo spot. But I don't need another solo or my own poster or a raise. What I told Robyn wasn't a lie. I do need to figure out what I want.

You're the only one willing to risk it all for what you're feeling.

That's what Ricky said. He's right. I even wrote a stupid, sappy love letter. It's a good thing somewhere between the reception and the club, I lost it. I thought I was right. I thought it was love. Was it? I wanted Robyn. Every fiber in me wants her, still. But what do I give her? A man searching for himself? A man who isn't sure of his future? I don't know what I can offer her anymore. How can that be love?

As I shove clothes into duffel bags, Yaz barks at me, refusing to sit still. I've walked her four times and it isn't even noon yet. She sits at the door and whines, looking back at me with those sharp blue eyes.

"You don't want to leave?" I ask her, as if she could respond. I pick her up and carry her around like a newborn baby. "We have to, girl. I think you'll like Boston. We have a big park. Better hot dogs."

I laugh. This is my new life. Talking to my dog.

Ricky texts me.

Ricky: *You're still going to do the last set tomorrow, right?*

Me: *Yeah, why?*

Ricky: *Gotta be sure. Need an official head count.*

Me: *I gotchu.*

Staying away from Robyn is the hardest thing I've ever done. At random intervals I can smell her, hear her, see her. She's a living ghost around me. It doesn't help that her voice drifts from her upstairs every now and then.

She's giggling with someone. I wonder who is up there with her. It's been a day since I watched her walk away, *told her* to walk away, and I'm too much of a coward to go and apologize. Talk to her. Fix things.

So, I'm not going to Vegas. I'm going to Boston.

Stop that, I tell myself. I unfold another box and shove my clothes in it. My costumes, all of it, I put in a separate box to give to Ricky.

When I get to a red, white, and blue sequin thong, I hold it up for inspection. I don't see any incident where I would wear this ever again. But I put it in the box I'm taking with me because I like the memory attached to her. It reminds me of her and the whole reason she came into my life. Every single moment around us brought us together. And every other moment tried to pull us apart.

20

Crawling Back to You

FALLON

It's my last show. I'm backstage getting ready for my solo. I'm not doing the bedroom scene. I want to keep it simple. Just me and a girl plucked from the audience.

The house is packed for the final night, even for a Saturday. We oversold tickets, and added chairs to tables to make room for everyone.

"You ready, brother?" Ricky asks. He slaps my shoulder. I pat down my body. My shirt, my pants, a big-ass buckle she'll take off.

"I was born ready."

He winks at me, which is off because he never winks at me before a set. Ricky is nothing if not ruled by his regimen of performance superstitions. I suppose it has to do with the fact that I'm leaving.

He struts onstage wearing his emerald-green blazer that looks like he's the motherfucking Wizard of Oz. He gets the crowd hyped up to the point I'm pretty sure people across the river can hear us.

"We've got a huge surprise for you, girls. As most of you know, tonight is our last night here in the Big Apple. You've been mighty good to us. Now, we're headed to Veeeeeeegas! Make sure if you're out there to come and see Mayhem City at The Royal." Ricky does another sprint across the stage and the crowd cheers and hollers at him. "This next performer has been part of Mayhem City for ten years. Tonight, he's dancing his last dance. So I'm going to need a very special girl to send him off right. Do I have any volunteers?"

Aiden sidles up beside me. "I've never seen a crowd like this, man."

I slap his arm. "Wait until Vegas."

Ricky's voice fills the room again. He leads a blond woman up the steps and sits her center stage. "Give it up for my boy, Fallon!"

The lights go dark and I line up on my mark. The DJ cues up my song. It's dark, and sensual, and everything that reminds me of Robyn. I know I shouldn't be thinking of her on my last night, but it's my last shot to remember. And I know I'll give my best performance with her on my mind.

I walk across the stage. The blond woman sits on a black chair that faces the audience. Her tanned legs are thick and muscular. My heart thunders in my chest at the sight of them, a memory of Robyn straddling me on the Wonder Wheel. I stand in front of the woman and swerve my lower body toward her.

A smile creeps up on her lips, obscured by the shadows of the stage. Fueled by the screams from the crowd, I rip my shirt into shreds and throw them toward the audience. I throw my body at her feet and thrust my pelvis against the stage, slowly, hard.

I get back up on my knees, grab her thighs, and part them open. She holds on to the chair. I can't read her like usual. Most women are shy in this moment. They need to be coaxed into it. But maybe she's been here before and knows the routine. Because she seems to be expecting my moves.

"Hold up, hold up," Ricky says, stepping back onstage.

Confusion riddles my thoughts. I stand back up, Ricky getting between the blonde and me. I look to the stage, slightly out of breath, and smile.

"I said before this is Fallon's last night here! Why does he have to do all the work?" He waits for the hollers and screams from the crowd, who encourage him. Then, Rick Rocket turns to me and says, "So, all the boys got together and figured out a way to wish you bon voyage on your next adventure. Get it, girl."

That's when the blonde stands. Aiden appears behind me and slams me down onto a chair, strapping my arms behind my back with silk ties.

The track slows, scratches, then changes. A familiar song, a song I've danced to before.

ROBYN

The lights are hot and bright against my skin. The last time I was on this stage, I wasn't sure what to do with my hands. I let Fallon lead the way, and now he kicks off the set with me. Only he doesn't know it's me.

It's the same song he danced for me and I wonder if he chose it on purpose. His body is a ripple of muscle and skin and I love watching every second of it.

But it's my turn.

Rick walks back up onstage and stops the set. Fallon is a deer in headlights, looks from Ricky to me to the audience. For a moment, I can't even hear what Rick is saying. My heart thunders, adrenaline surging through my body as I find my mark, and Aiden appears from behind stage and ties Fallon to the chair.

I'm not going to try to replicate his moves, because Fallon can pop and lock his body in ways that I can't. But I spent all day yesterday with Ricky to get the movements right. Fallon's smile is undeniable as the light hits me center stage, and the song changes, blasting Warrant's "Cherry Pie."

I dig under the seam of my blond wig and pull it off. I can almost hear Fallon gasp as I turn and shake my hair into his face. I wind my lower body, and he watches me like I'm a cobra rising to meet his eyes. He's struggling against his restraints. I take off my sunglasses, like the guys did the time they performed at Lily's bachelorette party. I can almost hear her and Anise screaming from the audience.

I throw the sunglasses to the side and sit astride him, my back against his chest. I grab my tank top. Ricky made a little cut at the collar, and I rip it down the middle. My bikini top is covered in sequins, red, white, and blue.

I stand, and slam back down onto his lap, lining up our best parts together. I grind against him, then bend forward and flip my hair from side to side, letting my body glide against his naked torso.

I drop down, get on my knees, and spread his legs open the same way he did to me. I turn to the audience at the same time as I rake my nails up and down his thighs.

I get up to my feet and spin. As their voices crescendo, I land across his lap. Then the lights go dark.

"Robyn," Fallon calls out after me, but I'm already racing behind stage.

FALLON

The crowd goes wild. In the dark, I can feel someone untie my hands. Robyn isn't anywhere backstage.

"Where is she?" I ask.

They all point out the back door that leads to the main area. I don't care that I'm shirtless and in a pair of pants I never got to take off. I don't care that my heart is racing a thousand miles per hour. I don't care that Ricky tricked me right onstage. All I want is to get to Robyn.

I run out the side door that leads toward the bar area. She's there, surrounded by Lily, Anise, and a couple of the brides-maids I remember. They all high-five her. Rachel pours a round of drinks. She's got the best eye in the whole club because she looks up at the exact same time that I march toward the bar.

Rachel smirks, and when Robyn notices it she spins around. She's still in her bikini top. Her body is slick with whatever shimmer the makeup artists put on her. How didn't I recognize the second she was onstage? The wig, the glasses, the way the lights were adjusted to keep her face hidden.

I pick her up by her waist. I revel in the scent of her, the feel of her skin, lower her against me until our mouths are lined up.

An overwhelming sense of relief crashes over me as she kisses me harder than she ever has.

"I'm sorry," I say.

"I'm sorry, too," she says. "I got your letter."

"I love you, Robyn."

"I know." She digs her fingers in my hair and I pull on those long dark strands she teased against my face.

The spotlight turns on us. Ricky is standing on the side of the stage closest to the bar. The boys are lined up ready to do their next set, but he takes the time to put us on blast.

"Let it be said, ladies, that when you're with Mayhem City, we give everyone their happy ending."

21

Love You Like a Love Song

ROBYN

One Month Later

I put most of my things in storage. On the last day of school, I didn't look back. I don't know what's to become of Lukas, but I hope he gets what's coming to him. I had more things to take care of in New York than I expected. I found a subletter: Sebastian's sister Daya needed a place closer to work.

Fallon and I spent days making up and making love. We wished the boys farewell. I created an Instagram account to keep track of their everyday shenanigans. But so far, they're having fun, breaking hearts, and preparing for their shows on the Vegas strip.

Fallon left for Boston first. That part of our plan never changed. He needed to be there for his family. And he needed to be there to find us a place.

A few days after Lily's wedding I came home to an acceptance letter from a creative writing program at Pine Manor College just outside of Boston. It was the only creative writing program I had applied to, and the only one I got into.

My dad says it's a sign that I'm on the right track, no matter the plan, no matter what I had set out to do in the first place.

When I'm packed, I say good-bye to my city and promise that

I'll return. Then, I get on the train to South Station where a certain man is waiting for me.

FALLON

I've made a lot of mistakes, but quitting the group wasn't one of them. Letting the world get in between Robyn and me, that was a mistake. One I'll never make again.

My pop is doing better. I think what he really missed was shouting at me from one floor up. I found a place for Robyn and me in the North End. Somewhere she can look at the water from her office and where I can figure out my next step. I'll never be tired of our lives turning, our places changing. It keeps me on my toes. At the end of it, I know that I want her to be there. I want her to be the first person I see when I wake and the last person I see when I sleep.

Mary Lee helps me get the apartment ready for when Robyn shows up, and Pop pulls me aside after we're done clearing up the trash.

"Here you go, Zacky," he tells me. His stiff, arthritis-ridden hand presses something cold against my hand. "When you find the right girl, you keep her, you hear? You keep her and you do right by both of you."

I look at the ring on my palm. It's a pale gold with an emerald surrounded by diamonds. Simple, but stunning, and one of a kind. It was my mother's.

ROBYN

South Station is confusing, but eventually I find Fallon. He's waiting for me amid a sea of people, but I see him. I can always find him, no matter how many people are in the room.

If my backpack wasn't heavy, I'd run to him. Instead, he runs to me. I unhook my arms from the straps and let them fall. He picks me up and spins me in the air, and I laugh and cry because I didn't realize it was possible to miss someone like this.

After I kiss him long enough to make onlookers uncomfortable, I pull away and look around. "So, this is Boston. I brought my Mets cap."

He takes my backpack from me and shoulders it. "Don't start. We'll have none of that."

He threads his fingers through mine and takes me for a walk through Boston Common. It's lush and green, and the sun is setting, the water alight with a starburst of colors. We walk across a little bridge right over the water. I nestle myself into his arms, strong and loving and safe.

"Do you have a verdict yet?" he asks me, setting my pack down while we enjoy the warm summer breeze.

"I only just got here," I say, "but I know that I'm going to love it as long as I'm with you. And as long as you feed me lobster rolls."

I keep walking but he tugs on my sleeve. When I turn around, he's down on one knee. I cup my hand on my mouth.

"Robyn Flores, when we met, we were both a little bit broken. I think something in the universe was driving us together. Working to get us to that moment."

"To when I stole your laundry?"

"The very same moment. And I was wrong. I think that when we're together, our broken pieces do fit." He takes my hand. The ring is brilliant and green, unlike anything I've ever seen. "Will you marry me?"

"Yes," I say, breathless as I get down on my knees to meet him and he slides the ring into place.

We reach for each other at the same time, and kiss until the sun has long finished setting.

Acknowledgments

A huge thank-you goes out to my agent, Adrienne Rosado, and my editor, Norma Perez-Hernandez. You both believed in these characters. I owe you a trip to Vegas. Thank you to the Kensington team and everyone who had a part in creating this series.

To the wonderful romance community and those who try to give a HEA to all. Special thanks to Channing Tatum and the greatest modern fairytale ever told—*Magic Mike XXL*.

Finally, to the readers. I hope you all find your Happily Ever Afters.

Connect with 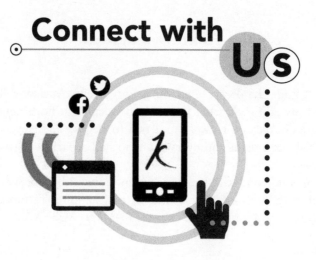 U S

Visit us online at
KensingtonBooks.com
to read more from your favorite authors, see books
by series, view reading group guides, and more.

 Join us on social media
for sneak peeks, chances to win books and prize packs,
and to share your thoughts with other readers.

facebook.com/kensingtonpublishing
twitter.com/kensingtonbooks

Tell us what you think!
To share your thoughts, submit a review,
or sign up for our eNewsletters, please visit:
KensingtonBooks.com/TellUs.